PIECES
&
PARTS

DAWN HOSMER

THE BITS & PIECES SERIES
BOOK 2

ISBN: 978-1-7374695-0-6 paperback
1st edition: September 2021

Cover Design: Rebecca F. Kenney
Interior Design: Nicole Scarano
Editing: Kate Yelland

To Alayna
You have the power to change the world.
You've already brightened ours beyond measure.

We are all sculptors and painters, and our material is our own flesh and blood and bones. Any nobleness begins at once to refine a man's features, any meanness or sensuality to imbrute them.
~ Henry David Thoreau

PART I

JULY

CHAPTER 1

Sharp, angular brush strokes cover the canvas in garish shades of red, orange, yellow, purple, blue, and green. I stand back to examine the painting now that I'm confident it is complete. It takes a moment for my eyes to adjust and see past the colors, but all at once it comes into crystal clear focus. I've painted Liam with his boyish face twisted in agony. Something black, like a club, plummets toward his head.

I stumble backwards into a chair. What the hell did I just paint, and why? Bile rises in my throat as my mind searches for a way to make sense of it. A thought from nowhere reverberates through my mind —*Liam is in danger. Someone is going to kill him.*

"Jonas!" I shout.

"You okay?" He stumbles into the studio, rubbing sleep from his eyes.

I point at the painting without saying a word.

Jonas squints and moves closer. "It looks nice."

My throat is so thick that I can barely spit out the words. "Do you not see what it is?"

Again, he rubs his eyes and peers closer before shaking his head. "You woke me up so I can't see too clearly yet. The way you screamed —I thought something was wrong with you."

I inhale a shaky breath. "Something *is* wrong. That's Liam. Someone is going to kill him."

Jonas leans over the back of the chair and wraps his arms around me. "Tess, honey, it's late. You're tired. I don't see Liam. Please come to bed."

Maybe he's right. I've been working hard lately to get commissioned paintings out, and the lack of sleep must be getting to me. "Okay, I'll be there in a few minutes."

Jonas kisses me on top of my head and goes back to bed. Before I can sleep, I need this painting out of my house. My heart pounds so hard as I carry it downstairs. I glance at it one more time before heaving it into the outside trash can and slam the lid closed as a shiver races up my spine. I haven't thrown many of my paintings away, but this one must go. Chaundra can never see it—she'd immediately recognize her son's face.

Before heading upstairs, I chug a glass of water. Some sloshes over the edge because my hands are so shaky. I haven't been in that type of painting trance for a long time—back to when I used to have the flashes—one so deep that I have no knowledge of what I've painted until I'm finished.

As I undress and climb into bed, I debate whether I should mention the painting to Chaundra this weekend at Lily's birthday party but decide it's probably best if I don't. Like Jonas said, I'm just overly tired. But why did I have the distinct feeling that someone was after Liam, intent on killing him?

I curl around Jonas and tell myself to stop obsessing over a silly painting that doesn't mean anything. Questions continue to creep into my thoughts. Why did I use those particular colors? Why did Liam's panic and fear race through my body? Who was holding that club?

I repeat *it was only a painting* over and over in my mind until finally, Jonas' warmth pulls me into sleep.

CHAPTER 2

"... Happy Birthday, dear Lily. Happy Birthday to you!" the off-key chorus sings, while Lily sits beaming in front of her princess cake with eight candles. Liam stands next to her, singing at the top of his lungs. A shiver works its way through me, remembering my painting, and his face contorted in pain. I shake my head to clear the memory of the painting.

How is Lily eight already, and Liam almost a teenager? These past five years have flown by. Sometimes it feels like Chaundra and the kids have been a part of my life forever, but then other times, like now, I'm reminded that I've only known them for a short time. This found family of mine, including Jonas, has made my life complete. They all love and accept the real me. The person who was hidden beneath all the bits and pieces I'd picked up from other people through the years.

"Don't forget to make a wish, honey!" Chaundra says and squeezes Lily's shoulder. Her voice pulls me back to the room.

Lily closes her eyes for a second and blows all the candles out with one breath.

"What did you wish for Lily?" I ask, stooping down to look in her eyes.

"You know I can't tell you that, Aunt Tessa. Not if I want it to come true."

I stick out my bottom lip in a fake pout. "Well, okay then. Can I at least have a birthday hug since you won't share your wish?"

Lily giggles and throws her arms around my shoulders. I kiss her on the cheek, and she stiffens in my arms. I pull back to see what's wrong. She's staring at me, but she's somewhere far away.

"Hey, Lily. Earth to Lily!" I snap my fingers in front of her face. She finally blinks and smiles, but it seems forced. "What's wrong? Are you okay?"

Her eyes shift around the room as she nods. She leans close and whispers. "Can you, Jonas, and Mommy come in my room a minute?"

"But honey, all your friends are here. It's your party—you can't leave."

"It'll just take a second," she says and bounds over to where Chaundra scoops ice cream for all the party goers.

I work my way through the sea of children to Jonas. He's in the back corner of the kitchen talking to one of the other kids' dads. As soon as he glimpses me, his face breaks into a smile.

"Hi there, beautiful!" He grabs me by the hand and pulls me close.

I turn toward the gentleman standing with him. "Could you excuse us for a moment?"

"Sure thing. I need to get some cake anyway! Nice talking with you, Jonas!" he says and walks away.

"What's up, Tess?"

"Lily said she needs to talk to us and Chaundra in her bedroom for a second."

Jonas' brow wrinkles in confusion. He holds out his hand to indicate the kitchen full of children. "Right now?"

"That's what I said, but she promises it will only take a second." I shrug and grab his hand.

When we get to Lily's room, she and Chaundra are already sitting on her bed. Chaundra looks like she's been attacked by an ice cream monster with bits of it drying all the way up her arms. Her hair is coming out of her braid, and she seems plain worn out. I can't help but laugh.

"Yeah, I know. I know. I'm a hot mess!" Chaundra chuckles as she smooths down her hair. "Okay, Lil, spill it. We've got a house full of people."

"Well, I've got some good news." Lily grins and turns to Jonas and me.

"Okay…" I say slowly, more confused than ever.

She jumps up from the bed and smiles. "You're gonna have a baby!"

"What? How…" I say as my hand instinctively goes to my stomach.

"Are you serious, Lily?" Jonas asks, resting his hand on top of mine.

She nods. "I know when, too, and whether it's a girl or boy. Do you wanna know?"

Chaundra grabs her by the arm. "No, little miss! Keep that to yourself unless they want to know." Chaundra eagerly scrutinizes us with raised eyebrows. "Do you want to know?"

I gaze at Jonas, and he shakes his head, which is a relief. I want to do all this the normal way, other than having a psychic little girl tell me I'm pregnant.

Tears fill my eyes. I am pregnant. *We are going to have a baby.*

"Just tell me one thing. How far along am I?" As I think back, I realize I'm at least two weeks late for my period. They've always been so irregular, though, especially now that I'm off the pill.

"Not very," Lily says. "When you hugged me, I knew."

Jonas pulls me into his arms and kisses me.

"Congratulations, guys! Lily and I will give you a few minutes alone." Chaundra grabs Lily's hand, and they both stop to give us hugs on the way out of the room.

Once the door closes, Jonas pulls me back into his arms, and we stand in stunned silence for a few moments. Chaundra and Lily talk quietly on the other side of the closed bedroom door. I can't make out most of the words but hear Chaundra say one thing clearly—*do not tell them. Do you understand?*

"A baby! We're going to have a baby!" Jonas whoops, drowning out their voices. "Are you ready to be a mommy?"

Lily's declaration hits me again. *A baby!* Tears of joy spill down my cheeks. "You know I am! What about you, Daddy?"

"There is nothing in the world that will make me happier."

After a few minutes, we head back downstairs to the festivities. My mind swarms with all the things I need to do. Make a doctor's appointment. Decorate a nursery. Pick out baby names. Find out what else Lily saw during our hug. And what she is not supposed to tell me.

CHAPTER 3

"Hey! Why so quiet?" Jonas squeezes my hand and draws my attention back inside the car instead of into the darkened tree line.

"Huh? Oh, sorry. Just thinking."

"I'd say you were lost somewhere deep in thought. I've been rambling on over here, and I'd venture to say you didn't hear a word," Jonas says with a chuckle. "You okay?"

I don't know how to answer this question honestly. *Am I?* A million thoughts swirl around in this brain of mine, and I don't think I can verbalize it in a way that will make any sense.

"Yeah. I have a lot on my mind with Lily's announcement."

"All good stuff, I hope. You're excited, right?"

I take a deep breath and twirl my hair around my finger. "I am, but I'm also scared, which I know is silly because we are ready for a baby. We've talked about it for the past year." I pause and gaze out into the night sky. "I have a lot of doubts, too. First off, what if Lily is wrong? I'd hate to get my hopes up and then find out I'm not pregnant after all."

Jonas laughs. "Lily, wrong? You know better. She's not wrong."

I nod. He has a valid point. She never is.

"What else is going on in that pretty little head of yours? I know that's not it."

"You know me too well." I lean back into the seat and shut my eyes. "Okay, here goes. What if we're not as ready as we think we are? What if I'm a terrible mother, like my mom? What if I can't do this?"

Jonas pulls the car off the road and throws it into park. He turns to me and grabs my chin, forcing me to look him in the eye. We've been married for a little over two years now and those big brown eyes of his still make me swoon.

"Tess, honey. You are nothing like your mother. You will do a great job. No, scratch that... *we* will be wonderful parents. Remember how well you did with the kids at the preschool? They loved you! You're a natural. We're as ready for this baby as two people can possibly be." He cups his hands around my face and pulls me close for a kiss.

I clear my throat several times. "There's one other thing that's bothering me. I heard Lily and Chaundra talking outside the bedroom door. I couldn't make out much of what they said, but I caught Chaundra telling Lily to keep something from us. What did she see that she's not telling us?"

Jonas slumps back against his seat and drums his fingers on the steering wheel. "Well, I'm not sure what you heard, but maybe it wasn't about us or the baby. Or, if it was, and it's something we need to know, I have no doubt that Chaundra will tell us in time."

Even though the right words come out, his facial expression doesn't match them. The exuberance that was there before this declaration of mine is now replaced with apprehension. I shouldn't have told him. I don't want him to carry the burden of worrying with me.

I force myself to smile. "You're right. I'm sure I misheard them. It's probably got nothing to do with us." I lean over and kiss him on the cheek.

"How about you call tomorrow and get a doctor's appointment scheduled? I think we'll both feel better after that."

"I will. Now let's get home." I pat him on the leg.

We ride quietly along the winding roads to take us to our log cabin tucked in the forest at the edge of town. I only wish my thoughts would quiet, too. By the time we pull in our driveway, I've decided that in addition to scheduling an appointment with the doctor, I also need to make one to see Ophelia. And schedule a lunch date with Chaundra to figure out what secret she's keeping from me.

CHAPTER 4

The smell of coffee finally pulls me from bed at six, as the sunrise looms beyond the horizon. I barely slept last night as my thoughts were spinning around about a million miles per hour. One minute, I'd be elated about Lily's revelation; the next, I'd be so full of worry I felt like I was going to puke.

I pull on my robe and slippers and make my way to the kitchen. My eyes feel like sandpaper. Jonas meets me in the doorway with a steaming cup of coffee.

"Morning, love!" He kisses me on the cheek. "You look tired. Did you sleep?"

I chuckle. "Whew! I was worried my tossing and turning kept you up all night. I guess not, huh?"

"Sit," he says, holding out his hand toward the leather chair in front of the fireplace. "What was keeping you up?"

"Oh, you know. The usual. My overactive imagination and racing thoughts." I take a drink of coffee. Every muscle in my body relaxes.

"Oh, hon. The pregnancy?" Worry lines fill the corners of his eyes.

I nod. "I'll be okay, though. I'm going to get a doctor's appointment and one with Ophelia. Since I'm almost done with my commissioned pieces, I'll be able to catch up on sleep if need be."

Jonas raises his eyebrows. "Ophelia? It's been a while since you've seen her. Do you need me to go with you?"

Over the past couple of years, I've been able to cut back to seeing Ophelia once every other month or so. Those appointments were more to check in and make sure I kept the lines of communication open. Sure, there were a few times I went to her in freak out mode over wedding planning and my family issues, but I can count those on one hand in the past five years.

"I'm okay. And no, you don't need to come with me. The thought of being a mother is bringing back some of those old, ugly childhood memories, I think. Nothing major but it may help me to talk through it."

"You know, I'm always here if you need to talk, too," he says with a wink.

"I know, babe. I promise it's nothing more than what I've said. Maybe we both should go a few times before the baby comes."

Jonas nods. "Agreed. Therapy never hurt anyone, that's for sure." He stands and stretches. "Anyway, I've got a full class schedule and office hours today, so I'll be gone until this evening. Let me know when you can get into the doctor. If you want, I can pick up a pregnancy test on the way home to ease your mind."

My heart swells as I once again realize how much I love this man. I couldn't have asked for a kinder, more caring, or more handsome husband. "I'll text and let you know. I may have to go into town to meet with Ophelia, if she can fit me in. Or maybe lunch with Chaundra. But, if not, I'll have you stop."

He leans forward and kisses me. A deep, passionate kiss that tells me how much he loves me, wants me, needs me. Finally, he pushes away.

"Okay, I've gotta go or I may have to take you back to bed."

I wiggle my eyebrows. "That works for me."

"Ugh. Don't tempt me. I've got to go, or I'll be late for class. But, raincheck, okay?"

I grab his hand and give it a gentle squeeze. "Anytime."

~

As I FINISH my cup of coffee, I call Dr. Weyman's office. They can get me in next Monday. Waiting an entire week might kill me. I grab my phone to let Jonas know about the appointment.

Hey, babe! Appointment with Dr. Weyman, Monday at 9. Love you and have a good day.

I also shoot a text to Chaundra asking if she has time in the next couple of days for lunch and leave a voice mail for Ophelia, telling her I need an appointment. I sit and savor my coffee for a few minutes before the phone rings.

"Hi, Ophelia!"

"Good morning. I'm returning your call. Is everything okay?" Ophelia's voice fills with concern. It's been a long time since I've had to request an impromptu appointment with her.

"Yes, everything is good. I wondered if I could come in to see you sometime this week to talk through a few things."

"Certainly. I had a cancellation for two this afternoon if that works for you."

"That would be perfect. I'll see you then."

I take a long, hot shower. My worries and concerns melt away, down the drain with the water. I leave early enough for my appointment with Ophelia, so I have time to stop at the pharmacy to buy a pregnancy test. I can't wait until next week to confirm what my heart already knows.

I enter Ophelia's waiting room with ten minutes to spare. I sit and try to let the peace fill me as it normally does when I'm here, but I can't relax knowing that the test is in my purse waiting for me to take it.

"Screw it," I say out loud to the empty room and rush into the restroom.

I tear open the packaging and peruse the directions, which are easy enough to understand. I pee on the stick and then place it back in the enclosed plastic baggie. I really should've waited until I got home with Jonas to take the test, but it's too late now. It says to wait five minutes, so I set the alarm on my phone and go back to the waiting room.

Five minutes have never felt so long. Each second seems to take an eternity. Right as Ophelia opens her door to call me in, the timer on my phone beeps.

"I'm ready, Tessa," she says.

I hold up a finger and pull out the plastic bag with the test. A plus sign. Lily was right, as always. Tears fill my eyes—I'm not sure if they're ones of relief, anxiety, or joy. But I guess that's why I'm waiting to talk to my therapist.

"Is everything, okay?" Ophelia asks, walking toward me.

I nod and hold out the pregnancy test. Ophelia laughs with delight and then gives me a huge hug.

"I'm ecstatic for you guys! Come on in, and let's talk."

I grab the box of tissues before I take a seat in my favorite eggplant chair.

"So, are you having mixed feelings?"

I nod. "I'm a bit overwhelmed. Lily told us last night at her birthday party and, like usual, I'm way over thinking it. I bought the test just to confirm, although I should've known she was right."

"Talk to me about being overwhelmed."

I swallow the lump in my throat. "What if I'm a terrible mother, like mine? What if a baby changes Jonas and my relationship? Are we really ready?"

"Let's back up a bit. Your first question is, what if you're a terrible mother?"

I nod.

"Let's focus on your history with children a bit to examine that realistically. Close your eyes and think about your relationship with Lily and Liam. And about the teaching you did at the preschool. And your relationship with Cyle's children."

I picture all the children she mentions and open my eyes. "Okay, point taken. I'm ready to be a mom. I am good with children. I guess it's more the fear of what if I turn out like my mom? Perhaps she had a maternal instinct at some point, yet she still did a really shitty job with all of us."

"I've met your mother, both through your stories and in person. You are nothing like her." Ophelia says, matter-of-factly.

My parents and siblings actually came to our wedding. Ophelia spent quite a bit of time talking with my mother. I spent hours in therapy before the big event preparing for my family to show up. While Ophelia never said a bad word about my mother, she told me that Mom was exactly what she expected. That I'd painted a vivid and accurate picture of my family over the years.

I know in my heart she's absolutely correct. Any parts of her I had in me at one time were because of my gift. Thankfully, I lost those when I dumped everything into Matthew, the sadistic bastard that tried to take over my mind and threatened my life, as well as my sanity.

"You're right," I say. "The person in my family I'm most like is Cyle, and he was a great dad."

Ophelia smiles. "Lastly, you said you're worried it's going to change your relationship with Jonas. On that, you're correct. It *will* change your relationship, individually and as a couple. But it will change it for the better."

An image of Jonas with Lily and Liam fills my mind. He's so good and patient with children. He will be the perfect father and would have ten kids if I were up for it. I nod and smile.

"Again, you're right." I laugh. "Remind me why I'm paying you to sit here and tell you how correct you are about everything."

Ophelia chuckles. "It's a perfect scheme, huh? All kidding aside, it's normal to feel overwhelmed and emotional during major life changes, especially a pregnancy. Then, add in some of your remaining childhood issues, that makes it even more stressful. I'm here to help you figure out the truth on your own by asking the right questions. The ones your brain won't allow you to ask yourself when it goes into panic mode."

"Are you up for seeing me and Jonas a few times through all this? I'm sure this won't be the last time these insecurities rear their ugly heads."

"I'm always here whenever you need me. You both know that."

I take a deep breath and let that truth settle my spirit. We've got this. We will be fine. I have the best people in my corner to see me through this pregnancy.

∼

As soon as I'm in the car, I call Jonas, hoping that he's not in class. He picks up on the first ring.

"Hey, babe! How did your appointment go?"

"It went well. It always helps to talk with Ophelia. So, listen... I stopped at the pharmacy on the way to my appointment. I know I should've waited until we were together to take the test, but..."

Jonas interrupts. "Spill it!"

"Lily was right!"

Jonas laughs, and I can hear his smile. "I knew she was. I can't wait to be a daddy."

"You will be the best one ever," I say, and mean every word.

PART II

JANUARY — FEBRUARY

CHAPTER 5

A kiss on the forehead wakes me. I force my eyes open despite still being exhausted. I didn't sleep well at all last night. I couldn't get comfortable now that my belly is growing, and the baby decides to do somersaults whenever I lay down.

"Hey, I didn't mean to wake you. Just wanted to kiss you good-bye," Jonas whispers.

I smile. "Love you! Don't forget, I have my counseling appointment at four. Hopefully little one will let me get some more sleep."

Jonas pats his hand on my stomach. "Let Mommy sleep! I felt you tossing and turning all night."

"Ugh. I'm sorry. I tried not to wake you."

"Hey, it's all part of parenthood, right? Anyway, I gotta run. Have a good day. My schedule is jam-packed, but text or call if you need me. I love you both." Jonas kisses me and then my belly.

"Love you too. Have a good day!"

As soon as Jonas leaves the room, I pull the covers over my head and drift back to dreamland.

I ONLY MANAGE to sleep until nine since baby has decided it is time to eat. I devour some yogurt and fruit—and, of course, a cup of coffee which seems to appease little one for the time being. Since I have nothing on my agenda today besides my appointment with Ophelia, I head upstairs to my favorite room in our cabin in the woods—my studio. It has floor to ceiling windows on three of the four walls, with a view of the surrounding forest, the mountains, and a stream. Not only is it the perfect spot to find motivation to paint, but spending time here is a balm that soothes my soul. I'm surrounded by nature yet protected from the elements. This winter has been colder than usual, and the ground is covered in snow. Outside the windows lies a winter wonderland.

I exchange my robe for a smock, fill my palette, tell Alexa to play classical music, and set to work on an empty canvas. I'm lost in my painting when the ringing phone interrupts me.

"Hi, Ophelia!"

"I wanted to call to confirm that you're still able to come in today. The roads are a bit rough with the snow."

I peer out the window and see that the roads are, indeed, covered. "I'll be there. A little snow doesn't scare me. I grew up in New York, remember?"

Ophelia laughs. "Ah, yes. So, this little amount of snow is nothing for you. Alright, I will see you at four, and be careful."

I laugh. Ophelia worries about me more than my mother does. "Will do. See you then."

I hang up and return to my painting. Ever since the incident with that demented sicko, Matthew, my paintings have been less abstract, but this one has those elements peeking through. I've painted the winter scene outside of my window. While the trees have no leaves remaining, the stream has reflections of them in all different colors. It's quite lovely even though I have no idea why I painted it in exactly this way... abstract. The reflection of the red, blue, purple, yellow, green, and orange leaves. All the colors that used to dictate my life are now represented in the reflection of the stream, except for the green, of course.

I pause for a moment and stare at the painting. Why did I choose those colors for the leaves? I peer out the window to the stream below. There are no leaves in the water. What was going on in my mind to make me paint them there? I shake my head to try to clear thoughts I shouldn't even spend a second on. It's a lovely painting and, for the past five years, since my flashes went away, I've tried really hard not to analyze my work in the same way. To not stifle my creative process with overthinking. I write the title *Winter Wonderland* and the date on the back.

I laugh to myself as I head to the bathroom for a shower. Back in the day, a painting like this would've made me analyze it for hours, trying to figure out what I was trying to portray emotionally through my work. I'm so relieved that I've come such a long way that I can appreciate the beauty in what I paint rather than always searching for the deeper meaning. I've learned to trust that if there's something hidden there, it will reveal itself to me in time. There's no rush for me to figure it all out. Yet, a nagging feeling in my gut won't go away.

"Stop it!" I shout, which is one way I've learned to cope with intrusive thoughts that I don't want. The thoughts vanish with the steam.

Gratitude fills me as the warmth of the water flows over me. I place a hand on my stomach and smile.

CHAPTER 6

I leave at two-thirty for my appointment with Ophelia since the roads aren't the best. Usually, it would only be about a fifteen-minute drive, but snow has been falling steadily all day—thank God for four-wheel drive. If I make it early enough, I'll grab a coffee for Jonas and stop by to see him for a few minutes since he should be in his office for advisory hours. I debate sending him a text to let him know I'm leaving, but the thought of possibly being able to surprise him makes me smile. So, I decide against it.

I crank the heat and head down our steep driveway with a prayer that I don't skid. One of the few bad things about living this far out is the awful road conditions in the winter. I don't think they've ever seen a snowplow, which is one of the main reasons Jonas insisted upon each of us getting a four-wheel-drive vehicle. Usually, North Carolina doesn't see too much snow, but it seems we've had more the last several years than ever before.

Once I make it out of the driveway, I turn on the radio to listen to a podcast on my drive into town. Music sometimes allows too much time for my thoughts to wander into places they shouldn't go, whereas podcasts help me increase my focus on driving rather than my own crazy ideas. With how treacherous the roads are, I can't be distracted for a second by my wandering thoughts.

I grip the wheel and make it down the first hill by our house without a skid. I breathe a sigh of relief as I go around the bend to the right where the road runs parallel to the stream. The drive from this point on should be much better, without so many steep hills or twists and turns.

I turn up the volume and relax my shoulders. Little one kicks or punches me, and instinctively, my hand flies to my stomach. *Whoosh!* Out of nowhere, a green flash consumes my vision, overtakes my mind, invades my soul. *A green flash? What the hell?* I've never had this color flash before. I gasp in shock but don't have time to ponder the meaning or the reasons. As though an unseen hand is steering my car, it veers off the road. I fight against the wheel, trying to pull the vehicle back onto the road or at least away from trees in my path. My actions have no consequences. I pump the brakes, but they fail to respond.

What the hell is happening? I think as my Jeep rams into a large tree right in front of the stream that I painted earlier.

I'M IN A FOG. I open my eyes to try to figure out where I am, but the world is upside down. Before I can figure out why or how, my eyes drift closed again.

Voices call to me, and the sound of sirens fills the air. Someone familiar is nearby. Jonas? No, a woman. *Ophelia?* I try to say her name, but no words will come out. My eyes are too heavy to pry open, to see what's happening. Sleep calls. I shut my eyes and give in.

I'm moving. Perhaps I'm dreaming. I float down a river in a boat. No, wait... a stream. Something about a stream fills me with panic and screams at me to open my eyes. But the lull of the boat rocks me gently, drifts me away to a deeper sleep despite the voices calling out to me.

I JERK awake to a kiss on my cheek. I squint against the brightness.

"Tess, oh my God!" Jonas leans down and rests his cheek against mine.

My head feels like it's in a vice, gripping tighter and tighter. So taut that soon it may crush my skull. *Where am I? Why do I hurt so badly?* My eyes scan the room and I realize exactly where I am. The hospital. My hands fly to my stomach. *My baby! Is my baby okay?*

"The baby is fine," Jonas says and rests his hand on top of mine. "The doctor just had you hooked up so we could hear the heartbeat. It's still good and strong."

"What happened?" I say even though I'm still so, so tired. I want to sleep.

"Why don't you get some rest for now? We'll talk later," Jonas offers a forced smile, but his forehead scrunches in worry.

I want to say no. To insist that he tell me what's going on, why I'm in the hospital. But my head hurts so badly. I'm exhausted. I grasp his hand and shut my eyes.

WHEN I AWAKEN AGAIN, it's dark. Jonas' hand is still linked with mine, but he's dozing in the chair next to me. My head throbs, but I feel a bit clearer than the last time I woke up. Then, it hits me. I was in the car. I crashed.

"Oh my God!" I gasp.

Jonas jolts awake. "What? You okay?"

"I just remembered the wreck. I crashed into a tree. That's all I can recall. Was I there until you came home?"

Jonas shakes his head. "No. Thankfully, Miss Lily got a vision of your accident while she was at school. She said she was sick so she could go to the office and call Chaundra. Chaundra jumped in her car to get to you and called 911 on the way." A shudder works its way through Jonas' entire body. "You hit a large tree, and the Jeep was on its side in the stream. Thank God it's so shallow this time of year! You must've been going pretty fast to flip it."

His words open the gate to my memory, and it all comes back like a flood, forceful and unrelenting. Tears fill my eyes.

"Babe? What's wrong? You're okay. The baby's okay." Jonas wipes a tear from my cheek.

I shake my head and try to find the words. "You don't understand… I think the flashes are back."

Jonas' face goes ashen, and he wraps his arms around himself. "What?"

"I had a flash. In the car, before I crashed. A green one, which is weird and new. Then something made the car drive into that tree. It wasn't me."

What I don't say is how confused I am and that none of this makes sense. Why are the flashes back? More importantly, how? I wasn't touching anyone. And why do I now have a new color?

CHAPTER 7

After my revelation about the flash, Jonas tries to convince me, and himself, that it is a fluke. That maybe my concussion is making me mis-remember. I offer comforting words, smiles, and nods to assure him I agree, but I *know* it was a flash. I am certain because I felt it in every part of my body, exactly like I used to.

Jonas also tries to convince me that when a vehicle slides on ice or snow, it can feel like you have no control as the driver. Again, I pretend as though I agree to keep him from freaking out along with me, but that isn't what happened at all. Since I grew up in New York, I've driven on much snowier and icier roads, and I've done my fair share of sliding on them. My car was being controlled by something other than me.

I can't figure out why. Or how?

I am discharged from the hospital after twenty-four hours of observation. Besides a concussion, I am covered in bumps and bruises, but everything else is fine about me physically. Emotionally, it is a completely different story. The doctor does an ultrasound to make sure everything is okay with little one. She offers to tell us the gender of the baby, but we say no, agreeing that we want it to be a surprise.

On the drive home, I am finally able to see where my Jeep went off the road. My entire body freezes as we slowly make our way past that spot. I am terrified that again something weird will overtake the car and pull us back toward the stream. But it doesn't. Once we reach the house, I can finally breathe again.

～

WE'VE BEEN HOME for a few days, and Jonas is waiting on me hand and foot. Per doctor's orders, I'm supposed to take it easy for at least a week, until I can get an appointment. I would never tell him, but I'm relieved that he has to go into work tomorrow—I need a bit of a break so I can sort out all the thoughts whirling through my mind.

Since I missed my appointment with Ophelia, she was kind enough to offer to come to the house tomorrow to meet with me while Jonas is at work. With the events of the last week, I *really* need to see her.

For the first time since I've been home, I'm able to sneak away from my spot on the couch, and Jonas' watchful eye, while he showers. I head upstairs to my studio. Something has been eating away at me, other than the obvious with the flash and wreck. Since we've been home, I've felt compelled to peer out the windows upstairs to more clearly see where I crashed from a bird's-eye view.

I flip on the lights and make my way toward the front windows that overlook the stream. I have the perfect view from here. I see where my car went off the road and how it missed several trees on the way to the large one I ultimately crashed into. The ground has deep ruts at the edge of the stream, where the car finally came to a stop. Jonas was right—thank God there wasn't more water in the stream or I could've drowned. I shiver at the thought. There's something else here, though, that I need to see. I don't know what, but I sense it throughout my body. I lean closer to the window and study the area, but there's nothing I hadn't noticed before.

As I fight to clear my mind of these notions, I catch a glimpse of the painting I did the day of the wreck out of the corner of my eye. As it comes into focus, goosebumps cover my entire body. The spot where my car crashed is the *exact* place where I painted all the multi-colored leaves in the stream. The ones that weren't there. Now, I wonder if they aren't really leaves at all but something else. Something represented in the same colors of the flashes I had for years. I shudder and force myself to walk away when I hear the shower stop.

Besides talking with Ophelia tomorrow, I know what else I need to do, even though I shouldn't. I'm going to take a walk down to the stream to see what is in that spot. What drew my painting, and my car, to it.

CHAPTER 8

"Are you sure you're okay?" Jonas sits next to me on the bed.

I yawn and nod. "I'm fine, other than being tired. I'm going to rest until Ophelia comes around noon."

Worry creases his face. I know he hates to leave me. "Keep your phone with you at all times, even on your way to the bathroom. Okay? And call if you need anything."

I squeeze his hand. "I'm okay. Promise. And I'll keep it with me."

He leans forward and kisses me. "I love you!" He moves a hand to my belly. "And I love you, my little bean."

I can't help but smile. He's going to be such a wonderful daddy. Even though I still have anxieties about being a mom, I have no doubt in his ability to be a caring and involved father.

As Jonas leaves, I look out the windows and consider getting out of bed, but the day is dreary and seems as though it will snow at any moment. Instead, I set the alarm on my phone for ten, snuggle under the covers, and drift off to sleep.

~

MY ALARM JARS ME AWAKE. I'm tempted to hit snooze but drag myself from bed to take a shower before Ophelia comes. I was right about my earlier prediction—the snow is really coming down now. I sure hope Ophelia can make it. I also hope that the snowfall doesn't completely cover the area where I wrecked because I need to explore. Not that there's any way I will forget where I ended up. I'll head down after I meet with Ophelia, or maybe I can convince her to explore the area with me.

Because I'm still sluggish and sore, everything takes me longer than usual. I typically spend ten minutes in the shower. Today, I let the warm water flow over me for at least forty-five minutes. It helps ease my pain a bit. I zone out while I shower, remembering the wreck, the flash, how out of control I was in that moment. I've never had a flash that wasn't connected to touching someone else. And I haven't had one in over five years. Yet, with that simple green flash, a lifetime of memories with my gift came back in an instant.

After overthinking it, as is my specialty, I finally pull myself from the shower, throw clothes on, get a fire going, and make a pot of coffee. About twenty minutes before noon, Ophelia's SUV rounds the bend in front of our house. I laugh. She's so predictable with always being early.

I walk out and stand on the deck, breathing in the fresh winter air. Our land is so beautiful in the snow. We were fortunate enough to find this perfect little slice of heaven on earth for a reasonable price. Our log cabin home sits on five acres, but all the surrounding land is protected and will never be developed. Our closest neighbor is about a mile away. It's the kind of place I always dreamed of living. To be able to raise our child in such a beautiful setting is truly a blessing.

I take in the quietness and serenity of how pure everything feels. The coldness doesn't bother me unless it gets to below zero windchills, which rarely happens in our area.

Ophelia's tires crunch up the driveway and snap me from my reverie. I walk to the steps so that I can help her up if need be.

Before Ophelia is even out of the car, she yells, "For God's sake, Tessa. You shouldn't be out in this cold. Get inside."

I laugh. "I'm fine. I want to make sure you make it in okay."

"I'm fifty-five, not ninety-five!" she says as she walks toward me.

Once she's on the porch, I open my arms to her. As always, the scent of vanilla and cinnamon fills me.

"Come on in! I've got fresh coffee and a fire."

She takes off her coat and boots once she steps inside. "This place is amazing—even better than the last time I saw it. You guys have done such a beautiful job with it!"

I glance around the room. It *is* beautiful. Thankfully, Jonas and I have similar decorating tastes which makes it conflict-free when choosing décor or furniture.

"I love it here so much. Have a seat in front of the fire and warm up. I'll get us coffee. Still cream, no sugar?"

Ophelia nods.

Once I've gotten our coffee, I sit in the chair across from her. "Thanks for coming all the way out here. I'm sorry for the inconvenience."

"Pfft. First off, no worries. I love an excuse to get out of the office once in a while. And second, you're in no condition to drive. What happened?"

I take a deep breath, followed by a drink of coffee. "Well, now that's a story." To hide my shakiness, I twirl my hair around my finger. I recount the events exactly as they unfolded.

Ophelia sits silently and nods for a few moments before responding. "Wow! I can see why you're shaken up. A flash, out of nowhere? And a new color?"

"Yep." I continue to wrap my hair around my finger. "Weird, right?"

"It is. You haven't had any other flashes that you haven't told me about?"

I shake my head. "Nope. Just that one."

Ophelia taps a finger against her lips. "Maybe all the extra hormones your body is producing right now with the pregnancy caused the flash."

I shudder. "You could be right! Does that mean I'll have them through the rest of my pregnancy? Oh, God! I don't want to go through that again!"

"I wish I could answer that, Tessa. But you and I both know that we don't really understand your gift or the way it works. The why's or the how's. As much as I hate to say it, I think it's going to be a matter of waiting to see what happens."

I wrap my arms around myself to quell my shakiness, trying to suppress my urge to vomit.

"Maybe it only happened the one time and you won't experience it again. Try not to borrow trouble by preparing mentally for something that may not happen."

I chuckle despite my uneasiness. "Seriously? That's what I do best, and you know it!"

Ophelia smiles. "Yes, I know you overthink everything, but we need to come up with ways for you to deal with your worries differently. Especially while you're pregnant. Stress isn't good for the baby, or you."

"I know. I've been doing better with that, but not so much right now..."

"Have you been painting?" she asks.

I nod. "Speaking of painting, can you come up to my studio so I can show you my most recent piece?"

"Certainly!"

We make our way upstairs. With all the windows, it's as though we're in the middle of a snow globe with flakes swirling all around outside.

Ophelia gasps. "Wow, what a view! It is gorgeous up here, especially with the snow."

"I know, right? Talk about the perfect place for inspiration."

She walks toward the easel that holds my latest painting. "This is gorgeous, Tessa! More abstract than some of your recent work, but beautiful all the same."

"Thank you! I called this one *Winter Wonderland*. But this is what I wanted to show you. Can you see that I was painting the landscape even though it's abstract?"

Ophelia nods.

I point at the pile of colorful leaves I painted in the stream. "So, I

34

painted those for some reason. There were no leaves in the stream, whatsoever. I thought it was interesting at the time, especially given my color choices. But, with the flash and the accident, now I think there's something more there."

I pause to give her a moment to see if she can figure out what I mean.

She tilts her head to the side and purses her lips as she studies the painting. "I'm not sure I understand."

"Look outside, to see where that spot with the leaves is," I say and point.

Her eyes peruse the area and then stop. She gasps and covers her mouth with her hand. "That's where your car crashed?"

I nod. "Yes. That's *exactly* where something forced my car to land during the wreck. I was pulled to that same spot."

We both stand silently for several moments inspecting the place near the stream compared to the painting.

"I need to go down there. To see what's there and why I was pulled to that particular place. Will you come with me?"

"I understand your desire to go down there, but it's not a good idea with your recent injuries and your pregnancy. You're supposed to be resting, remember?" Ophelia crosses her arms and peers intently at me over the top of her glasses.

"So, is that a yes or a no?" I ask, knowing what she meant but needing her to say it.

"That would be a no. I'm not going down there today, and neither are you," she says sternly. For someone who never had children, she sure has the motherly tone and glare down pat.

I pace back and forth a few times. "Well, in all honesty, I'm going down there with or without you. I need to see what's there."

Ophelia lets out an exasperated sigh. "Dammit, Tessa. You're so stubborn sometimes. Too much for your own good. Jonas would kill me for this but," she pauses and runs her hand through her wild, curly hair, "I'll go with you. I can't have an injured, pregnant woman traipsing down a snowy hill without assistance, now can I?"

I rush to her and throw my arms around her. "Thank you. I really do want you there with me. To be honest, I'm a little scared of what I'm going to find. And you're right, Jonas would kill us both, so let's not tell him unless he needs to know."

Ophelia tsks and shakes her head. "I don't know how I let you talk me into such things."

I head out of the studio and down the stairs. "I'm going to get ready. I'm glad you brought your boots."

OVER THE NEXT FIFTEEN MINUTES, we both bundle up and head down the driveway. We debate about driving down and walking on flatter land, which would've been the easier route. But, for some reason, I feel like this is a journey we need to take on foot. We only slip and slide a little as we make our way down the steep driveway. Then, instead of walking along the road, we cut across the hillside in front of our house that leads down to the stream.

Several deer are tucked in among the trees. This snow-covered world is breathtaking. Ophelia and I walk in silence, taking it all in. My head throbs with the activity, but there's no way I'm going to admit that. I have to get to the stream. I can rest later.

The land finally flattens out as we approach. In the spring and summer, the stream overflows its current banks and fills up the entire little valley. I quicken my pace to make it to the edge where my Jeep ended up. My tires dug into the earth as evidenced by the deep ruts. A bit of the bank has been flattened where my car toppled on it. This is the spot in my painting.

I stoop down and put my hand in the ice-cold water. The chill doesn't have a chance to register before I am bombarded by intense flashes of all colors. Red. Yellow. Blue. Purple. Orange. Green. They hit me rapid-fire, and I fall back, yanking my hand from the stream.

"Tessa!" Ophelia cries out, rushing toward me.

I want to answer, but I can't. The colors stopped as soon as I removed my hand, but they're still coursing through my veins. Throbbing inside my mind. Overtaking my voice. Overpowering me.

Ophelia places her hand on my shoulder. "Tessa, what happened? Are you okay?"

My entire body trembles, but not from the cold. From a knowing deep inside my soul that hasn't yet worked its way into my mind. There's something here, in this water. Something I need to find. Something that's already found me. Questions start to form but then flit away before they become a full thought.

"You're scaring me," Ophelia says, stooping down to meet my gaze. "Tell me what's wrong or I'm calling Jonas." She pulls her cell phone out of her pocket.

I can only utter two words past the tightness in my throat and my chattering teeth. "Flashes. Water."

Ophelia steps away from me, toward the water. She bends down and puts her hand where mine was moments earlier. She stays stooped for a moment, but I can't tell what she's doing. I am unable to focus on anything.

Until she gasps. "Oh my God! We need to call the police!"

CHAPTER 9

I fade in and out of reality, lost within a sea of colors that has once again invaded me. I remember bits and pieces of Ophelia's phone call to the police and words like *bones* and *stream*. I also recall hearing her talk to Jonas, telling him to come home quickly. The whole time I sat on the cold ground, with my arms wrapped around my knees, and rocked back and forth. Images flitted through my brain, but nothing I could grab a hold of.

Several times, Ophelia tried to get me to my feet, to make me walk back up to the house, but I was too stuck in my mind to budge. Now, a flurry of activity surrounds us as police cars and ambulance sirens break up the silence of this snowy day. Even so, I sit.

Two paramedics lift me to a gurney and carry me to the ambulance waiting on the road. Ophelia stays behind to talk to the police. *What did she find? Why are the flashes back?* The two phrases play on repeat in my mind. I don't feel cold—in fact, I'm sweating—chills sweep through my entire body and my teeth chatter. I can't answer the simple questions that the paramedics spew at me. They check my vitals and say words I can't comprehend while covering me with blankets.

Ophelia's voice finally rises above the cacophony, and I try to raise my head to call out to her. I want her to come to me, to tell me what she found. To help me figure out why these damn flashes are back. But my head is too heavy—a jackhammer pounds inside of it. After a moment of talking with her, a paramedic comes back in and elevates my head. I reach out and grab his arm, trying to say Ophelia's name. When the words won't come, I point out the back doors of the ambulance.

"You want her to come in with you?" he asks, and I nod, which sets off an explosion inside my head. "You got it. Ma'am, she's asking to see you. Don't let her move around much or get her too worked up."

"I understand." Ophelia's normally calm voice sounds strained, shaken.

She sits on the bench next to the gurney and squeezes my arm. "You're okay, Tessa."

Her words ring hollow. A single tear escapes down my cheek, which she promptly wipes away.

"What..." My voice trails off before I can finish the sentence with a myriad of possibilities, from what did you find to what is happening to me?

"You need to rest right now. Jonas will be here any minute. We can talk about all of this later."

I try to sit up, furious that she won't tell me more. I need to understand what's going on.

"Flashes," I manage to say.

Ophelia nods. "I know. We'll talk about it later, though."

My eyes plead with her to tell me more, but she turns away, unable to bear the weight of my gaze. She grips my hand, but it seems as though it's to comfort her, ease her fear. We sit silently even though I want to talk, to hammer her for information, to beg, plead, and cry.

"Tessa!" I hear Jonas call out before I see him.

Ophelia drops my hand and moves to meet him at the back doors of the ambulance. She murmurs, but then he interrupts and pushes past her to get to me. He leans down and pulls me into an embrace. My thoughts and racing heart instantly calm in his arms, even though tears continue to stream down my cheeks.

"Are you okay?" he says, leaning back to peer into my eyes. He grabs a tissue and wipes my tears as I shake my head. "Oh, babe. I want to know what happened. Can you talk about it?"

"Touched the water. Flashes. Lots." Those few words exhaust me.

He shudders, then stares out the back door of the ambulance toward the group of police officers near the stream. He sighs. "We'll get through this. The important thing right now is making sure you and the baby are okay. You're going to need to go to the hospital to get checked out."

I shake my head so hard it feels like my brain is going to come out of my ears. "No!" I shout.

He rests a hand on each of my cheeks and looks into my eyes. "I know you don't want to, but you have to with everything today, especially given your recent injuries. Don't worry, I'll be right there with you the whole time. I won't leave you."

His promise calms me some, but I don't want to go back to the hospital. I just got out. *Why did I walk down to the stream today? What was I thinking?*

As clear as day, a voice fills my head. "You needed to see."

"See what?" I yell. I didn't see anything other than the flashes. *Whose voice is in my head?*

Jonas' brow scrunches in confusion. "What do you mean, hon?"

Instead of answering, I shake my head and grip his arm tightly against my chest, as though he's my life preserver in a raging sea. He leans forward and kisses me on the forehead as a paramedic climbs back in and slams the doors closed behind him.

The motion and sirens tell me where we're headed. Back to the hospital.

CHAPTER 10

I've been drifting in and out of sleep, so I do not know how long I've been in the hospital. It could be hours or weeks—I have no sense of time. The colors invade my dreams, along with images just out of reach. When I can finally pry my eyes open, it is dark outside and Jonas is asleep in the chair next to me, clutching my hand. According to the giant clock on the wall it's only six-thirty but, of course, it's black as midnight since it's winter. My mind feels less muddled, but confusion still swarms. They've got me hooked up to an IV.

Part of me wants to wake Jonas so that I'm not left with my own thoughts but, instead, I stare at the ceiling and try to bring some of the visions lurking in my mind to the surface. Something is keeping them buried.

The door slowly creaks open, and Chaundra pokes her head around the corner. She whispers, "You up to visitors?"

I force a smile and a slight nod—even that slight movement makes it feel like my skull is going to split open. She pushes the door the rest of the way open so that she, Liam, and Lily can enter. I don't miss the look exchanged between Chaundra and Lily. Jonas opens his eyes and stretches before I have the chance to question it.

"Oh, hi guys! Hello, beautiful," he says, turning to me. "Sorry I drifted off. Have you been awake long?"

"No, only a few minutes," I say. "Hey, since these three are here, why don't you run down and get us both some coffee? And grab yourself some dinner, you have to be starving." I don't want him in the room for this conversation.

"Are you sure?" he asks, and I nod. "Will you guys stay until I get back?"

"Of course," Chaundra says with a smile while Lily gapes at me.

Liam rushes over to give me a hug before planting himself in the chair in the corner and pulling out his phone. Normally, Lily would've bounded over to give me a hug by now. Something is definitely up.

"Alright. I'll be back soon, and I'll bring you a decaf, my dear," Jonas says with a wink.

The worst part of pregnancy so far is reduced caffeine intake. Thankfully, the doctor said I can still have a cup of regular coffee each day, which is nowhere near enough. As Jonas walks toward the door, Chaundra comes and gives me a hug. Lily moves to the foot of the bed.

"How are you?" Chaundra asks.

I wait to respond until Jonas shuts the door. "I've had better days, that's for sure. The past week has been hell. The important question is what in God's name is going on with you two? I saw Lily's face and the fact that she won't touch me isn't going unnoticed."

Lily peeks through her hair at Chaundra, rather than me. Chaundra gives a slight nod.

"Aunt Tess, your rainbow is back. But it's different."

I gasp, trying to wrap my mind around her words. "What do you mean, it's different? Do you see it Chaundra?"

Chaundra bites her bottom lip, then gives a slight nod. "Maybe we shouldn't talk about this now, though. You've been through enough."

I laugh, but it holds no joy. "Nope, nice try. What's different?"

Chaundra sighs. "You're so damn stubborn! It's almost like it's more muted, darker somehow. And the colors blend together more if that makes sense."

"What you're describing makes logical sense. What I don't understand is why. Can you guys see my face or is it completely consuming me like before?"

Lily chimes in. "If I focus really hard, I can see past the colors to your face. The colors before were pretty. These are kind of scary." Her voice quivers.

Hearing her fear breaks my heart. "Oh, honey! I'm sorry. It's still me. I'm the same person."

"I know," she says quietly, but she doesn't sound sure.

"You guys need to help me figure out what in the world is going on. Why the flashes are back."

"Oh, so you had flashes?" Chaundra asks.

I nod. "A green one the day of the wreck, which was weird because that's a new color. And then I was bombarded by them today when I touched the water in the stream near our house. But I have no idea why."

I talk for what feels like forever explaining the painting, my car being pulled toward the stream, the flashes, Ophelia calling the police, and being brought here.

"I have no idea what they found in the stream, though. Do either of you know?" I ask, hopeful they can give me some information.

Chaundra shakes her head as Lily clears her throat. "I know what they found," she whispers.

"What was it?"

Lily leans against her mom. "Mommy, should I?"

"I don't know what you see, but I know your Aunt Tessa will not let you off the hook without telling her, so go ahead."

Lily stares at the ground and picks at her fingernails. Quieter than a whisper, she says, "Bones. They found bones."

As soon as the words come out of Lily's mouth, memories invade my mind. A boy, no older than thirteen, struggling against a man's hand gripped tightly around his arm. Pushing and pulling, trying to get away. Panic rising in his chest as he realizes what's coming. The man's other hand raised with a large rock, barreling toward his head. The only feature I can make out on the man is his piercing blue eyes, filled with rage, anguish, and need. The boy's thoughts scream out in my mind, *Mommy, Daddy, help me! Please help me!* His shrieks echo inside of my head until the rock finally strikes him, quieting him forever. His fear cracks my heart in two.

I gasp for breath as the images change. Now, I'm in someone's body with their memories as they saw off a leg below the knee and carefully place it in a plastic tote, resting on the forest floor beside him. It's a small leg, and I know, without a doubt, that it's the boy's. I'm now looking through those blue eyes as thoughts rattle my mind. *Accept this sacrifice. Use it to make him whole.* These two thoughts play on a loop as the man works to pull the boy's body into the nearby stream. Bile rises in my throat as I get another glimpse of the boy's face. He is so young and innocent.

"Tessa!" Chaundra's voice snaps me back to now.

I'm hyperventilating. What in God's name is happening? Where did this come from? Even though the questions race through my mind, somewhere deep inside, I know. These memories came from the bones they found in the stream.

"Do you need me to call the nurse?" Chaundra asks.

I shake my head and try to breathe normally. Finally, my breath is calm enough to spit out words. "The bones. His name is Tatum."

Chaundra's mouth drops open, and it seems as though she's struggling to find her voice. Finally, she says, "Can you tell me what you just saw?"

I swallow the lump in my throat. "I'll try. It was like I had memories from two different people. The person being killed. A boy—Tatum. And the man killing him. Tatum was trying to get away, but he couldn't. The man was too strong. He wanted his parents, cried out to them, right before…" I can't finish the sentence. Chaundra squeezes my arm.

"Then, once Tatum was dead, it was like I switched places and went into the killer's mind. Watched him cut off Tatum's leg below the knee and then drag his body into the stream. There was so much blood. He was so young."

Chaundra shudders and shakes her head. "You've never had this before, have you? Where you get flashes from touching *something* instead of *someone*?"

"No. Never."

Lily moves to my bedside. She reaches out and places her hand on the top of my head. She closes her eyes and doesn't say a word. Her entire body starts to tremble, but still, she keeps her hand there. Finally, she falls back against Chaundra and exhales loudly.

"Honey, what happened?" Chaundra wraps her arms around Lily, trying to calm her tremors.

She glances at Chaundra and raises her eyebrows. "It's happening, and it's all different now," she whispers.

"What do you mean, Lily?" I ask, afraid to hear the answer.

She shrugs. "I can't really explain. Your gift has changed."

I reach out and touch Lily's arm, thinking that if I can still get flashes from anyone, it would be her. Nothing happens. There are no flashes whatsoever.

I withdraw my hand as Jonas walks back into the room. "Hi ladies! Did you miss me?"

I quickly plaster a smile on my face. "Always!"

He places a cup of coffee on my bedside table. "Decaf. Sorry but baby demands it." He turns and must catch sight of Lily's ghost-white face. "Did something happen while I was gone?"

The three of us remain quiet and look at each other. Finally, I say, "Just girl talk. Right?"

Lily and Chaundra both nod, but it's not convincing in the least. Liam is so absorbed with whatever game he's playing on his phone that I doubt he's heard a word that's been said.

"Tessa, what's going on? I can tell by Lily's face that it wasn't only girl talk. What happened?"

I sigh. I don't want him to be stuck in my crazy world again. He's been through enough with me. "Please, Jonas. Can we not talk about this right now? Please."

He narrows his gaze, slowly looking at each of us. "You gotta give me something. I can tell you're upset, and Lily looks as though she's seen a ghost. Well... you know what I mean," he says, catching his error since Lily does, in fact, see ghosts.

Which reminds me. "Lily, is Cyle here?"

She nods and points to the other side of my bed. "He's been here the whole time. Aiden too."

I look to where she pointed, but of course see nothing. If I have to get these crazy flashes back, I could at least regain the ability to see my brother, too. Lily has only seen him a few times in the last five years, one of which was at my wedding.

"He says he loves you and congratulations about the baby," Lily says. "He also says that you need to be careful."

Jonas paces. "Careful? About what? Someone tell me what the hell is going on!"

I have to give him something. It's not fair to keep him totally in the dark. "The flashes. They're back."

CHAPTER 11

Soon after my revelation to Jonas, Chaundra and the kids leave, promising to come check in on me tomorrow, be it at home or at the hospital. Lily doesn't give me a goodbye hug for the first time in a *long* time. My heart aches, realizing she's once again terrified of whatever's looming inside of me.

Jonas pounds me with questions after they leave. I give him as little information as possible to keep him from worrying any more than he already is. He confirms with me that Ophelia found bones in the stream and that crime scene investigators will be working outside of our house for a while. He has no more details than that, though. I withhold the knowledge I gained from the images in my mind. Part of me thinks holding back is to protect Jonas, but maybe it's to protect me. I still need to sort that out.

I agree to start seeing Ophelia again on a more consistent basis, as well as painting more often. Jonas is convinced that the flashes aren't here to stay. Or, at least, that's what he's saying to me, probably as terrified as I am of any other possibility.

Jonas eventually drifts off in the chair next to my bed, but I can't get more than a few minutes of sleep at a time. Whenever I start to nod off, one of the images from my flashes jolts me awake. Each one gives me another piece of the puzzle. Even awake, the visions continue to assault me. The boy, Tatum, runs through the woods, trying to get away. His feet slip and slide on the leaf-covered ground. It looks like spring, based on the amount of sunlight streaming through the treetops and the greenness of the foliage. His hot tears burn my cheeks as they fall. The panic rises in my chest at realizing the bad man is so close. His screams slice through the air as despair crushes him, realizing no one can hear him. No one is coming. Tremors quake through Tatum's body as the man's hand finally grabs hold of his arm and an understanding settles over him that he's not going to be okay. Nothing will ever be okay again. I watch through his eyes as he peers into the deep blue eyes of the wicked man, begging and pleading for his life. Calling out for his parents. I watch the rock come down and hit Tatum, sending his world into blackness.

Once Tatum's world goes dark, I'm stuck in the man's brain—the one chasing Tatum, crushing his skull. The only things I can see of the killer are his eyes, from Tatum's point of view, and his hands, which are weathered and worn. His voice echoes in my brain, much as Matthew's did before. His thoughts are jumbled and don't make much sense. They come through in fragments. *Bring you back to me. Make you whole. Pay for my sins. Forgive me, Father.* They play on a loop over and over again as the man's hands strip Tatum's body and clean him using water from the stream as though preparing him for burial. The hands are gentle with him now, unlike when they raised the rock over his head to crush his skull. There's a tenderness and many whispered *I'm sorry's* as he washes each body part carefully. Even though I know it's coming, my entire body goes rigid as the man scrubs Tatum's left leg. I try to stop the rest of the images from coming. But, again, they do. The man struggles against a hand saw, working his way through flesh and bone to remove the leg. I wonder why he doesn't use a chainsaw, but I have a sense that a part of him enjoys this process. Or it's healing for him somehow to physically struggle to remove Tatum's leg. While he is sawing and straining, his thoughts go blank. The actions quiet his raging soul.

A hand on my arm rips me out of that world and back into the present. "Tess," Jonas whispers in a shaking voice, one that emanates fear.

I turn to face him—my entire body quivers. My voice fails me as I try to speak.

"Honey, are you okay?"

I shake my head and let the tears race down my cheeks. I don't even have the words to explain what is happening in my mind. Jonas pulls me into his arms. He gently rocks me back and forth, telling me it will be okay. But he's wrong. It won't. The one thing I know for certain is that this is only the beginning of a new nightmare.

CHAPTER 12

The doctor comes in before sunrise to check on me. I'm so sleep-deprived that I can barely concentrate on what he's saying. I hope Jonas is paying attention because only pieces are making it through the fog in my mind. The one thing I hear that I cling to is that the baby is okay. I rub my stomach, thankful that our little one is nestled safely inside of me, instead of in this cruel world.

Doubts race through my mind as the doctor continues speaking. *How can I raise a child? Especially now that part of my gift has returned. What if he or she is cursed with this same thing? Why would I bring a child into such an evil world where young boys can be chased through the woods and murdered?*

"Tess," Jonas says as he places a hand on my arm. "Did you hear the doctor? You get to go home today."

I shake my head and stare at the ceiling to keep my tears from falling.

"Are you okay, Mrs. McCafferty?" the doctor asks. "Is there a reason you don't feel safe going home?"

"I'm not safe anywhere. You don't understand," I say.

"Would you like your husband to leave the room for this conversation?"

A laugh full of bitterness escapes me. The doctor suspects I'm being abused and that I'm afraid of Jonas. I reach for Jonas' hand and clutch it tightly within my own. "No, Jonas is not hurting me. I can't explain. I'll be fine to go home. I'm sorry."

My laugh is gone, replaced by a sob. The doctor raises his eyebrows, looking back and forth between Jonas and me. Finally, he signs the papers on his clipboard and says a nurse will be in shortly to go over my discharge instructions.

As soon as the doctor leaves the room, Jonas sits on the bed next to me and envelops me in his arms. "I know you're scared and that there's a lot of confusing stuff going on. I promise you're safe, and we'll get through this together. I'll do whatever I need to do. I can take a leave of absence or something."

I shake my head. "Please don't. You've worked so hard to get where you are. I don't want to ruin everything."

Jonas sighs. "How about we take things a day at a time and figure it all out as we go? Sound good?"

I nod and bury my head against his chest. I love this man so much. I hope that whatever's going on in my head doesn't destroy our marriage or hurt our baby.

WITHIN TWO HOURS, we're loaded in the car and headed home. Perhaps I'll feel more at ease in the safety of our house, my sanctuary. I try to focus on the important things and, each time a memory or a voice calls out to me from the flashes, I make a mental list of things I'm grateful for in an attempt to stop them from manifesting. Jonas must notice my quietness, but he lets me be and doesn't force conversation.

My mental exercises work for the most part until we are almost home, and the crime scene tape wrapped around the place I found the bones comes into view. A dozen investigators scour the area around the creek. I gasp as a chill zooms through me.

"I'm sorry they're still here, hon. I know this can't be good for you."

With shuddering breaths, I finally ask the question that's been plaguing me. "Have they... identified him yet?"

Jonas takes a deep breath. "The only thing I know is what I've seen in the paper. They know it's a boy, most likely in his early teens. They haven't released his name or any other details yet. I don't even know if they have that info at this point."

As we pull into the driveway, my eyes are glued down the hill to Tatum's final resting place. A green flash envelops me, and his voice echoes inside my head. *Help them find me. Help me go home!*

"Jonas, we have to help the police. We have to get this boy back to his family."

"For now, let's get you inside, okay?" Jonas says as he opens his car door.

I fling mine open and storm out of the car. "Jonas, his family needs to know. We have to help them. Not later. Now!" I yell.

"How exactly are we going to do that, Tessa? Am I supposed to march up to them and say you know this kid's name? They will not believe you. There's no way to explain it so that they'll understand," Jonas says as tears of frustration and anguish build in his eyes.

"We have to try. Tatum is screaming inside of my head to go home," I say in a whisper and grab his arm. "Please."

Jonas shivers and closes his eyes, his face upturned toward the falling snow. "Okay, okay. Let's get you inside and I'll walk down to ask one of the investigators to come talk with us."

I throw my arms around him. "Thank you."

ONCE INSIDE, Jonas builds a fire while I put on a fresh pot of coffee. After getting a cup, I sit on the couch per Jonas' instructions while he walks down to talk with the investigators. As I wait, I watch the dancing flames and let the voices in my head out to play for a while. To talk and to reveal whatever pieces of information they can.

Tatum's voice is the loudest in my mind—begging, pleading, and crying to go home. For his mommy. My heart fractures listening to his pleas. His pain and fear rumble throughout my body. The man's voice chimes in too every once in a while. Sometimes it's filled with anger, other times with remorse and sadness. It's such a strange sensation because when Matthew was inside of my head, there was no doubt he was pure evil. That his actions were despicable and only to fulfill his sick needs and desires. This man is different. Yet I know he killed this innocent boy.

"Who are you? Why did you do this?" I say out loud, wishing the man in my head could hear me and answer my questions.

Instead of receiving an answer, the front door opens, and Jonas enters with a man who looks to be about my age, along with a blast of cold air.

"Have a seat," Jonas says, pointing toward the family room. "Would you like some coffee?"

"That would be wonderful. It's pretty cold out there."

Jonas heads to the kitchen, and the man leans down, extending his hand to me. "I'm Detective Oliver, one of the crime scene investigators."

"Hi! I'm Tessa McCafferty. Thank you for coming to talk with us."

He chuckles. "Your husband didn't really leave me much choice. And it's nice to get out of the cold for a while."

Jonas hands Detective Oliver a warm mug before taking a seat next to me on the couch.

The detective takes a sip and then says, "So, your husband said you have some information that might be helpful to our investigation."

I wrap my hands around my mug and nod. "I do. I don't know if I can explain it so that it makes sense." I pause and he nods as if to tell me to continue. "I have this gift. It's kind of like being a psychic, but a little different."

Detective Oliver raises his eyebrows and sighs. I'm sure he's encountered his share of whack jobs in this line of work. I can't blame him for doubting.

"You don't have to believe me, but I have information that could be helpful, so please listen without judging. Please," I pause, and he holds out a hand to tell me to continue. "Do you know whose bones you've found?"

"All I can tell you is what we've released to the public. They belong to a male, probably pre-teen to teen. I can't really divulge any more information than that."

I nod. "I know it is a teenage boy named Tatum. I don't know his last name. He was hit in the head with a large rock which killed him. His lower left leg was then removed by a man with blue eyes."

Jonas squeezes my hand so tightly that I'm afraid he's going to break my fingers.

Detective Oliver's eyes narrow, and he takes a long drink of his coffee before speaking. "How do you know this?"

"Like she said, she has a gift that allows her to see these things. She just wants to be helpful." Jonas' voice shakes as he speaks.

"I want to help him get back to his family. He wants to go home," I whisper as another green flash whooshes through me.

Detective Oliver raises his cup to take a drink but his hand trembles, and a bit of the coffee sloshes out onto his pants and the floor. "Shit! I'm sorry about that."

Jonas leaps up to get a towel and hands it to the detective. Once he's cleaned up the spill, he steeples his hands and rests his chin on them while staring into the fire. Several moments of silence pass.

Finally, he clears his throat and turns back to us. "I don't really understand how you know what you do, but I know for a fact some of what you said is true. I will take the rest of the information back to my team. It may prove helpful in identifying the body and the family members. Will you please make yourself available for further questions?"

"Of course," Jonas and I both say at the same time.

"Trust me, I know that a lot of this doesn't make sense. I wish I could make you understand, but I don't even fully grasp it," I say. "I only want to help get this poor child back to his parents."

"Understood," Detective Oliver says as he stands and reaches forward to shake our hands. "I've learned one thing in my life, and that's the fact that I don't have to understand everything. The world is full of strange things, some of which make no logical sense. So, thank you for sharing. But I guarantee we'll need to talk with you again."

I breathe a sigh of relief that at least it seems like he believes me. "Thank you. And we won't be going anywhere. You know where to find us. Please, please, please, help him get home."

The detective nods with a slight smile and heads back out into the winter day.

CHAPTER 13

We have been home for a couple of hours when I'm finally able to convince Jonas I feel well enough to paint. I'm desperate to get some of this madness swirling around in my mind onto a canvas. I may explode if I don't get it out of me. He agrees to get in touch with Chaundra while I paint to see if she can come over to stay with me. Jonas has a heavy class schedule for the next couple of days, and he doesn't want to leave me alone until I feel better. At least that's how he phrases it, but I know he means until we figure out what is going on with the flashes and whether I'm mentally stable enough to be alone. I understand his concern, but I'm also a bit resentful that he thinks I need a babysitter. How quickly I've been thrown right back into the lunacy to which I once was so accustomed.

I smock up and, rather than paint to music as usual, I decide to paint in silence today. Well, not silence exactly, rather to the voices and images in my mind. To let them flow through me and out my paintbrush onto the blank canvas. I have no idea what is going to emerge, so I begin painting with no plan in mind.

I'm quickly lost in a world of color. Voices and images in my mind guide my hands as the paint flies onto the canvas. My mind is not in this room. I work frantically, trying to dump everything out before it vanishes. All that matters right now is getting this piece done. Deep inside, I am cognizant that this painting will help me better understand what's going on. It will be instrumental in coping with both the return of the flashes and the discovery of Tatum's bones.

A gasp from somewhere behind me snaps me back to the studio. "Tess!" Jonas says, his voice shaking.

I whip around. "What's wrong? Are you okay?" I put my palette and brush down and head toward him. His face is ashen, and his mouth hangs open in shock.

"What are you painting?" He points to my easel.

Based on his reaction, I'm terrified to look. Even though I've been working on this piece for hours, I haven't really absorbed what I've painted. I've let my mind guide each stroke without taking any of it in. I keep my gaze fixed on Jonas, terrified to turn around.

"Hon, look at what you've painted. Please." He takes my arm and gently turns me.

I raise my hand to my mouth to stifle a scream. "Oh my God!"

Jonas steers me to the sofa and we both sit. "Is that… Tatum?"

"No, it's not."

"Who then?"

I massage my temples and close my eyes. I have no idea. The painting is more like an abstract portrait of a young boy who looks to be twelve or thirteen. The setting is serene. He stands in a garden, surrounded by flowers. Half of his face is normal, a young boy's face painted clearly. He has sandy blond hair, big brown eyes, cheeks that haven't yet lost that boyishness, still a bit chubby. The other half of his face is a skull. Some of his body is normal in the picture, and other parts of the painting have bones replacing his body parts. His left upper arm a bone, while his lower arm is intact. His entire right arm is made of bone. His midsection is that of a normal child, dressed in a short-sleeved blue shirt and a pair of tan shorts. Beneath the shorts, his whole right leg is made of bone, including his foot. The left leg is normal to the knee and, then below it, only bone. Surrounding him on the ground are bones of various shapes and sizes. In the upper right corner, a blue-eyed man peers out from behind a tree. A tear trails down his left cheek. Those are the eyes of the killer.

What in the hell is this? I push away from Jonas and run to the trash can to vomit. He follows and holds my hair back. I heave until I have nothing left. I'm drenched with sweat even though I'm chilled to the bone. Finally, I collapse against Jonas. He gently leads me to the couch, where he holds me to his chest and strokes my hair.

When my racing heart has calmed, and my breathing has returned to normal, he finally speaks. "Can we talk about this?"

I whisper, "I can try."

"What do you think it is? You said it's not Tatum, so who?"

I shake my head. "I have no idea. It's gruesome though. And did you see the man peeking around the tree? That's the killer. Those are his eyes."

Jonas stands, walks to the painting, and leans forward, squinting. "I hadn't noticed that before. He's crying. What do you think that means?"

"I wish I knew, but I don't," I say and cover my face with my hands.

Jonas comes back to the couch and holds his hand out to me. "How about we let this sit for a while and step away? Maybe things will become clearer once you have some distance."

"That's a great idea."

I need to get away from this gruesome half-boy, half-skeleton, and those blue eyes that belong to a killer. I grab Jonas' hand and head downstairs, away from the ugliness of my mind.

AFTER EATING two peanut butter and pickle sandwiches, which fulfill so many of my pregnancy cravings, Jonas and I snuggle on the couch where he watches movies, and I listen since I'm not supposed to have too much screen time. It's a helpful distraction from the images in my mind and the painting upstairs, waiting for my interpretation or under-standing. I don't realize Jonas has dozed off until I hear his quiet snores. I slip out of his embrace and tuck the blanket around him. After turning down the volume on the television, I head upstairs. I need to get back to figuring out what in the world I've painted. I grab a note-book and pen from my desk to write down some of the thoughts and feelings the painting evokes in me.

I flip on the light and feel nauseated as soon as I catch a glimpse of the picture. *Get control of yourself. Stop it!* I pull a chair close to the canvas and force myself to study it, even though I desperately want to look away. I take a deep breath and write.

> *Bring you back*
> *I'm sorry*
> *Forgive me*
> *Atonement*
> *Heartbreak*
> *Seven to go*
> *Come Home*
> *Sacrifice*
> *Put in it the pieces, every good piece, the thigh and the*
>   *shoulder; fill it with choice bones.*
> *Choice Bones*
> *Choice Bones*
> *Choice Bones*
> *Ezekiel*

My breathing becomes shallow, and I feel light-headed. I toss the pen on my desk and read through the list. None of it makes sense. Ezekiel—is that the boy's name? Or the killer's? And that sentence—what does it mean? It sounds familiar but I have no idea why.

I throw the notebook to the floor and bury my face in my hands. I don't know what any of this means. Why is this happening again? Why now when I'm pregnant and want to just enjoy this phase of my life? Why?

CHAPTER 14

Surprisingly, I manage to get a good night's sleep despite my inner turmoil. There's a knock on the door as Jonas and I finish our breakfast. My nerves are so frazzled that I jump at the intrusive sound. Jonas rushes to answer.

"Hello, friends!" Chaundra says, way too cheerfully. She scurries over and squeezes my shoulder. "I come bearing gifts."

She puts a huge pan of lasagna, a salad, and garlic bread on the table.

"I thought you all could use some dinner. We need to keep that baby fed, don't we?"

I can't help but smile. "Thank you. You know I love your lasagna! This will be perfect for dinner tonight."

"Yes, I do. Plus, I wanted to check on you. I thought you could use some girl time," she says as she pours herself a cup of coffee.

"Uh, that's my cue to leave. I'll go do some work," Jonas says. He plants a kiss on top of my head. "I'll be upstairs in my office. Yell if you need me."

Chaundra and I sit in silence until we hear the office door close. "How are you? You look rough."

I rub the back of my neck, trying to loosen up the muscles. "Are the investigators still outside?" I point to the window. I haven't been able to bear checking for myself.

"Yes. Have you heard anything?" she asks.

"I talked to a detective and told him about Tatum and the man with the blue eyes. He seemed to believe me, which caught me off guard."

Chaundra sighs. "Let's hope they take it seriously. I know a lot of cops deal in black and white and don't believe in unknown things, like our gifts. So, back to you."

How am I? That's a loaded question—one I'm not sure how to answer.

I blow out a breath. "I'm a mess. I need them to find Tatum's family. Get him home. You gotta see this screwed up painting I did."

I rise, and Chaundra follows behind, up the stairs to the studio. She heads straight to my easel and studies it in silence. I sit on the couch and watch her, trying to figure out what's going through her head. Finally, after what feels like hours, she joins me on the couch.

"Well, that's pretty disturbing. Who's the boy?"

I shrug. "I wish I knew. Did you see the eyes?"

She nods. "I'm assuming that's the killer. But he's crying, which is weird. Any ideas?"

I hand her the notebook where I jotted down my thoughts. She reads the list and gasps.

"What's wrong?"

She pulls out her phone and begins typing something in. She holds up a finger, telling me to wait a minute.

"I knew it. I thought that part of what you wrote looks familiar, and here's why. It's in the Bible. Listen, in Ezekiel 24:4 *Put in it the pieces, Every good piece, the thigh and the shoulder; fill it with choice bones.*"

I grab her phone. "Let me see that!" It's right there in front of me. A scripture that fits what was going through my head. "Wow! So, what does it mean?"

"I don't know. But it's kind of applicable to the painting. Some parts of the boy are whole and other parts are bone. The question is why? And, looking at what you painted, it seems the bones are of different shapes and sizes—like pieces of a puzzle that don't necessarily go together." She heads to the painting and points. "Like look at this left upper arm, it's a daintier bone than what makes up the right arm. Even these bones in the right arm don't seem to match per se. It's as though pieces of different people are put together to make up missing parts of this boy."

I creep closer to the painting and see exactly what she means. "You're absolutely right. Weird, huh? And why?"

The doorbell rings before she can answer. I peep out the window but can't see the porch from this angle. A large crew is still searching the area by the stream.

"Tess! Can you come down?" Jonas yells.

Chaundra and I go downstairs to find Detective Oliver and a woman seated at the kitchen table.

"Hi. This is my friend, Chaundra Raines." I extend my hand to the female. "And I'm Tessa McCafferty."

"I'm Detective Garson."

Detective Oliver rises and extends his hand to Chaundra. "And I'm Detective Oliver. We have a few questions for you, Mr. and Mrs. McCafferty."

"Is it okay if Chaundra stays?"

The detectives exchange a look and finally Detective Garson says that it's fine. We all sit at the table.

"Detective Oliver filled me in on your conversation the other day and we have some follow-up questions. How long have you and Mr. McCafferty lived on this property?"

Jonas answers. "We've lived here since we got married two years ago."

"And did you own the property prior to then, or how did you come into possession of it?"

I shake my head. "We got a substantial amount of money as a wedding gift from my parents. We used it to buy this property and build our cabin."

Detective Oliver jots something in his notebook. "When is the first time you saw this land?"

Jonas and I look at each other, trying to remember. "My parents wanted us to be able to move into the house as soon as we were married, so we bought the property beforehand. I believe it was August 2018 when we first saw the land. We purchased it in late September and construction started in late October."

Again, Detective Oliver scratches notes down.

"What made you look at this particular property?" the female detective asks.

"Our realtor showed us several locations throughout the area. We knew this was the one for us the moment we saw it. It's protected land on three sides, so we knew there'd be no other construction in the vicinity," Jonas says.

Detective Garson nods. "Tell us about Tatum. Where did you come up with this name?"

I take a deep breath. I should've known that my answers to Detective Oliver wouldn't suffice. "It's hard to explain, but I kind of have this gift. It used to come when I'd touch people, I'd pick up pieces of them. I lost this ability about five years ago during the whole incident with Matthew James, which you probably know about." I pause, and both detectives nod. "Anyway, after that, my gift went away. Then, out of nowhere, it came back. I reached into the water the other day, and my brain flooded with images. Part of what I saw showed me that the bones belong to a boy named Tatum. And that the killer has blue eyes."

A hush falls over the room. The only sound is the scratch of Detective Oliver's pen as he presumably writes down everything I say.

Finally, Detective Garson leans across the table and peers directly into my eyes. "See, the thing is, you were right about a couple of things you shared with my partner here. You told him the lower left leg of our victim would be missing. Exactly how did you know that?"

"I saw it in my mind. I saw him die. I watched the killer remove the lower left leg."

Detective Garson's brow furrows. "That doesn't make any sense."

"I know," I say, barely louder than a whisper.

"Help me understand," she says with a raised voice, now laced with frustration.

Jonas forcefully pushes his chair back and stands. "Whoa! You need to calm down. If you're going to question my wife, perhaps we should get an attorney. She wants to help you figure out who this boy is and find the killer. That's it. She's been through hell lately, and she's pregnant, as you can see. So, unless you can keep it calm and civil, I'm going to need you to leave."

Detective Garson stiffens, and Detective Oliver places his hand on her arm. "We understand, Mr. McCafferty. We're trying to make sense of all this. Thank you for allowing us into your home," he says as Detective Garson finally relaxes and slouches back in the chair.

"If I may," Chaundra says. "I am a psychic who has helped with several cases locally. You can talk to Officer Morel and Detective Stanley to check me out. I know it's hard to accept that people like me, and Tessa, exist in the world, but we do. Tessa isn't a psychic, but she has the ability to pick up pieces of other people. It doesn't necessarily make sense to her, to me, or to you, but it is what it is. You need to decide if you want to let her help you or not. If not, that's fine and good luck. She did nothing wrong other than touch water where bones happened to be."

She pauses and takes a drink of her coffee. "Ask yourself... does what she told you line up with what you've found so far? If the answer is yes, regardless of what you believe or don't believe, then have a little faith in what she's saying. Just go with it and figure out who this boy is. Get him home."

A slight, lopsided smile pulls up the corners of Detective Oliver's mouth while Detective Garson's eyes narrow and she crosses her arms over her chest.

"We can't divulge anything that's not been made public yet, but we have located what we believe to be the boy's family. Testing still needs to take place to confirm this, but about ten years ago, a boy, Tatum Wright, went missing from the area. Going with what Mrs. McCafferty told us, we are closely looking at that case."

I take a deep breath, thankful that they've listened to at least a little of what I've said. Now that I've heard his name, I have zero doubt that it is, indeed, Tatum Wright, and they are going to get him back to his family.

"Speaking of which... how long have you and Mr. McCafferty lived in Chandlersville?" Detective Garson asks.

"I've lived here for about ten years," I say.

"I did my PhD program at Cardell, so a little over eleven years," Jonas adds.

"Interesting," Detective Garson says, and raises her eyebrows.

Jonas slams his hand on the table. "No, not interesting. We have nothing to do with this other than we bought property where a young boy's bones were found. That's it. The end."

"Understood," Detective Oliver says. "We'll be going for now. Thanks for answering our questions." He stands, but Detective Garson stays seated with a scowl so vicious that it looks like she could attack at any moment. It'd be laughable if we weren't in such a tense and serious situation. She obviously has more she wants to say.

Without giving her the chance, Detective Oliver taps her on the shoulder, and she rises. He flashes a smile at us and offers another thank you as they leave. As soon as the door shuts behind them, we all release a collective breath.

"Well, that was interesting!" Chaundra says. "What do you think?"

"I'm pissed," Jonas says with his fists clenched at his sides. "How dare they come in here and insinuate that either of us had something to do with this? Tessa doesn't need any more stress."

I wrap my arm around him and lean my head on his shoulder. "It's okay, Jonas. I'm difficult to understand, that's for sure. At least it sounds like they may have figured out who Tatum is. I'm relieved about that. If going through this crap the past couple of days helps me get that poor child home, then it's all worth it."

Jonas kisses me on the cheek. "I love you. You're a beautiful and kind person."

"I love you too. Now, I want to look up the case about Tatum Wright. You wanna help Chaundra?"

"Sure, as long as you think you're up to it."

I grab a water bottle and the jar of pickles as Chaundra picks up my laptop.

"Well, ladies, I'm back to work. Let me know if you need me."

"Love you, babe. Thanks for looking out for me," I say as he heads upstairs.

"Always!"

As soon as Jonas is gone from sight, a devious smile beams across Chaundra's face.

"What's that look for?" I ask.

"You know who I want to look into besides Tatum?"

I shake my head. "No idea."

"Detective Oliver. He's handsome! I need to know more about him."

I laugh. "He wasn't wearing a ring."

"Yeah, I know. I've got some checking to do."

I chuckle. Chaundra's reaction gives me hope that maybe some good could come from this devastation, besides getting Tatum home. She hasn't dated anyone since I've known her, and the thought of a possible budding romance between her and the detective brings me joy. She needs a little love in her life.

CHAPTER 15

C haundra and I find several news articles about the missing boy, Tatum Wright. After seeing his picture, I have no doubts left that he is the boy in the stream. His face is the one that has invaded my mind. His screams echo in my head. That poor, poor child. Knowing how he met his end sickens me.

Apparently, Tatum lived less than two miles from where we now live. It was a spring day, March nineteenth, 2010, and he was cutting through the woods between his house and his best friend's, who lived about a mile away from him. His parents were quoted in several articles saying it was something he'd done hundreds of times before, that those woods were his second home. Tatum never made it to his friend's house. His friend's mother called after two hours to check on Tatum, to see why he hadn't made it. His parents reported him missing immediately and started searching the woods. They knew something was horribly wrong when they found his shoe and a swatch of his green shirt on a tree branch.

Extensive searches of the area were held for weeks after he went missing, but nothing else turned up, and there were no leads. Other than an occasional interview with his family or a memorial held each year on the date of his disappearance, there was no other information. It was as if Tatum vanished into thin air. I know, however, that he didn't. He ended up hit in the head with a rock, killed, and had his leg sawed off before being dragged to the stream in front of our house.

We both scour news clips and articles to see if they ever named any suspects, but they only stated a few times they were interviewing persons of interest. No names were given. No pictures to compare to the visions in my mind.

When my frustration grows and my head starts to pound again, I slam the laptop shut and toss it onto the couch next to me. Chaundra grabs it and, with a grin, suggests we switch gears by looking up Detective Oliver, which is a welcome and needed break. She finds him on Instagram, Twitter, and Facebook and follows him on all three. He almost instantly follows her back. From studying his profiles, it appears he is unmarried. Before Chaundra leaves, she sends him a direct message, asking if he'd like to meet for coffee. He quickly agrees, and they set up a coffee date for tomorrow. Of course, she promises to call me with all the details as soon as it's over.

I'M LYING IN BED, trying to decide between getting up or sleeping a few more hours, when the smell of coffee wafts in the air. Decision made! As I throw on my robe and slippers, I realize I was actually able to sleep soundly last night. Knowing Tatum would soon be returned to his family allowed me to be at peace. Perhaps that's why the flashes came back—so this family could get some closure.

Jonas sits at the kitchen island, scrolling through his phone and drinking a cup of coffee. I tiptoe over and wrap my arms around him from behind.

"Shit! You scared me!" Jonas says and shuts off the screen on his phone.

"Sorry," I say as I nuzzle his neck. "Good morning! That delightful smell woke me up. One cup won't hurt, right?"

Jonas sighs and leans into my arms. "You know the answer to that. One cup is fine."

I squeeze him. "Yay!" I kiss him on the cheek and head to the coffeepot.

"What time is Chaundra's coffee date today?"

I glance at the clock. It's nine-thirty. "Actually, right about now, I think. Chaundra is so excited."

Jonas smiles. "Yeah, I could tell. He seems like a nice guy. I'm sure she'll give you all the details."

"Uh, she better!" I sit next to him at the island. "What's your plan today?"

"I got my TA to cover class, so I'll be working from home. You?"

"Not much other than enjoying every moment of this cup of coffee," I say and take another drink.

"Tess, a cup of coffee, not a carafe!" He grabs the extra-large cup from my hands and dumps half of it into a normal sized cup.

I stick out my bottom lip in a pout. "You weren't supposed to notice that. Meanie."

"We don't want our baby coming out already addicted to coffee, do we?"

I shake my head. "I suppose you're right, although I kind of hate you for it."

He takes the cup from me and puts it on the counter. He leans forward and kisses me passionately, slipping a hand inside my robe.

"Do you still hate me?" he whispers against my ear, circling his tongue around the lobe, which he knows drives me crazy in a good way.

I stand and guide him to the bedroom. Coffee and work can wait.

BREATHLESS, we collapse back against the pillows after spending some quality time together between the sheets.

After a few moments, Jonas says, "Since you didn't get to finish your *one* cup of coffee for the day, I'll go make some fresh and then I must get to work. No more distracting me with that body of yours."

"Are you complaining? Because it seemed like you rather enjoyed yourself."

"You know I'm teasing. Hell, you could convince me to blow off the rest of the day if you promise more of that." He laughs.

"If I didn't need coffee so badly, I would take you up on that offer, but baby and I need our caffeine."

He throws on a t-shirt and heads out the door. "Your caffeine is on its way, my precious."

I grab my phone from the nightstand and head downstairs after him. I'm so relaxed and satisfied I could just stay in bed. God, I love Jonas.

My phone vibrates in my hand before I've reached the kitchen. It's a text from Chaundra.

OH MY GOD! CALL ME ASAP!

I can't help but smile as I sit at the island where my perfect cup of heaven awaits.

"Wow! I must have done a really good job if you're still smiling," Jonas says.

I laugh. "You always do, but I'm smiling about this text from Chaundra. I need to call her."

Jonas clutches his hands to his heart. "You crush me."

I pull him close and kiss him. "Look at me! That was amazing. I would take you back to bed right this minute, in fact, but I need coffee and you need to work. Trust me, my whole body is smiling right now because of you."

A slight blush rises to his cheeks, which is so damn cute and charming. I can still make his cheeks redden.

The corners of his mouth lift in a smirk. "Call Chaundra. Come tell me what she has to say. We can do that again later if you'd like."

"Absolutely, Professor McCafferty." I bat my eyelashes and pucker my lips, attempting to look seductive.

He kisses me on the cheek and heads to his office. I take a big swig of coffee and dial Chaundra.

"Oh my god! I'm in love!" she squeals into the phone.

I laugh. "Good date?"

"Uh... yeah. We've got a real dinner date scheduled for this weekend, if you don't mind Lily hanging out with you. Liam has a birthday party to go to, or I'd just let them hang out at home."

"Of course, she's always welcome. So, tell me about Detective Oliver!"

"I thought he was sexy in his work get-up, but, boy, oh boy, was I wrong. He showed up in tight-fitting jeans and a shirt that showed off his muscles. I was practically panting. I think it's been too long since I've been with a man. I truly was ready to drag him off to some seedy motel and jump his bones."

"You need to get laid, girlfriend. Speaking of which, I just had delightful sex," I say, and can't help but smile.

"No fair! I'm dying over here," she pauses. "Anyway, Detective Oliver's name is Micah. He is most definitely single, no children, been married and divorced for six years, and did I mention he's sexy?"

"You may have indicated that," I say with a laugh. "Does he seem like a nice guy? Is he okay that you have kids?"

"He seems really nice, which probably means he's too good to be true. He's lived in this area his whole life. Comes from a long line of cops and a big family—six kids total. He would love to have the same. He's my age, so we best be getting busy with making some babies, huh?"

I laugh so hard that I spit coffee out all over the counter. "Whoa, there. Slow down a bit."

"Don't ruin my fun! You know I'm kidding... partly. Anyway, can Lily come over Saturday evening and spend the night in case I get lucky?"

"She can come for as long as you need her to."

"Thank you, Tess. I may need your help picking out an outfit and getting ready. It's been such a long time since I've had a real date."

"I'm so excited for you. You need this." After a moment, I say, "Did the psychic thing come up at all?"

"Actually, yes. He's a believer. He said he's encountered enough in his lifetime to know that not everything makes sense and that people have extraordinary abilities beyond what others can see," she says and laughs. "He even asked if I had a vision of a handsome man named Micah Oliver crossing my path."

"I love that. Have you had that vision?"

"No, but trust me, I'm having all kinds of visions of Micah Oliver now. Even though most of them have nothing to do with being psychic."

I shake my head and stifle a giggle. "Oh, Chaundra. I want this to work out for you."

"You have no idea how much I need this to work out. Okay, I gotta run. We'll talk before Saturday and make a plan for Lily."

"Sounds good. Love you!"

"Love you, too!"

I have the biggest smile on my face when I hang up. I've never seen or heard Chaundra be so giddy. I hope and pray this works out for her. After the hell Adam put her through, she needs a good man.

CHAPTER 16

It's impossible for me to relax, which I've been instructed to do as much as I can because of my concussion. What the hell are people supposed to do if they can't read, watch TV, or play on their phones?

"Hey, hon! What'cha doing?" Jonas says as he leans over the back of the couch.

"Looking through baby name websites. I know I'm not supposed to be on my phone too much, but geez, I'm bored," I say.

"Any good names?"

"Well, for a girl, I love Gabriella and Alayna."

"I really like both of those. I also love the name Zoe. What about for a boy?" Jonas plops down on the couch and pulls my feet onto his lap.

"So far, Gabriel, Zander, Josiah, and Alexander," I say and pause. "No matter what, I'd like the middle name to be some form of Cyle... girl or boy."

Jonas squeezes my foot. "I am one hundred percent in agreement with that. And those boy's names rock. I notice you stayed as far away from the letter c as possible."

I laugh. "That I did. I didn't even look at any names that start with that dreaded letter. So, if it's a girl, do you think we should stick with Cyle as the middle name or maybe Cylie?"

"Either works for me. It's entirely up to you, my love," Jonas says and pulls his phone out of his pocket. "Did you happen to see the news update?"

I shake my head. "About?"

He pushes a few buttons on his phone and then hands it to me. "They found his family."

I gasp and read the article. They identified the bones found in our creek as the missing boy, Tatum Wright. The article quotes his parents, Monica and Jared Wright, as saying they're relieved to finally be able to bring their son home, where he belongs. The article goes on to state they are seeking any and all information about what happened to Tatum and pleading for people to call in with any relevant tips. It doesn't mention his missing leg bone but says that local police wonder if it may be linked to some other cases of missing children around the state.

A tear falls down my cheek. "I'm glad they found his parents and got him home. But how heartbreaking." My hand goes to my stomach. "I can't even imagine their pain."

Jonas rests his hand on top of mine. "I know. Me either. I'm glad you could help get him back where he needed to be. Maybe now your flashes will end."

"God, I hope so. If I went through all this to help that poor family, then I'm grateful it happened. I really don't want any more of those images in my head, that's for sure," I say and pause. "But I'm curious about why they think it could be linked to other cases. Maybe the missing bone?"

Jonas shrugs. "Maybe. Let's hope if it is, they find the sick bastard that did this."

"Indeed. Oh, and by the way, Chaundra's date with Detective Oliver went well today. They're going to dinner this weekend and Lily will be coming over to spend the night."

Jonas smiles. "Good. Chaundra needs to have a break once in a while. I hope it works out for her."

"Me too. Do you have to go to work tomorrow?"

He shakes his head. "My TA is covering the rest of this week, so I can stay right here with you. I've got enough grading to keep me busy."

"Professor McCafferty, your students will be so disappointed that you're not in class." I sit up and straddle his lap, which isn't easy with this baby bump. "Your wife, however, has some plans for you."

Jonas kisses me deeply and makes me forget all about baby names, missing boys, and disappointed students.

~

SINCE JONAS DOESN'T HAVE to go into the office, he and I both sleep in on Thursday morning. My ringing phone finally rouses me around ten.

I answer, seeing that it's Chaundra. "Good morning," I say, stifling a yawn.

"Were you still in bed? I'm sorry," she says.

"It's okay. I've slept late enough. Jonas has the week off, so we are spending as much time in bed as possible," I say and rub my hand down his bare chest.

"Good for you. I'm jealous. I need some time in bed with a sexy man," she chuckles.

"Oh, dear lord. Detective Oliver isn't gonna know what hit him, is he?"

"Speaking of the sexy detective, that's why I'm calling. He has to cover shifts this weekend and wanted to see if we could do dinner tonight instead. Lily doesn't have school tomorrow, so could she come over and spend the night?"

"It sounds like he couldn't wait for his date with you! And of course. Is she okay with it? She got a bit weirded out in the hospital. Liam is welcome, too." Jonas is now fully awake and kissing my neck. This man's appetite is insatiable, I swear.

"She's okay. We've talked about it, and she knows you're still you. I told her you'd probably be much better now that they located Tatum's family. You saw that, right? Oh, and Liam already made plans to stay with a friend."

"Hold on," I say and cover the mouthpiece of my phone. "Jonas, give me a minute. I'll be all yours in a second." I return my attention to the phone. "Sorry… someone's feisty this morning. Yes, I did see that, and I'm doing much better. Tell her we'll have fun. I think I'm allowed to watch a little bit of TV now, so we'll watch some movies and paint our nails."

"Awesome. I'll bring her over at five. In the meantime, spend some quality time with Jonas," Chaundra giggles.

"Sounds good!" I hang up and turn toward Jonas.

"Have I ever told you how sexy you are pregnant?" he says, running his hand over my belly.

"I'm not sure how you see it that way, but I'll take it," I laugh and lean in to kiss him.

He breaks our kiss. "I don't know how you can't. You're sexy as hell. Now, let's have a little morning lovin' to get this day off to the right start."

I could get used to starting my morning like this. Pregnancy has done crazy, unexpected things to my libido. I bury myself under the covers, where Jonas is ready and waiting for me.

CHAPTER 17

I hear the crunch of Chaundra's tires on the gravel at four, an hour earlier than she said she'd be here. I walk out onto the deck to greet her and Lily, which is a good thing because Chaundra's arms are loaded down with clothes.

"Are you moving in?" I ask as I grab an armful to help ease her load.

"I need your help! I can't decide what to wear. Do you know how long it's been since I've been on a date?" Chaundra asks, breathlessly.

"Let's get inside and ease you of this burden. Hi, kiddo! I'm glad you're here," I say and lean over the bundle in my arms to kiss Lily on the head.

"Mommy's a disaster!" Lily laughs.

"Yeah, I can see that. We'll get her taken care of, won't we, Lil?"

We dump the clothes into a pile on the table, and Chaundra starts frantically digging through it. "Sit down and take a breath, okay? We'll get this sorted out."

Jonas' footsteps pound down the stairs. "What in God's name? Are you two moving in?"

I can't help but laugh. "That's what I asked. Chaundra is having a bit of trouble deciding what to wear on her date."

"I will never understand women. Don't you know we don't notice things like that?"

"Oh, you guys notice when things fit in all the right places. I guarantee that," Chaundra says, plopping in the chair.

Jonas holds up his hands in defeat. "Okay, you may have me on that point. Lily, do you want to hang out with these two or do you want to play with my VR? I've got some really cool, new games."

Without hesitation, Lily bounds toward Jonas. "Your VR, definitely. I've been dealing with Mom stressing out all day!"

"Great. Ladies, Lily and I have a date with virtual reality. Let us know when it's safe to come back."

"Have fun," I call out as they quickly make their escape up the stairs. "Do you need some coffee or a glass of wine?"

Chaundra shakes her head. "I don't have time. Look at me. I'm a hot mess! He's going to pick me up at six. Help!"

"We have plenty of time. This reminds me of the days when you would help me get ready for dates with Jonas," I say. "And you are one hundred percent correct, Jonas absolutely noticed my curves hiding underneath my outfits."

She laughs and nods. "Part of the problem is I have no idea where he's taking me. He said to wear whatever I want. Doesn't he know how unhelpful that is?"

"Men can be clueless sometimes, that's for sure. But a surprise date is pretty romantic."

Redness creeps into Chaundra's cheeks. "I know, right?"

"Well, let's find something that's both sexy and comfortable!"

For the next hour and a half, we work together to get her ready. I help do her hair and make-up and we find an outfit that emits the right amount of sexiness and comfort after digging through her pile of clothes and my closet. She looks hot. It's so weird to see her all made up because normally she's dressed in leggings and a t-shirt without makeup and her hair in a messy bun.

"Lily! Come kiss me goodbye," she yells up the stairs.

Little and big feet pound down the stairs in unison.

"Mommy!" Lily gasps. "You look beautiful!"

"She does, doesn't she?" I say.

"You look very nice, Chaundra. I'm sure the detective will be pleased," Jonas adds.

"Thank you, guys. Tess, I couldn't have pulled myself together without your help." She pulls me into a hug, then stoops to make eye contact with Lily. "You, be good. I'll come get you tomorrow afternoon. Listen to Aunt Tessa and Uncle Jonas. And go to bed when they tell you to."

"I will, Mommy! Promise!"

I walk Chaundra to the door and lean close to whisper before she steps out onto the porch. "Hoping you get lucky tonight. I think you're about to."

She raises a hand to her chest in mock surprise. "A lady never puts out on the first date. But I never did claim to be a lady." She laughs. "Call if you need me, but I hope you don't."

I wave and shut the door against the winter chill.

"Alright, guys. We're making homemade pizza!" I turn to Lily and Jonas.

"Sounds delicious!" Jonas whoops.

WE SPEND the evening crafting and devouring our delicious homemade pizzas, watching *Beauty and the Beast,* eating ice cream sundaes with all the fixings, and then giving each other manicures and pedicures. Jonas even joins in to get a hot wax treatment on his hands and feet. It is the perfect night.

Watching Jonas interact with Lily only makes my excitement grow about having a baby. Despite my anxieties, we will be great parents. Thankfully, there's none of the weirdness remaining on Lily's part that was there in the hospital. It's just a normal night of fun.

At about one in the morning, while watching *The Little Mermaid,* Lily's head nods against my shoulder.

"Hey, Jonas," I whisper and point at her while mouthing the words, "Is she asleep?"

He nods. "Let's give her a few minutes and then I'll carry her upstairs."

I give him a thumbs up and wrap my arm around Lily. I can definitely get used to having a child around all the time. My eyes grow heavy with her deep breathing and sleeping sighs.

Jonas flips through the channels before choosing a show on The History Channel, and my eyes finally drift closed.

"HON. Let's go up to bed," Jonas says, and I bolt upright, feeling beside me for Lily.

"I already carried her up. I put her in your studio on the pullout."

I rub my eyes and nod. "Thanks, hon. Sorry I fell asleep. Your history shows bore the crap out of me."

Jonas laughs and pulls me up. "I know. C'mon sleepyhead."

"What time is it?" I ask amid a yawn.

"It's three. I can't seem to turn off those shows you find so boring."

I fall into bed and curl up to Jonas. I'm back to sleep within seconds. It seems like I just drifted off when a loud, shrill scream yanks me awake. Jonas bolts out of bed and pulls on his sweats. We both run toward the studio and Lily's shrieks. She stands in front of the painting of the little boy made from bones. Tears stream down her face, and her entire body trembles.

I run to her. "Lily, it's okay. It's okay." I pull her against me and shield her face from the picture. It does nothing to calm her quivering or screeches.

"What can I do?" Jonas shouts.

"I don't know. Lily, honey, calm down. What's wrong? What can we do?"

She looks into my eyes and pulls away from my hug, clutching my hand tightly in hers while pointing at the painting. "Look."

At that moment, another flash like lightning courses through my entire body, electrifying every nerve ending and seeming to magnetize Lily's hand to mine. Her mind to mine. Images and sounds bombard me. A young black boy lying dead in a pile of leaves, his left arm removed. A girl with auburn hair and lifeless eyes lying on the forest floor with her left foot gone. Another dead girl with short brown hair, with her lower right arm removed, thrown into a ravine like trash. Then a boy with sandy brown hair with his entire right arm gone. Two more boys and a girl that all blend together in my mind, each missing either their entire right leg and foot or parts of it. A boy whose hair has been shaved so that part of his skull can be removed, his brain showing through the right side of his head.

Names echo in my mind. Dominick. Chase. Anna. Scott. AJ. Leah. Stephanie. David. Tatum. They play on repeat, along with the images —a thunderous chorus in my mind.

A man's voice rises above the cacophony. *Forgive me. I will make you new. A broken spirit dries up the bones. I will carry your bones up from here. O, dry bones, hear the word of the Lord. Rise up. You will be whole. I will make you whole. I will fix what is broken. Forgive me. Forgive me.*

I cannot see the man's face, but his pain, agony, and heartbreak consume me, crush my soul. I need to pull free from Lily's hand. I need this to stop. But I can't. I'm stuck. Names, screams, the man's chants play over and over on a loop in my mind. I can no longer hear Lily's wails. I'm no longer in this room. I'm in the middle of the forest with bloody hands holding a bone. I have become the blue-eyed man who did awful things to these poor, innocent children.

Suddenly, my hand and Lily's are forced apart. I fall to the ground where darkness and quiet engulf me.

CHAPTER 18

"Tessa, can you hear me?" A voice calls out to me from somewhere.

I force my eyes open. It's Chaundra, leaning down to meet my gaze. Somehow, I'm now sitting on the chaise in my studio with Lily curled up next to me.

Jonas stoops next to her. "There you are. I didn't know what to do to help Lily calm down, so I called Chaundra."

"Mama," Lily says and hoists herself into Chaundra's arms. Her entire body quivers.

My eyes frantically search the studio for the painting, but it's gone from the easel. "Where is it?"

Jonas sits next to me and pulls my hand to his. "I moved it for now. Can you make it downstairs?"

Tears stream down my cheeks. "I... don't know."

Chaundra carries Lily from the room as Jonas hoists me to my feet. "Let's try to go downstairs so we can all talk. Okay?"

My legs are so wobbly that I must cling to him for support. Jonas and I carefully make our way down the stairs where Lily and Chaundra are cuddled on the couch and Detective Oliver is seated at the kitchen table.

"I hope it's okay that I brought him with me. We were... uh...

together when I got the call. I drank a bit too much wine, so he offered to drive me."

I nod, unable to force any words out. Nothing makes sense. Nothing matters. Jonas leads me to the sofa where we both sit, and he pulls me close to him.

"Do you need anything, Tessa, Lily?" Detective Oliver asks.

"Water," I whisper and Lily nods.

"There's bottled water in the fridge," Jonas says.

Detective Oliver brings a bottle to each of us. "I can step outside if you'd like. I don't want to intrude." His comment is directed toward me.

"It's fine, detective. You can stay," I say.

"Please, call me Micah."

I nod. Silence falls like a heavy blanket.

Finally, Chaundra breaks it. "What happened?" She looks between Lily and me, but neither of us speaks.

Jonas clears his throat. "We put Lily to bed in the studio and she woke up screaming. We both ran into the room where she was standing in front of the painting Tess did the other day. She and Lily linked hands and then… I'm not sure what happened. Tess?"

"Another lightning flash. And so many kids. Those poor, poor children." Sobs overtake me.

"What kids?" Jonas gently prods.

"The man killed them. He cut off parts of their bodies," Lily declares.

Detective Oliver rises from the table and comes to sit on a chair in the family room. "What do you mean, Lily?" he asks.

She shakes her head and burrows her face into Chaundra's side.

"The painting. Each of the bones was from a child. Each one a different child," I say, feeling like I'm about to puke.

"Lily, honey. Can Mommy get up a minute to show Micah the painting?"

She nods and sticks her thumb in her mouth, something she hasn't done since she was four.

"I put it in the corner of the studio turned toward the wall," Jonas says.

Chaundra and Micah leave the room as we sit in silence. I want to offer to snuggle with Lily, but I'm terrified to touch her again. Jonas rubs circles on my back and kisses me on the head.

After a few moments, Micah and Chaundra return. Chaundra pulls Lily back onto her lap.

"To make sure I understand, you and Lily held hands and then you had a lightning flash?" Chaundra asks, and I nod. "Lily, did you feel it too?"

"Yes. Through my whole body. It hurt," she sobs.

My heart breaks for Lily—the last thing I ever want to do is cause her pain. "I'm so sorry, honey. I would never hurt you on purpose. I'm sorry." Again, sobs overtake me.

"What did you guys see?" Chaundra asks, gently.

"Dominick, Chase, Anna, Scott, AJ, Leah, Stephanie, David. Dominick, Chase, Anna, Scott, AJ, Leah, Stephanie, David. Dominick…" The same names that fill my mind pour out of Lily's mouth on a loop.

"Shh, honey. It's okay. Shh…" Chaundra says and pulls Lily tighter.

"The bad man hurt them all. He killed them. Then cut them up," Lily says.

"He wants to make them new. Make them whole," I say, not even sure what this means. "He wants forgiveness. He's broken. Sad."

"So, this bad man is killing kids. Cutting them up and saving their bones? And he's sad about it?" Chaundra asks.

Lily and I both nod.

"Mommy, he's going to hurt Liam if we don't stop him."

As soon as she says the words, I remember. I had blocked that part out. Liam will be his next victim. His bones will become a piece of the puzzle if we don't stop him. I pull away from Jonas and run to the bathroom to vomit, but he follows behind.

After I've thrown up, I sit back against the wall. "I saw it too. Liam with the right half of his skull missing." Once the words escape me, I throw up again as Jonas holds my hair back.

"We will stop him. He's not going to do a thing to Liam." He sounds so much surer than I feel.

Liam is twelve, about the same age as the other children I saw in my mind.

"We need to find him now. Chaundra can't lose another child. I won't let him hurt Liam." I hiccup a sob as a sense of determination rises within me. "I also saw something else. I don't know why, amid all the other faces, I saw another one. Our child's."

Jonas gasps. "Being hurt?"

"No. I'm not sure why she was there," I say and realize my mistake. I put my hand over my mouth.

Jonas' whole face breaks into a smile. Joy replaces his earlier fear. "We're having a girl?"

I nod. "Sorry I let that slip and that you have to find out this way instead of like any normal person would get to."

Jonas places his hand on my stomach. "Who needs normal? Which name do we go with?"

I hesitate, not sure if I should take away all the surprises but give in when Jonas raises his eyebrows in anticipation. "Zoe. Our little Zoe."

Jonas leans down to my stomach. "Hi, baby girl. I'm your daddy. I love you already. I'll do whatever I have to do to keep you and Mommy safe."

My heart bursts at his love for our little girl, but it breaks at the same time. How can we bring a child into this world full of monsters? And Liam—how do we save him?

"Let's go talk to Chaundra and Micah to see if we can figure this out," I say. "We've got to stop him."

CHAUNDRA HAS BREWED a fresh pot of coffee by the time we make our way back downstairs. I look at Jonas with raised eyebrows to see if he'll object to me having a cup, since I'm certain she didn't make decaf.

"I'd say you've earned a cup, as long as you don't think it will make you more anxious," he says.

I walk toward the kitchen. "Nothing could make me more anxious right now."

"Sit, Tess. I'll get it," Chaundra says and grabs my favorite mug from the cupboard while I take a seat at the dining table next to Micah.

"Chaundra showed me the painting and explained a bit more about your abilities," Detective Oliver says.

I nod and brace myself for his disbelief. Chaundra places a mug in front of each of us. I can't miss the quiver in her hand. She must be an absolute wreck with hearing the news about Liam, even though she's a master at hiding it.

"I'm sure you've caught quite a bit of flack over the years about it, huh?" he says.

I nod and take a drink.

"Tessa, you said a name that caught my attention. Anna. What can you tell me about her?" Micah says.

"She had short brown hair and dark brown eyes. She had dimples in each cheek. After he killed her, he cut off her lower right arm. He threw her in a ravine where she was hidden amongst fallen branches and leaves." Nausea fills me as I stare into my coffee mug.

Micah blows out a loud breath. I look up to see what caused his reaction.

"I... uh... need to step outside for a minute if you don't mind." Detective Oliver rushes out onto the deck.

"What's going on? What's wrong?" I ask Chaundra. "And are you okay?"

She takes a deep breath. "Actually, I'm freaking out. You guys saw Liam? I can't even..." She picks up her cup, takes a drink of coffee, followed by a deep breath. "Anyway, we'll deal with all of that later. I don't know the whole story, but Micah's little sister was murdered when she was twelve. Her name was Anna. Hopefully, he'll be able to tell us more when he comes back in. I think we should give him a minute."

We sit in silence and drink our coffee. Images of the children continue to batter my brain. *His* voice echoes in my mind, begging for absolution, pleading for forgiveness. Lily has managed to drift off on the couch, which I'm a bit envious of. I wish I could get these thoughts out of my mind long enough to rest.

"Lily told me the news. A little girl, huh?" Chaundra asks.

Jonas' face breaks into a huge smile. "Yep. Zoe."

God, I hate that he couldn't find out about all of this like a normal father would, instead of this way. Why does my ability have to interfere with our lives, especially now? I don't want this back. The last five years have been so peaceful without it. Now, at one of the happiest times of my life, it rears its ugly head again. Why?

Cold air rushes in as Detective Oliver opens the door. "I'm sorry about that," he says and sits next to Chaundra.

"I hope it's okay, but I told them about your sister," Chaundra says.

Micah slowly nods. "Normally, I'd have a really hard time wrapping my mind around your gift, but I've had some encounters with people through the years who have made me question my beliefs. One was a psychic that worked with our family when my little sister, Anna, went missing. She was the person who helped us find her body."

I meet his gaze. No wonder he didn't act totally freaked out by some of the things I told him the first time he was here.

Micah clears his throat and takes a deep breath. "The little girl you described with the dark hair, brown eyes, and dimples. That was my sister. Her body was found, thanks to the psychic, in a ravine at the bottom of the Unaka mountain in Tennessee. She was missing her lower right arm."

"Oh my god!" I cover my mouth with my hand and try to push the image of Anna's mutilated corpse out of my mind. "When did this happen?"

"Thirteen years ago. She was twelve. I was twenty-four." He pauses to take a drink of coffee. "It feels like yesterday."

"I'm so sorry," Jonas says. "I can't imagine what that was like for you. Your family."

"It was terrible. It's one of the things that made me go into law enforcement because before then, I was determined to break the family tradition. I didn't want other families to ever go through what we did. It seems like my plan didn't work, though. It appears that he had many more victims than my sister."

"At least seven more and he's not finished," I say. "I've been in his mind. He's only halfway done. And, like Lily said, if we don't stop him…" I trail off without finishing the sentence as my gaze falls on Lily sleeping peacefully on the couch. I hate knowing that she saw the same things as I did—the atrocities Liam will suffer if this guy isn't caught. Jonas pulls me close, trying to shelter me in his arms.

"Then we need to figure out who he is and make sure he never hurts another child," Micah says, his jaw rigid with determination. "There's only so much I can tell you because of the ongoing investigation, but I think there's a lot you and Lily can tell me, which may help."

My voice comes out barely louder than a whisper. "I'll do whatever I can to assist."

"Lily will too," Chaundra adds.

Micah nods. "How about we all try to get some sleep tonight and talk more tomorrow? I'm beat and I can only imagine how drained you are."

He has no idea. These flashes have only been back for a couple of weeks, but it feels like a lifetime already. As exhausted as I am, though, there will be no real rest for me until we figure out who is killing these children and collecting their bones. I will not stop until we find him. I refuse to let Liam be one of his victims.

CHAPTER 19

After everyone leaves, Jonas leads me back to bed. I try to sleep but children's faces, their screams, their pain fill my mind and prevent me from drifting off. Jonas fought to stay awake until he was sure I was asleep, but before long, his snores fill the room, as the sun is starting to peek over the horizon.

Since trying to sleep is pointless, I ease out of Jonas' embrace and tiptoe downstairs. I start a fire, grab my laptop, and head to the chair next to the fireplace to do my research. I type in *Anna Oliver murder* and wait as pages of search results load. Her picture pops up and there is no doubt in my mind that she's the girl who Lily and I saw. I scour each article for clues as to what happened to Micah's little sister, finally grabbing a notebook to write down the important details.

Micah and his family were on vacation for spring break, and they had rented a cabin near the base of Unaka Mountain for the week. Micah and Anna were on the trip with their parents and some of their siblings. According to the many articles, on March nineteenth, the third day of their getaway, Anna said she was taking a walk to a stream that was less than a half-mile from their cabin and promised she'd be back for lunch at noon. The family knew something was wrong when she wasn't back by twelve-thirty, so they all split up to look for her. After hours of searching, the only thing they'd found was her pink backpack resting along the edge of the path leading to the stream. It was filled with rocks, feathers, and other little trinkets she liked to collect on their trips. Anna was gone. The family called the police to report Anna missing at three in the afternoon, and officers arrived on the scene within forty-five minutes.

Daily searches and press conferences were held for the next four days, but still, they couldn't find Anna. By this time, the family's vacation was over, and they were supposed to leave the cabin to return to their normal daily lives. But they couldn't leave without their daughter. They instead rented a room in a nearby hotel, where they were contacted by a psychic on the sixth day after Anna went missing, who said she could help them locate their daughter. None of the articles state the psychic's name. On the seventh day, the psychic led the family to the ravine where Anna's body was later recovered. The ravine was so deep and overgrown—the only thing the family could see that told them their daughter's body was there was her red t-shirt, as well as one of her jelly sandals about half-way down the slope of the ravine. The police recovered the body, but the case is still open. No suspect has been named.

I scan my notes and circle March nineteenth. My heart falls to my stomach when I realize that not only is it my due date, but there's something else familiar about it. I pull up websites about Tatum Wright and quickly make the connection. It is the same date he went missing. March nineteenth is the key to this. I type in the date starting in 2005, two years before Anna went missing, and scour news reports for that day but nothing comes up that is familiar or important.

"What happened on March nineteenth?" I whisper, asking the ghost in my brain for an answer. I don't dare pose the question of whether or not it's a coincidence that it's the same day that Zoe is supposed to be born.

As though in answer, a pain stabs me through the heart like someone has reached into my chest and tried to rip it from my body. A name courses through my mind at the same time—Sam. Along with the name, the sandy blond-haired boy with the brown eyes and chubby cheeks that I painted takes over my thoughts. Makes me gasp for breath and my heart shatters into a million tiny shards. I don't know who the bad guy is or what happened for sure, but I am certain that Sam is his son and something terrible happened to him on March nineteenth. Something that forever changed this man's life and made him kill these children. Something that turned him from a loving father into a monster.

"Hey, why are you up?" Jonas asks from halfway down the steps, as he rubs his eyes.

His voice snaps my attention away from the laptop and back to this room. "I couldn't sleep, so I did some searching."

He makes his way to the couch and moves my laptop to the coffee table, then rests his head in my lap. "Hon, you need rest."

I nod. "I know, but I couldn't. I needed some answers… which I found a few."

"Fill me in, please," he says, stifling a yawn.

I share what I found about Anna and about the date, March nineteenth, being the key. Jonas' eyes widen when I mention the date, but he continues listening attentively, successfully burying his shock at hearing that our baby's due date is important to this case.

Once I finish, he says, "You'll need to pass on that information to Micah. My guess is he's more apt to figure out the meaning than you are by doing random searches. Plus, I don't think it's a good idea for you to worry about all of this."

"I agree about sharing the information with Micah. Hopefully, Chaundra will call soon. Maybe they can both come back over later today. I feel awful about interrupting their get together. I also know it's impossible for me not to worry about it." I run my fingers through his hair. "I know you caught the date, right?"

He nods but doesn't speak, and instead rubs my belly, right as Zoe gives a kick.

"Hey sweetie! Daddy's here." He kisses my stomach and then looks up at me. "I'm sure no one cares about a ruined date right now.

How about you come back to bed with me for a bit? I'm still exhausted, and I know you have to be, too."

As the words tumble from his mouth, my whole body shuts down from sleep-deprivation. I yawn and nod. Jonas stands and holds out his hand to me. I grab my phone and follow him up to bed.

CHAPTER 20

The ringing phone startles me awake. I glance at the clock before picking it up—it's two in the afternoon.

"Hi, Chaundra," I say after checking the display.

"Did I wake you? I'm so sorry! Twice this week, ugh," she says.

I yawn. "It's okay. I need to get up. I was awake all night, but Jonas finally dragged me to bed about nine this morning. How are you?"

"It was a rough night for Lily. She kept talking in her sleep and woke up several times. I called and spoke with Ophelia about recommending a counselor. She referred me to someone she thinks would be a good fit for Lily—her appointment is next week. Micah ended up crashing on my couch and left only a little while ago."

"Oh, I totally forgot to ask. How was your date? Well, before my interruption."

"A-maz-ing. One good thing about everything happening the way it did is it kept me from breaking my no sleeping together on the first date rule." Chaundra laughs.

"Oh no! Details, please!"

"Things were getting a little hot and heavy when Jonas called," Chaundra says and then sighs. "But like I said, it's probably good you interrupted. I really like him and don't want him to get the whole package on date one."

I smile. "You sound happy. Do you have another date planned?"

"He's going to come back after his shift tonight for a nightcap, which will be nice because the kids should be in bed. He's a great guy. We have a connection. He feels it too."

"I'm happy for you, Chaundra. I'm sorry about all this weirdness on your first date. How was he after the revelations about Anna?" Jonas stirs at this question and reaches his hand out to caress my back before his eyes open.

"He was rattled. We talked about her quite a bit last night and I got more details," Chaundra says.

"Yeah, I did some searching after you left and found out more information about her. My heart aches for his family. I can't imagine how hard that was on all of them." I pause, not sure if I should unload the rest of my discoveries. I finally decide to reveal what I found. "One thing I think is important is the date Anna went missing, March nineteenth."

"Your due date? Why do you say that?"

"It was also the date that Tatum went missing, and I think it's the day that something happened to the killer's son."

Chaundra puffs out an audible breath. "Oh, wow! It sounds like there is a connection then. That's only a few months away." The anxiety in her voice is palpable.

Jonas stands and mouths that he's going to make coffee.

"Are you okay?" I ask.

Chaundra sighs. "I'm trying to be but, honestly, I'm scared to death. Especially now that I know his killing time is fast approaching. We have to catch this guy before…" She doesn't finish the sentence.

"We will. We have no choice. In the meantime, make sure Liam is safe. Please share this with Detect… I mean Micah, to see what he thinks. We can talk more about it later. I really need to wake up a bit."

Chaundra takes a deep breath and then laughs. "You mean you need coffee first."

"Yeah, well, whatever. Same thing." I chuckle.

"Okay. Go get your coffee. I'll make sure to tell Micah. Please let me know if you figure anything else out. I'll try to talk to Lily some more today too."

I pull on my robe. "Okay, and Chaundra?"

"Yeah?"

"First, tonight is officially your second date, so you wouldn't be breaking any rules if you seduce him. Second, I'm here for you, and I'll do everything in my power to keep Liam safe. You can always be real with me and talk about what's going through your head. Don't suffer in silence."

"Trust me, I've already thought about that with the whole second date thing," she says with a laugh. "And I know you've got mine and Liam's backs. I promise to be real with you. Okay, get coffee. We'll talk later. Love you both!"

"Love you, too."

The smell of coffee wafts through the air as I run a brush through my hair. The scent is so tantalizing, I decide to forgo making myself presentable and head down to get a cup. Thankfully, Jonas loves me even at my worst.

CHAPTER 21

Jonas and I talk over coffee. He convinces me to call Ophelia today to update her on my latest lightning flash and all it revealed. I call and get an appointment for this evening, which works perfectly since Jonas has to be on campus for his class. I'll ride with him and hang out after my appointment until class is over.

Finally, we're having a more normal winter day here with the temperatures creeping up to the mid-forties which is making the snow melt. Our ride to campus is uneventful, although I can't quell my anxiety about meeting with Ophelia and revealing all that's happened in the past couple of days. I hate that I'm back in this situation where I need to talk about my bizarre abilities that I inherited from God knows who or what. It makes my heart ache for Lily. How hard this must be to deal with as an eight-year-old. The images in my mind shook me to my core as an adult, so they must've horrified her.

Jonas walks me to Ophelia's office and pulls me into his arms. "Good luck. Hopefully, this will help. I'll meet you at *Monticello's* as soon as I'm done with class. You okay?"

I nod and stand on my tiptoes to kiss him. "As okay as I can be. Take your time. I know your students might need to talk after class since you've been so distracted by me lately."

"That's why they have my email and number. I'm not hanging around long after. You need me more than them."

I caress his cheek, overcome with love and gratitude for him. "I love you. Have a good class!" I wave as I open the door to Ophelia's office building.

As soon as I enter her waiting room, I sink into one of the couches and shut my eyes, trying to let peace engulf me. My thoughts continue to race, and my hands shake despite my efforts.

I jerk my eyes open when I hear the door to Ophelia's office open. A young woman walks out and gives me a slight smile as she passes.

"Hi, Tessa. You can come in," Ophelia says with a grin.

I try to match her smile, but I can tell it falls short of genuine. I plop down in my favorite eggplant chair by the windows. It's only six and already dark. I hate that about winter.

"I'd offer you coffee, but with the baby, not sure that's a good idea. Would you like some tea instead?"

I shake my head. "I'm good. Thanks, though."

Ophelia sits across from me, then grabs her notebook and pen. "What's going on? You seem rattled."

I laugh drily. "Yeah, a bit. Lately life has felt like a rollercoaster, that's for sure."

"I know about some of it. How about filling in the blanks for me?"

I start by telling her about the painting, Lily, the lightning flash, March nineteenth, and Micah. Once the floodgates open, I can't stop until I've blurted it all out. Tears pour down my cheeks as I go through tissue after tissue. *How am I in this mess again?* Ophelia's pen scratches out the melody of my nightmare as I speak.

Ophelia puts down her notebook and leans forward with her elbows on her knees. "Wow! I see why you're stressed. You've been through quite an ordeal, and then dealing with pregnancy on top of it all."

I nod and blow my nose.

"These new green flashes are interesting to me. It shows that your ability has somehow changed. Do you have any thoughts on what the green indicates?"

I shake my head. "Not really. I had it the day of the wreck and then a few other times. It's weird, huh?"

"I don't know that I'd use the word *weird*, rather interesting. Part of me wonders if the flashes coming back and the new color are because you're pregnant. Maybe the hormones are having an impact."

I shrug. "I've thought about that, too. But what an awful time for them to rear their ugly heads. I want to enjoy being pregnant and getting ready to welcome our child. Not be focused on dead children and stuck inside the mind of another psychopath." I wrap my arms around my stomach, trying to protect Zoe from this crazy world. "Oh, which reminds me, I left out some of the most important details. If this deranged madman isn't stopped, Liam will be his next victim. And it seems he does all of his killing and mutilation on my delivery date. So, we have less than two months to find and stop this monster."

Ophelia's mouth gapes open in shock. "What? Did you and Lily both see this?"

I nod.

Ophelia sits back and steeples her hands under her chin, staring out the window quietly. "Tessa, I know this is hard and you've been through so much in your life because of your gift. But I want you to remember that it enabled you to stop a serial killer and rapist. It served a purpose. I believe it is back for a reason. You will use it to find this man and stop him. You'll help bring justice to so many families."

I suck in a deep breath and nod as a weight lifts from my chest. "You're right. I forget how strong I am. I know these flashes are back to help catch this guy. And yes, there are so many questions rattling around in my brain, but in my gut, I know I will help find him."

Ophelia smiles and gives a thumbs up. "That's the Tessa I know. Yes, this is all overwhelming—I get that. But instead of focusing on the *why me* aspect of it all, let's focus on what you have power over and the blessing of this gift."

"I know that's what I need to do, but it's hard. I'd gotten used to being normal, something I'd never experienced other than the past five years. I don't know how to throw that feeling away and go back to living life, never knowing how I'm going to change. Or when I'm going to get a flash."

Ophelia nods and sits quietly for a moment. "Let's talk through some benefits of your gift coming back right now."

I slump back and try to switch the gears in my brain to focus on the positives. "Well, for one, this situation brought Micah and Chaundra together."

Ophelia nods. "And?"

"I helped get Tatum home where he belongs. Back to his family."

"Yes, and by doing so, you helped them bring an end to years of suffering and wondering."

My chin trembles. "I wish I could've done something to save his life. I feel like the help I provided was too late."

Ophelia tucks one of her unruly curls behind her ear. "You gave what you could when it was available to you. I'm sure his family is grateful for that."

"I guess you're right. Also, I've gotten some information about his other victims and hopefully will be able to help their families gain some closure as well."

Ophelia leans forward in her chair. "And you realize that, if you can help find him, you're not only saving Liam's life, but you will also help save other children, too. You'll be sparing so many families the pain of waiting and wondering."

Zoe squirms inside of me. My hand goes to my stomach, hoping she can feel my gentle caress. I rest it there as a protective shield for our little girl. I am willing to do whatever it takes and go through the hell of flashes again if it means she and Liam will be safe. And to keep Chaundra from experiencing the loss of another child.

A warmth spreads up my arm as a thought invades me. "I know this may sound crazy, but I think that finding the killer will somehow help him, too. Give him the peace he's so desperately searching for."

"Hmm… that's an interesting take on it." Ophelia jots something down in her notebook. The scratching of her pen against paper soothes me.

"You know one thing I wish with all of this, though?"

She looks up from her notebook. "What's that?"

"That I could see Cyle again. I want to get that ability back. He would be able to help me through all of this."

"That's understandable. He's always been your rock when things were out of control. Has Lily mentioned seeing him?"

I nod. "She said he's been around a lot lately. Is it crazy if I want to keep touching her to see if I can get that ability back from her?" I laugh because it sounds insane.

"It makes perfect sense to me. Of course, you need to make sure it's okay with Lily. It sounds like it's pretty intense for her, too, whenever you guys touch."

"Yes, it is. I hate that she has to feel all of this with me. Chaundra mentioned talking to you today and getting a referral for Lily. Thank you for that. She's going to need someone to talk to."

"Of course. Again, try to reframe part of what you said in your mind, please. You aren't making her go through any of this. It's outside your control. It's outside hers. You two are linked on this journey together for whatever reason. Together, you will work to end this madness."

I rub my stomach. "Yes, we will."

"Okay, let's meet again next week, unless you need me sooner. In the meantime, I want you to paint. Also, whenever your mind starts to spiral, write down at least one good thing that is going to come from having the flashes again. Focus on that. Take it in. Every time your mind tries to pull you back into the *why me* thinking, focus on gratitude. Think of all the people you're helping. Think of Zoe."

I give a curt nod of determination. "I will. Thank you for helping me see what power I do have in this situation that feels so out of control."

"I'm always here for you, Tess," Ophelia says as she stands. She opens her arms and raises her eyebrows.

I stand and embrace her. I need all the comfort I can get to continue on this journey. A blue flash fills me along with a feeling of peace.

I walk out of her office, into the crisp night air with a renewed sense of purpose and feeling strong. I'm also convinced that I need Lily to help me find Cyle again.

⁓

THE TEMPERATURE HAS DROPPED about fifteen degrees since the sun set. I pull my coat tightly around me and head across campus, towards *Monticello's*. Now that we live farther out in the country, I don't get to spend as much time on campus, and I miss it. I pass by several groups of students chatting about their classes or parties scheduled for the weekend. Being back here feels like home and brings back so many memories of when Jonas and I met. I don't know how he dealt with me and my craziness in our first several months of knowing each other. I would've run for the hills, as quickly as possible, if I were him. But he's a better person than I am. I may have been the one with abilities, but he knew from the start we were meant to be together. He's since told me he knew I would be his wife the moment he bumped into me in the theater. Perhaps he's a little psychic, too. That thought makes me chuckle.

Jonas and I spent so much time walking on these same brick side-walks, hand in hand, getting to know one another better. It was under these same trees where he proposed to me. Our lives together began here at Cardell, and it will always hold a special place in my heart. Yes, I went through my fair share of hell here but, in the end, it was worth every second. I know that someday I'll look back on this time, which feels so insane now, in the same way. I'll see the purpose in it and find the beauty in what feels so ugly right now. My session with Ophelia helped solidify all of this in my mind.

Finally reaching *Monticello's*, I head inside and request a table for two. Thankfully, the hostess seats me at a table right next to the fire-place where it's warm and toasty. I really could go for a glass of wine right now but order a sparkling water instead. I nibble on the warm bread and scroll through social media while I wait on Jonas.

"Hey, love!" Jonas says and leans down to kiss me on the cheek.

"Hi!" I say with a smile.

He removes his coat and sits across from me. "Perfect table for tonight." He looks into my eyes and grins. "You look like you've dumped about a ton of stress in the past couple of hours."

I nod. "You know I always feel better after meeting with Ophelia. She helped me gain perspective."

"Anything you feel like sharing?"

"Oh, she just reminded me that I'm a badass warrior and that I'll, once again, help catch the bad guy and be fine." I laugh.

"I must say, I agree with her one hundred percent. Although she forgot a few things," he says and leans forward across the table.

I raise my eyebrows. "Oh, and what's that?"

"You are an incredibly sexy, badass warrior. And I'm so glad you're mine." He grabs my hand and wraps it within his own.

Oh, how Jonas still makes me swoon. "And for that I am so grateful."

He laughs. "Are you and my little girl ready for some dinner?"

"Are we ever!" As if on cue, my stomach growls.

We both burst out in laughter. "I think little Miss Zoe told you off for the very first time!" Jonas says.

"I'd say you're right. We'll have to make sure to write this one down in the baby book. But, for now, she needs food!"

We place our orders, and Jonas shares stories about his students while we wait. I love listening to him talk about his students and seeing his passion for teaching. Being here, in *Monticello's*, ordering way too much food and chatting reminds me of the beginning days of us.

"What's that smile for?" Jonas asks while shoving a piece of bread in his mouth.

"I just love you."

He reaches across the table and wraps my hand in his. "I am so in love with you, Tessa McCafferty."

A blue flash envelops me, along with warmth through my entire body. If I must deal with these flashes again, at least I'm getting something pleasant from them. I don't know exactly what the flash is from, but I'm filled with a profound sense of love and longing from Jonas.

"Is everything okay?"

I nod as tears of joy fill my eyes. "A blue flash. And feeling loved."

He squeezes my hand. "Good. You deserve it."

CHAPTER 22

Chaundra, Lily, and Micah arrive at our house at eight in the morning, which is way too early. Why must people insist on doing anything before ten? When I lost the flashes, I became a morning person, but I still have no desire to talk to anyone this early. I'm upstairs trying to make myself presentable when I hear Jonas answer the door.

I throw on a sweater and head downstairs. Jonas has prepared a feast for us to devour while we research—omelets, bacon, fruit, French toast, and, of course, coffee.

"Good morning!" I say to the three of them and walk over to wrap my arms around Jonas. "Thanks for all of this. What time did you wake up?"

He kisses me, letting it linger longer than he usually would in front of guests. "I was quite energized after last night and knew we'd need lots of fuel for today."

Chaundra clears her throat. "Uh, do you need us to leave so you can have some special time?"

I laugh. "We had plenty of special time last night, so you're fine."

Lily is already filling her plate with breakfast. "Lily, shouldn't you ask first? Geez!" Chaundra says.

Lily pauses with a serving spoon in mid-air and looks at me and Jonas.

"Don't listen to her. You never have to ask at Aunt Tessa's!" I say, and she immediately resumes piling food on her plate. "Where's Liam?"

"He's with his dad today, which I'm not thrilled about. I'm having a bit of trouble letting him out of my sight, but court orders and all that jazz. I told Adam not to let him leave his side," Chaundra huffs. "Let's hope for once that he listens to me."

"Micah, Chaundra, help yourselves." Jonas holds out his hand to the island full of food.

"Thank you. I'm famished. It looks and smells delicious!" Micah heads to the island and starts filling his plate.

I grab coffee and catch Chaundra's eye. She's pointing upstairs with an enormous smile plastered on her face.

"I need to show Chaundra something in the studio a minute. We'll be right back," I say, catching her desire to get me alone for girl talk.

As soon as we're in the studio, she shuts the door and squeals. "Oh my God!"

I laugh. "Uh, care to expand on that?"

"Well, let's just say, my nightcap with Micah was incredibly satisfying and lasted until the wee hours of this morning. In fact, he went to his car before the kids woke up to make it look like he didn't spend the night."

I hug her. "No wonder you're beaming today!"

"Is it that obvious?" she laughs.

"You look happier than I've ever seen you. Sex must be good for you."

"Indeed. It had been so long I'd forgotten how fabulous it could be." Her smile is so wide, her face might break. "And, on a more serious note, I really, really like him. I think he may feel the same about me, too. We have this connection. It's... indescribable."

I hug her again. "I'm thrilled for you. I have a good feeling about the two of you."

"Me too. But nothing compared to how good I was feeling a few hours ago. Lily wouldn't go into details, but she says Micah will be around for a while. I tried to press her, but she just smiles and says she's not telling me. Little brat!" Chaundra laughs. "Okay, we better get back down there. I'm hungry after last night's workout."

"You know Lily is never wrong, but how are you doing with everything else?"

Chaundra looks out into the woods for a moment before responding. "I'm terrified, but I also trust that with all of us working together, we'll stop this guy. He's not getting my son!"

"No, he's not. We could form a new team of superheroes! All we need are some cool outfits and names." We both laugh. "All kidding aside, none of us will let anything happen to him."

She nods. "Last night was the distraction I needed."

I walk to the door and open it. "Before we head down, you might want to dial back that smile a bit."

"I'm trying, but man, it's hard."

As we descend the stairs, Micah and I make eye contact—he immediately blushes and looks away. He knew the exact purpose of our little escape upstairs.

"How's everything taste, guys?" I ask as I fill a plate for myself.

"Delicious!" Lily declares with syrup dripping down her chin.

"Lily, wipe your mouth!" Chaundra tosses her a napkin.

The conversation is light and fun during breakfast, which is good, because I'm sure the rest of the day will be filled with unimaginable heaviness as we try to get some answers on these children who have taken up residence in my mind. And the killer who is threatening to consume my soul.

AFTER EATING, we set up Lily with the VR and each of us spreads out with our laptops to do research. We divvy up the names we know so far. With those and the date of March nineteenth, we should be able to find some information even if it takes a little digging. Chaundra takes Dominick and Chase. Micah takes Scott and AJ. Jonas takes Stephanie and David. I take Sam because I believe he is the key to all of this. The first child who died and the one who made the killer begin his rampage.

We agree to share any information that comes up that may be useful to the others in their research. We spend the first hour in silence, other than the clacking of our keyboards.

"I have something," Chaundra announces. We all look up from our computers. "Dominick Mason. Twelve years old, went missing while walking home from Dillsboro Baptist church in North Carolina on March nineteenth of 2016. According to the articles, his mother, Carolyn, stayed behind to set up for a potluck that evening, but Dominick wasn't feeling well and decided to walk home, leaving the church at two in the afternoon. They lived less than half a mile from the church and, according to his mom, he would've walked home along the town sidewalks and main streets. She didn't discover he was missing until that evening at seven-thirty when she got home. She'd tried calling and texting several times in the afternoon, but figured he must be sleeping, so she didn't worry. She knew something was wrong when she got home, and everything was exactly as it had been when the family left for church that morning. None of his belongings he had that day were in the house—his phone, his Bible, or his clothing. To this day, he hasn't been found despite numerous searches of the area and questioning witnesses. Several said they spotted Dominick on his walk home but then it's as if he vanished into thin air."

I pull up a picture on my laptop of Dillsboro Baptist church and the surrounding area. It is a small mountain town, surrounded by forests. Dominick could be anywhere, awaiting discovery.

"Does it say where their search was focused?" Micah asks.

"No, there's not much information, only that all leads went cold."

"Guys, pull up the town. It's surrounded by forests. He could be anywhere. The whole area looks like the perfect place for our guy to operate, seeing as how he likes to leave his victims in the woods," I say.

Quietly, we all take Google map tours of the town.

"Mommy?" Lily yells from upstairs.

"Yeah, hon."

"Can you bring me a snack and drink?"

"My lord, how can that kid be hungry already? I still feel like I'm about to burst." Chaundra laughs, then yells upstairs to Lily. "You may come down to get a snack and drink. I'm not bringing it up to you."

Lily sighs as though she's been asked to clean the house from top to bottom. "Fine," she mutters as she stomps down the stairs and makes her way to the kitchen.

She grabs a soda and a bag of chips and heads back up the stairs.

"Young lady, sit down here and eat. You know that eating happens in the kitchen," Chaundra says and points to the dining room table.

Lily smirks and replies, "There's no table in the kitchen, so I guess I can't eat there either."

I stifle a laugh because, technically, she's correct. Since the living room, dining room, and kitchen are all part of the great room, there is, in fact, no table in the space defined as a kitchen.

Jonas chuckles, then whispers, "It's fine… really."

Chaundra shakes her head. "She knows the rules."

Lily pounds her soda can onto the table and flops into the chair next to me, all the while glaring at Chaundra, who rolls her eyes. "Lose the attitude, little miss. Teenage years are gonna be fun with this one."

Lily doesn't answer and instead loudly rips open the chip bag, crinkling it as much as possible. I can't help but laugh.

"Don't encourage her, Tessa," Chaundra says through gritted teeth. "Lily, sit there and quietly eat or no more VR today. You can read instead."

Lily crosses her arms and slumps back in the chair. After a minute, she reaches into the bag and withdraws some chips as dramatically quiet as possible. I reach over and ruffle her hair.

We all resume our map searches of Dillsboro. Lily softly hums while she eats.

"No wonder they gave up. This would be an incredibly difficult area to search," Micah says. "Especially if they didn't have any good leads."

He's right. Given what we know about the killer, Dominick could literally be anywhere.

Lily gasps and points at my screen. "Right there."

She points to an area in the woods that looks like every other part of the town.

"What's right there, Lily?" I ask.

She moves closer and zooms in on a thickly wooded part of the forest. "Dominick. He's right there."

Micah bolts to the table. "Can you take a screenshot of that, please?"

I nod and screen shot it.

"Tell me everything you can see, Lily," Micah says, leaning closer.

She closes her eyes. "There are lots of trees. One of them fell down. A huge one. It's kind of falling down a big hill. He's there, under that tree. His blue tie is sticking out a little bit. That's all I can really see, just a tiny piece of that blue tie."

"Thank you. That is very helpful," Micah says. "Tessa, can you email me that screen shot and link?"

I give a thumbs up and send the email.

Lily sniffles and wipes a tear from her cheek. I'm glad that Chaundra is getting her in to talk to someone about all of this. I wrap my arm around her. Flashes rapid fire consume me. Red, blue, green, orange. Lily tenses under my arm, but I refuse to let go. Finally, they stop, and Lily relaxes against me.

"He's exactly where she said. He wants to go home," I whisper.

Micah nods. "I don't know how I'm going to explain this, but I've gotta call this in. They need to find that poor child."

CHAPTER 23

Micah goes upstairs to the quiet of the studio to make some phone calls about Dominick's location while Chaundra and I continue our internet searches. Because Lily is rattled after seeing the map along with the images of Dominick's remains, Jonas heads upstairs to play video games with her so she won't have to be alone. After about forty-five minutes, Micah comes back downstairs, his hair disheveled and with concern in every crease of his face.

Chaundra walks to him and places her hand on his arm. "Are you alright?"

He shakes his head and drops down in a chair at the table. "Not really. They aren't taking me seriously. I talked to detectives that cover the Dillsboro area. They said they already searched there and that they don't have the funds to do another search."

"What? They don't have the funds to search for a missing child?" Chaundra yells. "That's bullshit!"

Micah shrugs. "I know, right? So, I then placed a call to our chief to talk to him about it. To see if our department could assist in any way. He said no because it's not in our jurisdiction, even though it could possibly be linked to Tatum."

"We know it's linked to Tatum and a bunch of other missing kids," I say.

"Which is why I then called a buddy of mine with the FBI."

"Good thinking! They really should be involved with this case," Chaundra says.

"Thankfully, they would agree with that assessment if another body was found. *We* know they're connected but explaining that without evidence is another story. I could tell half the people I spoke to today thought I was insane." Micah rubs the back of his neck.

"So, we go find the evidence they need," Chaundra says, matter-of-factly.

Micah and I both snap our heads in her direction.

"What?" he asks.

"Look. Dillsboro is less than two hours from here. Let's all load up and go find Dominick. Then, the FBI will have to get involved, right?"

Micah stares out the window while I pull up directions to Dillsboro. "They'd be much more likely to get involved if we could find him, but, as frustrating as it is, we can't interfere. Especially since I just made all those calls."

"You can stay in the car or something while we go to look. Tessa, what do you think?" Chaundra asks.

My gut screams at me to say no, to not go on this little adventure. But my voice has a mind of its own. "I think it's a good day for a field trip."

AFTER CONVINCING Jonas this isn't the worst idea in the entire world and bundling up against the cold, we pile in my SUV and head toward Dillsboro. Lily was much more eager to go and find Dominick than the rest of us. She said she could see exactly where he is, and I hope she's right. By the time we get into town, it will be around three. The sun sets between five-fifteen and five-thirty. We need to find Dominick's body before night falls, which may be tricky with only coordinates and the visions in our minds.

Lily falls asleep quickly once we're on the road, nestled up to Chaundra in the back seat. I keep sneaking glances to the back where

Chaundra and Micah hold hands and occasionally slide in a kiss or two. I'm elated to see her so happy.

"Are you sure you're ready for this?" Jonas asks and clutches my hand.

I shrug because I honestly don't know. "Someone needs to find this boy's remains. He's been waiting to be found for a long time now. If we don't do it, who will?"

"I love you. You amaze me." Jonas pulls my hand to his lips and kisses it. "You also frustrate the hell out of me sometimes, though."

"I love you, too. But really, I think I'm doing what anyone in my position would. As Ophelia beat into my head in our session, I have this gift for a reason. I probably should use it."

"Aren't you scared of how all these flashes will change you?"

"Kind of. But so far it seems different somehow. Yes, I'm having the flashes, but I don't feel as if I'm losing myself or that they're changing me—if that makes sense. Does it scare you?"

"Honestly?"

I nod.

"It does a bit. I remember how lost and consumed you were with everything when we first met. I've loved watching you become who you really are. I don't want to lose you to these flashes. And I'm worried about all of this stress and how it's going to affect our little one." Jonas' eyes brim with tears.

I lean my head on his shoulder. "I know this has to be hell, not knowing what's going to happen to me. I'm sorry you have to go through this again. I promise I'll do whatever it takes to stay sane and protect our baby."

Jonas nods, but I see the worry etched across his face.

AFTER A NUMBER of wrong turns and driving around aimlessly, Lily bolts awake from the backseat. "Here! Stop here!"

We are on a gravel road, surrounded by thick forests. Jonas carefully maneuvers the car to the side of the road and puts it in park. It's already four o'clock and we don't have much daylight left.

"Are you absolutely sure, Lily?" Chaundra asks.

Lily stares out the window and nods.

"Okay, let's do this," Chaundra announces, opening her door. "Lily, lead the way."

To everyone's surprise, Micah gets out of the car with us.

Chaundra raises her eyebrows. "Um, I thought you were going to stay behind."

Micah sighs. "I know. I shouldn't go with you, but I need to do this. For Anna."

Chaundra grabs his hand, and we all take off after Lily, who seems to be pulled forward by an invisible force. Her face is devoid of emotion and completely focused on the task at hand. I run to catch up to her, linking her hand with mine. A green flash devours me, and I can instantly see exactly where we're headed.

Lily looks up at me, and I nod to tell her I see and know. We quicken our pace through the woods. It's a treacherous uphill walk covered with fallen branches, patches of ice and snow, and shadows. Not the best terrain for a very pregnant woman to navigate, that's for sure. It's as if everyone and everything has fallen away, including Jonas, Chaundra, and Micah. Our only desire is to move forward, to find Dominick.

We get to the top of the hill and freeze in our tracks. There it is. The fallen tree that we saw in our visions, with a glimpse of something blue sticking out in contrast to the white and brown landscape.

I'm panting thanks to our speed walk up the hill. "Let's wait for them to catch up, okay?"

Lily nods as her entire body trembles. Or perhaps it's mine.

"Dang, you guys booked it up that hill!" Chaundra says, huffing and puffing.

"For a pregnant lady, you sure move fast!" Jonas laughs and catches my eye. "What's wrong?"

I point to the fallen tree.

"Is that it?" Micah says, already rushing down the hill with Chaundra and Jonas right behind him.

"Do you want to go down, Lily?" I ask.

Instead of answering, she moves slowly forward. I follow behind.

Micah instructs us all to stop when we are about ten feet from the tree. "Don't want to contaminate things any more than they've already been. You guys stay here. I'm going to see if I can spot anything other than the tie so we can call it in."

Jonas wraps his arm around me as a tear rolls down my cheek. I lean back against a tree trunk. Another flash of green and a young boy's screams fill my mind. *Please, please, no. Let me go! I won't tell!* Dominick's fear consumes me. He searches for a way to escape. To get away from the dangerous man who snatched him from the sidewalk on his way home. Who threw him in the trunk of his car and drove him out to the middle of nowhere. But there's no place to run and hide because he's lost. He does not know where he is, and nothing looks familiar. There's nothing around except for trees. Miles and miles of trees.

Then visions of a man's hands—my hands—wrapping around his throat and squeezing. Feeling the life leave Dominick's body. Feelings of serenity sweep through me—him—as I think that I've got another piece of the puzzle. I'm one step closer. Watching this man, myself, lift Dominick's body and place him gently on the ground. Hearing this man's voice come out of my mouth, saying, "I'm sorry. Please forgive me."

The wetness of the man's tears stream down my own cheeks as he stoops beside the now lifeless body. He pulls a hacksaw from the bag he carries and begins slowly and methodically removing the boy's arm, speaking softly and lovingly to the lifeless child as he does it.

"No!" I scream and lunge forward, away from the tree.

"Tessa, what's wrong?" Jonas thrusts forward and grabs my arm.

"I see... I see it all," I sob and sink to the ground. Jonas stoops next to me, caressing my back. "I was inside both of them..."

A green flash buzzes through me before I even finish the sentence.

Jonas flinches and starts to say something, but we're interrupted by Micah.

"I found him! He's here!" Micah yells.

Instead of feeling the relief that Micah obviously does, I'm devastated by not only the loss of Dominick and the fear that plagued him in his final moments on this earth. But, also, from the broken heart of the man who believed he had no other choice than to murder him. And the profound, heart-wrenching longing of the man to, once again, hold his son in his arms.

CHAPTER 24

We make it back to the car somehow, debating the entire walk about who should call this in. Chaundra didn't want Micah to do so because she was afraid that he'd get in trouble for coming out here and searching without his chief's approval. By the time we are back where we can get a signal, Micah says he's willing to take the risk to call it in. If he gets in trouble, so be it.

Before long, a flurry of activity surrounds us with police cars, ambulances, and detectives everywhere. Micah leads them to the location where we discovered Dominick's remains. I can't extinguish the chill from my body, so Jonas convinces me to get into the car with the heater, where I wrap myself in a blanket and lean against his chest.

"Talk to me, hon. What's going on?"

I try to explain everything I'm thinking and feeling, but it comes out in fits and starts, and I'm not sure how much sense it makes.

"He... or I... choked him. Wrapped my hands around his throat."

"Tessa, please don't say you did it. You didn't do it. Please don't own something that's not yours to own."

"I'm sorry. I'll try. It feels like it was me that did it." I pause and suck in a deep breath. "Anyway, he choked Dominick and was consumed by guilt afterward. He kept apologizing as he cut off his arm. And crying. It just doesn't make sense. If he feels so badly, why does he keep killing these kids?"

"It does seem strange. Have you picked up anything that might give you insight?"

"Maybe. It's like he thinks he'll get his son back if he kills these children. Not that it makes sense, but in my gut, I know he really believes that."

"I wonder what happened to his son. Do you think he killed him?"

I shake my head. "I don't know. I wish I could piece it all together, but it doesn't make sense to me."

The car door opens, and Chaundra pokes her head in. "Can we join you guys? It's freezing out here."

"Of course," Jonas says, as she and Lily climb in the front seat. "Are you doing okay, Lily?"

"I don't know. I'm glad we found him, but…" her voice trails off.

I lean forward and squeeze her shoulder. "I know, hon. It's all too much. Did you see anything that might tell us who the killer is? I can see his hands and know his thoughts, but that's it."

She nods. "He's got grayish brown hair and is a little shorter than Uncle Jonas. He's older than him, too. And he's got a bigger belly."

Chaundra grabs a notebook and pen out of her purse and writes down everything Lily says.

"Anything else, hon? A beard? A mustache?" Chaundra asks.

Lily nods. "A beard and mustache. His eyes are kind of blue with a little gray mixed in."

"Tessa, anything special about his hands?"

"As Lily said, they look aged and worn. Like he's older than us. And they're rough, a bit calloused. Maybe he works with his hands, like manual labor of some sort."

Silence falls as Chaundra writes down these additions. Jonas kisses me on the temple and pulls me close again. I look out the window, mesmerized by the flashing lights bouncing off the snow-covered ground.

"Oh, hell! That didn't take long," Jonas says.

"What?" I ask and he points out his window.

Media vans have arrived, lining the other side of the narrow road. Dread fills me. On one hand, maybe media attention will be helpful to the police with securing some tips or leads. On the other hand, I don't want to have anything to do with their investigation.

"We need to stay in the car and wait on Micah," Chaundra says, as if reading my thoughts. Hell, she probably did.

"Agreed," Jonas says. "Maybe they'll think we're ambulance chasers or something."

"Let's hope," I say.

No sooner than the words are out of my mouth, a female reporter and cameraman rush toward our vehicle. We turn away, trying to avoid their gazes. There's a soft rap on the window next to Chaundra. She rolls it down a half-inch.

"Yes?"

"Hi! I'm Lanie Adams from Channel Eight news. We heard reports that some hikers found a body. Are you all the hikers by chance?"

"No. We were in the area and stopped to see what's going on," Chaundra says.

"From what I know about police investigations, I don't believe that's true. They have the roads blocked off to everyone but the media and police personnel. Would you be willing to answer a few questions?"

"No, Ms. Adams. We would not be willing to answer any questions. We don't have any information." Chaundra rolls the window back up and turns away.

The reporter says loudly. "We heard rumors that perhaps it's the body of Dominick Mason. Do you think it is?"

My body trembles. "Make them stop. Please," I beg Jonas.

"I wish I knew how."

"Was it a child or an adult's body? Just answer a few questions," the reporter shouts again.

She pulls a picture from her bag and holds it against the window. Dominick Mason's smiling school photo peers in at us. Bile works its way into my throat as his screams fill my mind. His fear courses throughout my body and his voice calling out for his mom echoes in my head.

"Turn away. Don't look at it or them," Jonas says.

I choke back a sob. "It doesn't matter if I look at it. He's in my head."

"He screamed for his mom," Lily adds, tears streaming down her face. "He was so scared."

A voice booms from outside the car. "Step away from the vehicle." It's Micah.

A new person arriving on the scene is enough to distract the hungry vulture. Lanie Adams and the cameraman swoop toward Micah. "Sir, were you one of the hikers that found the body? Can you answer a few questions for us?"

Micah pulls his badge from his pocket and holds it up. "I'm telling you to step away from the vehicle."

"Can you just answer a few questions?" Ms. Adams is quite persistent.

"Someone will address the media shortly. For now, back off!" he yells.

The force in his voice finally silences her, and they retreat back to the other side of the road, next to the Channel Eight van. Micah opens the front door, and Lily scoots onto Chaundra's lap to free up a seat for him.

"Are you all okay?" He scans each of our faces.

"Better now that you chased the press away," Jonas finally answers.

"Yeah, I should've warned you guys. I'm sorry about that." He runs his hands through his hair. "I know this isn't what any of you want to hear, but we're going to need to answer some questions."

Dread bubbles up my throat.

"What do we say?" Chaundra asks.

"Well, I told them, we drove out here for a short hike and stumbled across the body. So, we all need to stick to that story, okay? That will probably work for all of you but, for me answering to my chief, that's a whole different predicament." He rubs his hands together in front of the heater. "I told them we were descending the hill and saw the blue tie sticking out from under the tree. Since I'm a detective, I knew it could be something of importance, so I instructed you guys to wait while I checked it out. You all stood back, and I moved in for closer inspection and saw the remains. It's not the best story, but it's the one we're going with. Okay?"

We all nod.

"I've given my statement. Who wants to go first?" Micah asks.

"I will," Jonas says. "Can I be there when Tessa talks to them? She's not feeling so well."

"I'm sorry, but no. They'll want to talk to each of you individually. I'll stay with Lily when they talk to her," Micah answers and tousles Lily's hair. "Okay, Jonas, you're up first. The rest of you hang tight. I'm sorry but it's going to be a long night."

Jonas opens his door and steps into the night with Micah toward the vehicle parked behind us. He's gone for what feels like hours. Thankfully, I manage to drift off for a bit while he's away. I don't awaken until the cold air wafts in with his return.

"Tess, you're next," Jonas says and holds out his hand to help pull me out of the back seat.

"Did it go okay?" I ask him.

"Yeah, the detective pressed a bit on why we chose this spot to hike. I told them it caught our eye, and we decided to pull over. I don't know if he bought it or not. You'll be okay. Just stick to what Micah told us."

Micah approaches. "Tessa, I'm going to take you to talk with Detective Wyland."

I nod and grab his hand to avoid slipping as we walk toward the car parked directly behind us.

"Just stick to what we talked about, okay? You'll be fine," Micah whispers.

He opens the passenger side door and holds onto my arm as I slide into the seat next to the detective.

"Let me know when you're ready for the next person." Micah leans his head in. The detective nods, and before Micah shuts the door, he gives my shoulder a slight squeeze.

"I'm Detective Wyland. I have a few questions for you."

I nod.

"I'm going to record this," he says and points to his phone sitting on the dashboard.

I nod again.

"Can you start by telling me your name?"

"Tessa McCafferty."

"Hi, Ms. McCafferty. Can you please tell me what happened today?"

I recount the story as Micah instructed us to. My hands tremble uncontrollably when I share the part about the blue peeking out from under the tree.

"You seem upset, Ms. McCafferty."

I nod and fight the urge to say *no shit*. "Well, I am. Ever since Micah told us he found remains under the tree, I can't stop thinking about it."

"One thing I find interesting is that remains of a child were found on your property recently, weren't they?"

I suck in a sharp breath. *What? Why is he bringing this up?* Micah didn't prepare me for these questions.

"Um, yes. Actually."

"I find it odd that within the last few weeks, you've stumbled across the remains of two different people."

I blow out a raspy breath. "It's more than odd. It's awful and traumatic. And not something I'd ever want or expect to happen."

"After Detective Oliver told me the names of everyone with him on today's *hike*," he says, using air quotes around the word hike, "I put all of your names into the computer to do some preliminary checking."

"Okay," I say.

"You're Jonas McCafferty's wife, I'm assuming?"

I nod. *Very astute, asshole!*

"Tell me about finding the remains on your property."

Despite the tightness in my throat, I recount the events leading up to the discovery of Tatum's remains. He listens intently without making a sound. After I finish, he grips the steering wheel and stares out into the night.

"See, the thing I'm having trouble with is this. Do you know the odds of just accidentally stumbling onto one body, let alone two?"

"I have no idea," I say.

"I don't know either, but it's highly unlikely. Most people go their entire lives without encountering a dead body in the middle of nowhere. Yet, you have come across two in the past several weeks. Don't you find that to be a bit too coincidental and strange?"

God, why didn't we all think of this? Of course, what he's saying makes perfect sense. "What are you implying?" My voice quavers with anxiety and anger.

He smiles. "I'm not implying anything, rather I am pointing out some things I find interesting."

I sigh. "I don't find it interesting at all. I find it horrifying."

"Horrifying and interesting. Do you have any idea whose remains you found today?"

I shake my head. "How would I know that?"

He leans closer to me and peers into my eyes. "I think you know a lot more than what you're telling me. As do your husband and Detective Oliver."

I don't break eye contact, even though I desperately want to turn away from his gaze. "Well, you would be wrong about that. I assure you we know nothing more than what we're telling you or than what we shared with the investigators on our property."

"How did you know the name of the boy who was found at your house?" He smiles and raises his eyebrows.

My voice fails me. If I tell him about my gift, he won't believe me and will think I'm insane.

He drums his fingers against the steering wheel. "Did you hear the question, Mrs. McCafferty?"

Finally, my rage boils over. "Yes, I heard your question. I'm done answering, though. I assure you that neither my husband, nor I, have anything to do with the remains that have been found. It's just an awful, terrible coincidence," I shout. I yank the door handle and cold air rushes in. "I'm done answering your questions."

He starts to speak, but I slam the door shut. Micah rushes over and grabs my arm.

"Are you okay? What happened?"

Detective Wyland opens his car door and calls out to me. "You'll be hearing more from us, Mrs. McCafferty."

"What in God's name?" Micah whispers, trying to keep up with me as I sprint back to our car.

"He thinks we have something to do with this. He knew about Tatum's remains," I say, breathless.

"Dammit! This isn't good. I let my emotions get ahead of me and didn't think this through. Wanting to catch the bastard that murdered my sister has clouded my judgement." Micah runs his hands through his hair. "Get in the car and I'll go talk to him."

I nod and try to open the door, but my hand is shaking too badly. Jonas opens it from the inside, and I plop into the seat, burying my head in my hands.

"What happened? You're shaking like crazy," he says and rubs my back.

I don't respond. I'm too angry and scared about the detective's insinuations. How could we be so stupid to not think they'd realize the connection between finding Tatum's remains and now Dominick's? How could we not see that they'd think we were involved?

"Tessa, what's up?" Chaundra says from the front seat.

With my face still covered with my hands, I say, "They know about Tatum's remains on our property. They think we have something to do with this. Or rather, Jonas does."

"Shit," Chaundra and Jonas say at the same time.

CHAPTER 25

After what feels like a lifetime, Micah comes to get Chaundra and Lily to talk to the detective. He doesn't offer any platitudes about everything being okay or give any updates about his conversation with Detective Wyland. The stress is killing me, and I can tell it's bothering Jonas too, with his stiff posture and clenched jaw. He hasn't said much since my declaration. He's lost in his own world of worry and frustration.

My body has shut down from pure exhaustion because of all this stress, so I manage to drift off again when Chaundra and Lily are gone. Doors opening and Micah's voice startle me awake.

"Do you want me to drive back?" he asks Jonas.

Jonas answers by tossing him the keys.

"Wait. We can leave?" I ask.

"Yes. I assured Detective Wyland that you and Jonas would be available for further questions if need be. I provided him with your phone numbers. He already has your address from the system."

"Are we in trouble?" Jonas asks.

"Hard to say. My guess is they'll want to question you more at some point, but for now, let's just get the hell out of here."

"Hey, are you okay?" Chaundra asks, placing her hand on his arm.

"I'm pissed at myself for dragging you guys out here. How could I be so damn stupid?" He pounds his hand against the steering wheel.

"You didn't know…" Chaundra begins.

"Yes, the detective part of my brain knew. I let my emotions run rampant even though I should've slowed down and thought this through. I'm so sorry, guys." His eyes meet ours in the rearview mirror.

"Don't beat yourself up, man. We all wanted Dominick to be found. None of us were thinking clearly, so don't put all the blame on yourself," Jonas says with more level-headed calm than I feel.

Micah exhales loudly and starts the car.

As we make our way back home, fatigue overtakes me. I snuggle back against Jonas and let my eyes drift closed.

OTHER THAN ONE bathroom break pit stop, I sleep the rest of the way back and don't awaken until the car tires crunch up our gravel driveway.

"Thanks for driving," Jonas says and shakes Micah's hand.

"No problem. I'm sorry about this mess."

"It's not your fault," I say, my voice raspy from sleep. "Do you guys want to come in for a bit?"

"Thanks, but not tonight. I gotta get this one to bed." Chaundra points to a yawning Lily.

"We're all beat," Micah adds. "Do me a favor and don't do any more investigating tonight. We all need to chill awhile and get back at it tomorrow."

"Sounds like a plan to me," Jonas says while looking at me with raised eyebrows.

I nod in agreement.

"Goodnight, all!" Chaundra waves as she opens the car door.

"Night, Aunt Tessa and Uncle Jonas. Goodnight, Cyle," Lily says while climbing into the backseat.

"What? Did she say Cyle?" I wrestle free from Jonas' grip and run to the car. I swing the door open. "Lily, is Cyle here?"

She nods. "He's been with us all day." She yawns and lies on the seat.

I close my eyes and reach forward to clutch her arm, praying I'll get a flash that allows me to see him. A red and yellow flash zip through me. I wait a moment with my eyes clenched shut, hoping that I'm able to see my brother again when they open. I slowly open them and look around. No Cyle.

"Lily where's Cyle?" I ask, my voice shaking.

She points right next to me. "He's right there, with his arm around you. He said it's all going to be okay."

I am unable to see anything but the darkness of the surrounding night. I try with all my might to feel his warmth, but only the chill in the air greets me. A tear races down my cheek.

"Am I ever going to be able to see him again? Can you help me get him back, Lily?"

"Honey, it's cold and late. They need to go," Jonas says quietly as he grabs my hand.

"But he's here. I need to see him and talk to him." I sob and fall against Jonas.

"I know, hon. Let's go inside." He leans to shut the door. "Goodnight!"

Lily calls out to me as the door closes. "Cyle said he won't leave you until this is over."

As we walk into the house, I decide that for now, just knowing he's here will have to be enough. I will keep touching Lily until I can find him again.

CHAPTER 26

I sleep fitfully through the night with dreams of Cyle and nightmares vacillating between being hunted children and being the killer that took their lives. I finally decide that trying to sleep is fruitless and get out of bed at five. I frantically search every corner of my house to see if I can find my brother lurking there. He remains hidden from me; I discover nothing other than emptiness. I could really use his calm voice and comforting embrace right now to convince me that everything will be okay. I trust what he told Lily is the truth, though. He said he'd be with me through this whole experience, so I know he's here whether or not I can see him.

I start coffee and talk to him, deciding he can listen to me despite my inability to hear him respond. "Cyle, I know you're here somewhere. I wish I could see you, hear your voice. I've missed you so much. Losing you five years ago was the worst thing I've ever gone through. I really need your advice right now." I stop and blow my nose.

"I never got to really thank you for seeing me through the chaos and craziness with the whole Matthew thing. And for never giving up on me, even when I drove you absolutely insane." A laugh escapes me, despite the tears.

"I'm sure you already know this, but my flashes went away. I finally found myself and have begun building such a beautiful life with

Jonas, and soon to be our baby girl." My hand cradles my belly. "I want you to be a part of this life. Be an amazing uncle to little Zoe."

I get up and fill a coffee mug before heading back to the table, where I imagine Cyle sitting to have a cup with me. "Now the flashes are back, but they're different this time. There's a new color—green. And they don't come only when I touch someone. And now, I'm stuck with all these murdered children in my head, along with the man who killed them. I don't know what to do with it all. I'm trying to convince myself I'm strong enough to go through this, but I just don't know. I'd started to like who I was. Now, I'm changing again."

I bury my head in my hands to stifle my sobs. I feel a hand on my back. I whip my head around, trying to see him, but I can't. Relief floods me that at least I could feel his presence for a moment.

"I felt you, Cyle. I promise I will find you again."

"Hon, you okay?" Jonas yells from the loft.

I nod, but don't turn to look at him because he'll be able to tell I've been crying.

He quickly makes his way down the stairs, then wraps his arms around me from behind and rests his head on mine. "Why are you up so early, after such an exhausting day yesterday?"

"My crazy mind wouldn't shut off."

He leans around and looks at me. "Hey, why are you crying? What's wrong?"

I shake my head.

"Talk to me, please."

"Cyle. I know he's here. I need to be able to see and hear him."

He tightens his embrace. "It's good to know he's here with you through this, but I know how badly you want to see him."

"It sounds crazy, I know, but I was talking to him. I felt him touch me."

"I sure wish I could've met him. Of course, I feel like I know him from all you've said. Even so, it would be nice to be able to thank him for getting you through some of the darkest times of your life."

I nod as more tears fall. "And he's here again to get me through this one."

"Let me grab some coffee and get a fire going. Then you and I can snuggle on the couch."

This is exactly what I need.

MY PHONE RINGING rouses us both from sleep. I look at the clock and we've been asleep for hours. It's Chaundra calling.

"Hi!"

"I wanted to call and see how you're doing."

"I'm okay, I think. Other than being completely emotionally and physically drained, that is."

"I bet. So, listen. I wanted to call you before it hits the news. They've preliminarily identified Dominick."

My hand flies to cover my gaping mouth. "Wow! How so fast?"

"I don't have all the details, but his mom was able to make a positive ID on the items found near him. Of course, it will take some time before they can identify him forensically," Chaundra says and sighs.

"I sense there's a but waiting for me."

Another deep sigh. "Well, yes. Micah is trying to get more information, but the police have said they have several persons of interest."

I gasp. "They don't mean us, do they?"

"That's what he's trying to figure out. And, if it is you guys, what does it mean? If it's not, then who is it? That'd be good information to have."

"This is scary. They can't think Jonas or I had something to do with this. Can they?" Jonas whips his head up and his face scrunches with worry.

"I don't know. Try to stay calm and hang tight. I'll let you know as soon as I hear more."

"Okay." My voice comes out in a whisper.

"I love you both. This will all get sorted out. Okay?"

"I love you, too. Thanks for the heads up." A sense of dread fills me.

"What was that about?" Jonas says, now fully alert.

"They preliminarily identified Dominick, and apparently, the police say they have several persons of interest. Micah is trying to figure out if they mean us."

"God, what a nightmare! They can't be referring to us. How could they even think that?" Jonas jumps up and starts pacing. "Even an allegation like this could destroy me and my career."

I hadn't even thought of that. Stress boils within me and the weight of anxiety suddenly feels like it's going to crush me. I hate that I've brought Jonas into this. He doesn't deserve to be sucked into this insanity. He's a good man who would never hurt anyone. The police have to see that.

"I'm so sorry," I say.

"What are you sorry for? You've done nothing wrong." He crosses his arms across his chest.

I wave my hand around. "For this mess. It's my fault you're in the middle of it."

"No, it's not. You didn't ask for this any more than I did."

"I'm pissed we didn't think about what it could mean if we were associated with finding yet another dead child's remains! What the hell were we thinking?" I chuckle sarcastically. "What am I even saying? We didn't think. That's the problem."

Jonas stops pacing and sits back down next to me. "Listen, stop blaming yourself. We're all trying to get these kids back home, to parents who are waiting and wondering. This will all work out. I don't know how or what kind of hell they'll put us through in the process, but it will work out in the end. The only thing I'm worried about is you and Zoe staying safe and healthy through this."

I grab his hand. "And I'm worried about you. Your job."

"Let's give Micah time to do some digging before we let ourselves get too derailed. Maybe they actually have a credible, realistic lead. If so, that's a great thing. They need to catch this monster."

I nod, but I have a much more pessimistic outlook than he does. I feel an overwhelming sense of dread at putting the man I love more than life in harm's way.

I grab my phone and type in Dominick Mason. Many articles pop up, all with a similar headline of *Missing Boy's Remains Found.* I click on the top article, which has an interview posted today with Dominick's mother, Carolyn. My chest tightens and tears pool in my eyes as I listen to her talk about her precious son and how relieved she is that he can come home where he belongs. Every word she speaks is laced with pain, grief, and heartbreak. I cannot even begin to fathom it.

"That poor woman," Jonas says, wiping his own tears away.

I nod and continue listening as Carolyn says she hopes the monster who took her son's life is caught. The reporter then eagerly recounts details of his abduction and shares with all the viewers that there are several persons of interest. The reporter assures the public that as soon as they have additional information about who those people are, they will share with the audience.

"I hope they have some real suspects," I say.

"Me too." Jonas tries to smile but his eyebrows draw together in worry.

We scroll through and read several of the other articles, which pretty much all say the same things. I had hoped there would be a new detail or something that would give me more insight into who killed all these children. I toss my phone on the table.

"I need to do something other than sit here and worry about cops showing up to question us. I'm going to try to paint for a while."

Jonas nods. "I've got papers to grade."

I march toward the stairs, but Jonas grabs my arm and then envelops me in his. "It will be okay, Tess."

I stand on tiptoe and kiss him.

As I walk up the stairs, I wonder if his words of comfort are an attempt to convince me or himself.

WHILE I USUALLY PAINT TO classical music, today I choose rock and crank up the volume. It feels like it matches my mood better. I'm a bundle of nerves and raging emotions—anger, confusion, fear, dread. I grab a fresh canvas and get to work. I quickly get into the zone and can physically feel myself relax as all my emotions pour out through the paintbrush. My jaw unclenches and my shoulders lower as color fills the canvas.

I paint until my wrist hurts and my legs threaten to give out. I stand back to study my latest creation, hoping it is something other than a complete disaster like my mind.

Again, it is more abstract than my paintings were before the flashes returned. It's a forest in the early spring. There's green everywhere, in the leaves, the moss, and the plants covering the ground. It's quite beautiful until I find the area where I've painted Dominick lying there with his eyes wide open, his blue tie a drastic contrast to the green. It's as though he's begging me to look through his eyes and see the man who killed him.

I close my eyes and try to see through Dominick's. Glimpses of a man flash through my mind. Without pause, I grab my paint brush despite my cramped hand. At some point as I continue to work, I hear Jonas enter the room. He doesn't interrupt, but I glance over my shoulder to see that he's watching me from the couch. I don't know how much longer I've painted before complete exhaustion overtakes me, insisting that I'm done for now. Without examining the painting, I sit in my chair and shut my eyes for a moment to clear my mind before trying to see what Dominick needed to show me.

I open them and let them re-adjust to the light before glancing up at the painting. He's there. I've drawn Ezekiel, the killer. Not with enough detail that it could pinpoint his identity. It's him all the same, though. His hands are red with blood. In his left, he holds Dominick's severed arm. In his right, he holds a photo of a boy. His son. The one he lost. My painting matches Lily's description of him—short, grayish-brown hair. Somewhat stocky with a beard and mustache. His blue eyes are speckled with gray and filled with tears. His mouth is wrenched open in a scream. His pain—that of losing his son—pierces my heart. Disgust that he took another life rages through him. Horror that he killed this young boy engulfs him. The emptiness that he's somehow trying to fill with these pieces of other children. And suddenly, I think I understand some of the reasons behind his actions.

I grab a notebook and pen to jot down my racing thoughts. Or rather, *his* thoughts bombarding my mind. They are coming so quickly that it's hard for my hand to keep up with them. Finally, after I've emptied everything onto the page, I toss down the notebook and sit back in my chair, exhausted.

"Hon, what's going on?" Jonas asks.

I study the painting a bit longer before answering and then hold up my notebook. "I think all of this is the key to telling us why he's doing this. I can't make it fit together in my head, but the pieces are right here, just out of reach."

Jonas reads through the notes and looks at the painting. "I don't know what you're seeing and feeling. I wish I could put it all together for you."

I take a deep breath and slump back against the chair, frustrated that the answers seem like they're lingering a millimeter beyond my reach. "It's like a puzzle that's missing one vital piece. Without it, it's impossible to make sense of the whole. I guess we'll give it some time. Maybe it will all click into place."

"Hopefully sooner rather than later," Jonas says.

I'll share everything with Lily and Chaundra. Maybe one of them can help fill in the gaps and make sense of all these pieces and parts.

CHAPTER 27

The next few days pass by in a blur. I try to research more about the children, but I can't handle it mentally, emotionally, or physically. So instead, I sleep and watch TV. I can't even force myself to go into my studio for fear of what will pour out of me. Several times *his* voice has invaded my mind, trying to take over my thoughts. I force it away. I don't want to know anymore. I don't care why he's hurting these children. His reasons and pain don't matter. He's stolen their lives, taken them away from their parents. Each time I start to feel a bit of his agony and suffering, it makes me want to vomit.

Today, my focus is on making dinner for Chaundra, Micah, and the kids, who will be here soon. Nothing sounds good to me. I'm not sure whether it's the pregnancy, knowing where the discussion will go tonight, or a combination of the two. I settle on Tortellini soup, which is one of Jonas' favorite meals. Jonas finally returned to classes today, so I've had the house to myself, which has been nice.

"Hey, hon." Jonas walks in the door followed by a burst of fresh, cold air. "It smells delicious."

He walks over and wraps me in his arms.

"I made it just for you. How was your day?"

"It was good. My students might have something different to say though, since I handed out some pretty hefty assignments."

"Which means you'll have lots of grading to do here soon."

"Ugh. How do I always forget that part?" Jonas laughs. "I'm gonna run up and change before they get here."

"But you look so handsome, Professor McCafferty."

Jonas leans in and gives me a deep kiss. "Oh, admit it. You find me yummy no matter what I'm wearing."

"True statement. Now, go change, they'll be here soon."

Jonas heads upstairs, and I've just finished setting the table when there's a knock on the door.

"Come in," I yell. The four of them step inside. "Why are you knocking? You know you can just come in."

"I don't know. With some of the stories you've told lately, I didn't want to catch the two of you indisposed," Chaundra says with a laugh.

"Good point. Dinner is ready so, go ahead and take off your coats."

"Hey, guys!" Jonas says as he comes down the stairs.

I ladle the soup into bowls and pull the fresh bread out of the oven as they all make small talk.

"Dinner!" I interrupt as I take my seat. Now that it's done, my appetite has returned.

"This looks and smells delicious," Chaundra says. "I haven't had this since you stayed with us."

"It does, Aunt Tessa. Please teach Mom to make it so we can have it at home," Liam adds.

I laugh. "I'll give her the recipe, or you can just come over more often and I'll make it for you."

"That sounds like the best plan," Chaundra adds.

"I figured you'd like that one seeing as how you hate cooking," I laugh.

We make chit chat throughout dinner and avoid the subjects of police investigations, Liam being in danger, and missing children. They are lingering the entire time though and settle as a knot in my stomach.

After dinner, everyone, except for Liam, goes into the living room while Chaundra helps me clean up. After asking politely, Liam escapes upstairs to play video games.

While we load the dishwasher, I whisper, "It seems like you and the detective are getting along quite nicely."

Her smile brightens her whole face. "I have so much to tell you. We are a perfect match. In all ways."

"I'm ecstatic for you. You're absolutely glowing. I'm assuming you two have spent some more quality time together," I say and can't help but laugh.

"Oh, boy, have we ever." Her cheeks redden. "Is it that obvious?"

I nod. "You're more relaxed than I've seen you in five years, even with all the current stress and worry. I kept telling you that you needed to get laid."

We both break out into laughter.

"You two okay over there?" Jonas asks.

"Just girl talk," I say as Micah blushes. He knows exactly what we've been discussing.

"Well, finish up so we can chat," Jonas adds.

My stomach drops again. I don't want to discuss anything to do with this case. I just want to relax and hang out with my best friend without this dark cloud lingering over us.

Chaundra wraps her arm around me. "I know. I feel it too. This all sucks. I want life to get back to normal."

I nod, and Chaundra jerks away from me.

"You okay?" I ask.

She nods, but her eyes are widened in horror or shock.

"What just happened? What did you see?"

"Nothing. I'm gonna run to the bathroom, then we can all talk." She rushes off.

What vision did she just get and why did it upset her so much? She's usually open with me about these things. Why is she keeping this hidden?

I finish loading the dishwasher and head over to sit between Jonas and Lily on the couch.

"Hey kiddo," I whisper so that I don't interrupt the guys. "Is Cyle here?"

Lily nods and points to the hearth. "Sitting by the fire with Aiden."

I search but only see the dancing flames. "Can we try something? Can I touch you so that maybe it will help me see him again?"

She holds out her hand, and I grab it. We link hands and I shut my eyes. A rush of color sweeps over me. The flashes come so quickly that they all blend together like a kaleidoscope. Finally, Lily breaks our connection.

Please let him be here, I pray with my eyes squeezed shut. I slowly open them and turn toward the hearth. Sitting there, smiling at me, are Aiden and Cyle. Tears fill my eyes, but I'm afraid to move. Afraid that if I do, he'll vanish.

"Hey, sis!"

I bolt off the couch and into his arms. "Cyle, oh my God! You're back."

"I never left," he says and squeezes me.

I can hardly breathe. He's here. He's real. I can feel him, see him, touch him. I burst into a sob.

"What's wrong, kiddo?" Cyle asks.

I hug him close again and let myself cry against his shoulder.

I hear Micah's voice, full of confusion, above my sobs. "What's going on?"

"Her brother is here. Long story, but I'm sure Chaundra can catch you up later," Jonas answers.

"Did somebody say my name?" Chaundra calls out, coming back into the room, followed by a gasp. "Lily, what's going on?"

"Cyle and Aiden are here. I helped Aunt Tessa find Cyle again," Lily answers with pride.

I finally release Cyle from my clutches and tousle Aiden's hair. "Hi buddy! It's so good to see you again!"

"I'm here all the time, Aunt Tessa," Aiden says. Even though he's older than Lily in reality, he's forever stuck in the body of a five-year-old.

Chaundra sits and tells Aiden to come snuggle with her. He bounds over and leaps into her lap. I know she can't see him, but I wonder if a part of her feels him there. She leans back and closes her eyes, a look of contentment on her face. I pray she can feel her baby boy in her lap.

"Cyle, I have so much to tell you. To ask you."

He nods. "I know, but let's save that until after you guys talk."

"But what if I can't see you then? I'm afraid you'll vanish again."

"Lily, will Tessa be able to see me and talk to me after you all talk?"

"Yes!" she says with a smile.

As scared as I am that he'll disappear again, I trust Lily. She wouldn't lie to me.

"Okay, fine, but I'm staying right here next to you the entire time and not letting go of you." Cyle laughs, and it's the most beautiful sound I've heard in a long time. I wipe the tears from my cheeks before responding. "So, a lot's been going on."

"I know, I've been here. Even when you couldn't see me, I never left your side. I know what's happening and I'm worried about you."

Of course, he's been here. Lily tried to tell me but hearing him say it fills me with love and gratitude. My big brother has never stopped watching out for me.

"I know this must be weird, Micah, but my brother's here. Please don't think I've completely lost my mind. We'll catch up later but for now, Cyle says we need to talk about everything going on."

Micah takes a deep breath and nods. "Okay, let's start with the good news. As I mentioned before, I was hoping the FBI would get involved if another child's body was found. They are now officially on the case."

With Aiden still on her lap, Chaundra leans back against Micah. They look adorable together.

"That's great news," Jonas says. "Right?"

Micah lets out another deep sigh. "Well, yes. It is because they have more resources at their disposal than any of our local departments, and we all know that there's a serial killer at work here, so we need all hands on deck. But..." his voice trails off as he caresses Chaundra's arm.

"But, what?" Jonas asks.

"I've been suspended for a week without pay for interfering in the investigation. My chief is not happy with me at all, but he understands

I believe this is all linked to Anna's murder." Chaundra kisses him on the cheek. "Also, the FBI requested the case files from Tatum and Dominick. Detective Wyland has shared his suspicions with the agents about your involvement in both cases."

"Which means what?" I ask as I reach up to twirl my hair around my finger.

"They will be questioning you guys in the near future. Probably the *very* near future." Micah clears his throat.

Jonas pounds his fist on the arm of the couch. "Damn! How can they think we have anything to do with this?"

"How can they not look into it, really?" I ask. "Given that we've been involved in finding two dead children, one of which was on our property. We have to hope they investigate properly and realize quickly that we had nothing to do with the murders. They can't waste a bunch of time on us, or they'll not catch the actual killer."

"Exactly," Micah says. "One way we could help move that along much faster is if we figure out where one of the earlier victim's remains are. Someone killed before either of you was anywhere near this area. Of course, completely off the record for me."

"What about Anna?" Chaundra asks.

"I've shared my story with the agents and the details of my sister's case. They are looking into it but still aren't fully convinced that she's a victim of the same killer, given the different victimology from the two bodies already discovered. Since they were both boys."

"We need to figure out where some of the earliest victims are then. Or find a way to convince them that the same man indeed killed Anna," I say. "Or better yet, figure out what happened to Sam that started this whole thing."

"Exactly," Micah says. "But we have to work quickly to hopefully get them off your backs as soon as possible."

"Where do we even start? I've seen the murders happen, but I don't know in what order or what years each occurred in. Then there's the whole matter of figuring out where the remains are."

"I know," Micah says and rubs his forehead. "It's a lot. I wish we knew where to begin."

Chaundra leans back, and he wraps his arms around her. Unbeknownst to him, he encircles Aiden as well.

"I know who we need to look for," Lily says.

Chaundra's eyes widen. "Who, honey?"

"Chase or AJ. Chase was before Anna and AJ was after her."

"That kid's amazing," Cyle says.

"I know, right? Her powers are something else."

Chaundra rushes over to Lily to hug her. "You are the best! I wish I could see half of what you're able to."

"No, you really don't," Lily says quietly, her voice quivering.

Chaundra squeezes her tighter. "You're right, honey. I'm sorry."

Aiden plants himself on the couch next to Lily.

"Mom, when you stood up you knocked Aiden off your lap," Lily says with a giggle.

"Where is he now?" Chaundra asks and Lily points. Chaundra turns to his general direction. "I'm so sorry, buddy. I didn't mean to."

Jonas stands. "Well, sounds like we all have a busy night. I'm going to start the coffee."

CHAPTER 28

"I know we have a lot to do, but I need some time to catch up with Cyle," I say while squeezing his arm. I'm still in shock that he's actually here.

"Of course. You guys talk, and we'll get started," Chaundra says with a smile.

"Let's go up to my studio." I stand and hold out my hand for him. He takes it and follows me upstairs.

Cyle laughs as I close the door behind us. "I've never known you to leave before grabbing a cup of coffee."

"Yeah, well, I've never gone so long without being able to talk to my brother. You win over coffee every single time."

"I'm not sure that's true. In fact, I can recall quite a few times I dared not speak to you until you'd drunk a cup or seven."

I punch him lightly on the arm. "Whatever! Let's sit. We have so much to talk about."

We settle onto the couch, and I wrap myself in a blanket.

"So, did you know?" I ask, unable to meet his gaze.

"Know what?"

"That you were, um… dead?" A shiver races through me at using the word in relation to my brother. I still can't believe he's gone, especially now that he's right in front of me again.

Cyle takes a deep breath. "Actually, I didn't know until the hospital when you figured it all out. Hearing you say those words felt like a punch to the gut."

"God! I'm so sorry. I can't imagine. Well, I kinda can. But how did you not know?"

"Well, now, looking back, I can see it and remember everything about the accident. But, during that time, things felt strange and a bit off. It was like I'd think of my family and suddenly be there with them. Or think of you and then, voila, I'd be with you. But it's like I wouldn't allow myself to even consider the question of how it was all possible. I did wonder why Tara and the kids wouldn't answer my questions sometimes." Cyle laughs, but it sounds like heartbreak instead of joy.

I lean my head against his shoulder and let the tears flow freely down my cheeks. "Why didn't you listen to me about that day? Why did you go on that fishing trip?"

"Trust me, I've asked myself the same question hundreds of times over the last five years. I wish I had listened. I'm sorry."

The next question gets stuck in my throat, but I finally force it out. "Did you not believe me? Or did you want to die?"

Cyle pulls back and looks directly into my eyes. "Listen, I always believe you. Never doubt that. And, no, I didn't want to die. I wanted to see my kids grow up. Be with you. I know it doesn't make much sense, but I was convinced back then that if it was my time to go, it was truly my time whether or not I went on that trip. I guess I always believed we shouldn't mess with fate."

I grab a tissue and blow my nose. "But if I could've helped save you, it would've made everything worth it. My gift. Our parents' cruelty. Everything. I felt like maybe I was given this ability to help save you. But you didn't listen."

He wraps his arm around me. "I wish I could change it—more than anything. But don't doubt that you were given this gift for a reason because, I know you were. Look at what happened with Matthew. You stopped a serial killer. How many women's lives did you save?"

"I wanted to save you, though."

He squeezes my shoulder. "And now, I know your gift is back for a reason. To help these parents find their children. To stop this guy."

I cover my face with my hands and sob. "It's so much pressure. What if I can't find him? What if Jonas or I get in trouble? What if he hurts Liam? A million what ifs always race through my brain."

"Oh, sis. That's nothing new." Cyle chuckles. "You still have your orange box?"

I nod.

"Maybe in addition to putting all those pieces of yourself you didn't want into it, you should also add some of these what ifs. Get them out of your head and onto paper. Maybe that will give you the strength and courage you need to move forward and do what you know in your heart needs done."

"God, I've missed you. You've always known exactly what to say to make things better. Ophelia would completely approve of your idea." I laugh and swipe away my tears.

Cyle points at my belly. "Not to change the subject, but congratulations! I heard I'm going to have a niece."

"You really have been here, huh?"

He holds up three fingers and says, "Scout's honor. I wouldn't lie to you."

"Yes, a baby girl. Zoe Cylia is the name we picked out. After you. I wish she'd get the chance to know you."

"She will. Through you."

I cradle my stomach and nod.

"We have plenty of time to catch up. Let's head downstairs and see what they've figured out." Cyle stands.

I don't want to move. I don't want to leave this place out of fear I'll lose him again. He holds out his hand to me, and I reluctantly grab it, allowing him to help pull me to my feet.

"I'll be right here. I'm not going anywhere, for now."

"How about forever?"

"I can't make promises I'm not sure I can keep. If it were up to me, it'd be forever. But we both know we're not in charge."

I suck in a breath. "And dammit, how I wish we could be."

"Let's go see what's going on with the missing kids. Together."

⁓

EVERYONE IS QUIETLY SCOURING the internet for any information on Chase or AJ. I grab my laptop and sit next to Chaundra at the table, pointing to the chair next to me for Cyle to sit. I won't allow him to leave my side yet.

I open my browser and type in March nineteenth and missing children. Page after page of results fill the screen, but most of the articles have nothing to do with the information we're looking for. To be sure, I open each one and scan it before moving onto the next.

"Hey guys, I think I've got something," Jonas says.

We all snap our heads in his direction.

"I found articles about Chase McMann, a thirteen-year-old boy who went missing from outside of Brevard on March nineteenth of 2006."

We all type in his name at the same time. An image of a smiling Chase McMann fills the screen. He's standing next to a pond, holding up his fishing rod, complete with his fresh catch, and smiling from ear to ear.

"It's him," I say. This is one of the boys I saw in my mind. "The killer took his right arm, used the bone for his demented little project."

"According to this article, he's never been found," Jonas says. "From what I read, he was supposed to meet some of his buddies to go fishing not far from his house. But he never arrived. The only thing found during searches was his fishing pole and tackle box, the contents of which were spilled throughout the surrounding area."

Micah's face reddens with anger. "That son of a bitch is crazy. These poor kids. My poor sister."

Silence settles over us, each lost in our own thoughts. I can't imagine Micah's pain digging into all of this. A shudder works its way through my body with the realization that we will all know his pain if we don't stop this guy before he gets to Liam.

"Does this dude wander around the woods in various places

looking for kids to kill?" Jonas asks. "We've got kids in North Carolina and Tennessee—most went missing from the woods. How does he find them? Is it planned or does he just come across them?"

Micah sighs. "I wish we knew. Do you have a detailed map of the United States or at least this region?"

Jonas and I both shake our heads.

"We need to get one of those and mark the locations we have for each of the bodies. Maybe that will tell us something. I have several at home," Micah announces. "I'll bring it next time. For now, how about we look through the articles about Chase to see if we can find out more?"

"Lily, honey," Chaundra yells upstairs, where she has joined Liam in playing video games.

Lily looks over the railing of the loft. "Yeah, mommy?"

"Can you come down and look at this to see if anything comes to you?"

Lily bounds down the steps and sits on Chaundra's lap. Chaundra flips between pictures of Chase and maps of the area where he went missing.

Lily shakes her head. "Sorry. I don't see anything."

"That's okay, sweetie. Thanks for trying." Chaundra tries to kiss her, but she wiggles away and rushes back up the stairs.

"So, how do we go about finding him? Which we need to do to keep us out of trouble." Jonas points back and forth between him and me.

"Let's look into the different articles and see if that adds anything to what we already know. Fingers crossed something clicks," Micah says, not looking up from his computer.

Defeat settles over me. How are the four of us supposed to find anything that the police haven't figured out yet by skimming articles? The only reason we were able to find Dominick is because of Lily's visions. Without that, it all feels hopeless.

"Did you say you had visions of Chase?" Cyle asks.

I nod. "Many. Plus, I know that his bone was included in my painting."

"I saw it. It's disturbing, that's for sure," Cyle pauses. "What about heading upstairs to look at the painting? See if that fills in any blanks for you?"

"It's worth a shot. As long as you come with me."

"Of course. I'll be right by your side." Cyle squeezes my arm.

With everyone's eyes turned toward me, I remember they can't see or hear Cyle and have no idea what I'm talking about. "Sorry, guys. I forget you can't hear him. Cyle and I are going upstairs to look at my painting. See if that helps me figure out anything."

"Do you want me to come too, babe?" Jonas asks.

"That's okay. You keep looking for information. Big brother will make sure I'm okay."

Jonas nods, but his brow furrows. This must be confusing and scary for him—entrusting me to the care of someone he can't see or hear. Plus, he's so used to being my rock that I'm sure it's difficult for him to pass that task to someone else.

Before heading upstairs, I wrap my arms around Jonas. "I love you, and I'll never stop needing you. I know this must be weird for you."

He tightens our embrace. "I only need you and Zoe to be okay. I'm glad Cyle's back for you. I really wish I could meet him face to face."

"I know. Me too." We kiss, and then I pull away. "C'mon, bro. Let's go look at this gruesome painting."

CHAPTER 29

I put the painting on the easel and we both stand back to study it.

"Tell me about it and what you know so far," Cyle says. "Talking through it may help."

I close my eyes and take a deep breath. Cyle grips my hand, which helps steady me. I slowly open my eyes and let myself absorb what I see.

I reach forward and touch the right side of the boy's skull. "This is David. I don't know much about him, but I've heard his voice in my mind. We haven't found any information about him yet."

I move my hand to the left upper arm bone exposed in the painting, and a knife plunges into my heart. "This is Dominick, whose remains we recently found. He was walking home from church when he was nabbed by this guy and taken to the woods. He called out for his mom right before he was hit in the head." His fear and sorrow threaten to shatter me.

"You're doing great, sis. I'm right here. You're okay," Cyle whispers.

I inhale a deep breath. "The whole right arm is gone, but he used two different kid's bones. This lower arm bone is from Anna, Detective Oliver's little sister. They found her body in a ravine. And the upper arm is from Chase, the boy we just…"

Zoe shifts rapidly inside me as though she's trying to force her way out. I put my hands on my stomach, trying to settle her as a green flash and jolt of electricity devour me. My mind fills with images of Chase running along a stream in the middle of the woods. He keeps looking behind him, slipping in the mud each time he turns his head. I want to scream at him to run, to get away. But I know it's too late. His thoughts invade my mind in little pieces of information, rather than full sentences.

Thought I could trust

Get away

Dad

Help me!

They all swirl together into a loud, shrill scream. As he tumbles to the ground, Chase shifts his gaze upward into the face of his pursuer. I'm looking through his eyes, seeing what and who he sees. I can't make out the details of the killer's face, but I see something else that gives me a vital piece of information.

I fall to my knees and fight for breath.

"Tess, what's wrong?" Cyle stoops down and puts his arms around me.

I feel like I'm hyperventilating and try several times to get the words out, but I need air.

Cyle rubs my back. "Cup your hands and put them in front of your mouth. Hold your breath for ten seconds."

It takes me several tries to follow his instructions.

"That's good. You're doing great. Hold it for a few seconds longer if you can." He continues rubbing my back. "Just a few more."

Finally, I'm able to breathe normally again. I lean back against him.

"We need to get downstairs. I think I know who this guy is and where we can find Chase."

CYLE HAS to help me to my feet between my shaky legs and my humongous belly. We stand for a few minutes to make sure I am steady before heading downstairs.

As soon as Jonas sees my face, he rushes to the stairs and grabs my arm, not realizing that Cyle is on the other side. "What happened? You're as white as a ghost."

"I'm okay. Let me sit first," I say and head to the couch.

Jonas grabs a glass of water for me as I huff and puff, attempting to catch my breath. He sits next to me and clutches my hand. "So, what happened?"

"I was talking through the painting with Cyle. I started at the head and was working my way down, explaining who each bone belonged to. When I got to Chase, something weird came over me." I pause and take a drink. "Well, not something weird... Chase took over my thoughts. I was looking through his eyes, seeing his final moments."

My hands tremble so badly that I hand the glass of water to Jonas to keep myself from dropping it. Jonas wraps his big hand around mine. "You're okay. Take your time."

I clear my throat. "I think I know who's doing this. Well, not exactly who, but how he finds these kids. I could see his uniform through Chase's eyes. He's a park ranger. His job places him in the woods where he can find his next victim."

Micah draws in a sharp breath. "Can you describe the uniform for me?"

I close my eyes and pull up the mental image given to me by Chase. "Dark green pants. A grayish shirt. A hat—kind of flat on top if that makes sense. And the insignia on the sleeve of the arm that says National Park Service. A badge of some sort, like a police badge. And," I gulp, "a name tag. He had a name tag on, but I can't see it."

"Hon, it's okay. You've given us a lot of information. Don't beat yourself up." Jonas wraps his arm around me.

"That's definitely a park ranger," Micah says. "What can you tell me about where Chase was when he was being pursued?"

"He was running along a stream. It was in a forest, but there was kind of a clearing on each side of the stream, like the trees didn't go up to the banks or it was cleared out. It was muddy. He kept slipping and falling when he was trying to get away. I think that's how the killer got him. Chase must've fallen, and the sicko was able to catch him." I cover my mouth with my hand to keep a sob from escaping.

Jonas leans close and whispers. "You don't have to talk about this right now if you don't want to. Do you need a break?"

Even though my heart threatens to pound right out of my chest, and I want to quit, I'm determined to press on. "I do, but I need to get this all out."

"If you're sure…" Jonas' voice trails off.

Micah grabs his laptop and sits on the other side of me. "I'm going to pull up some different streams. Tell me which one looks the closest in appearance to the one you saw, okay?"

I nod. Micah pulls up some pictures. My eyes rush over them.

"Those are all too rocky. There were some rocks in the water but not that many."

Micah types something in the search bar and shows me a different set of pictures. I shake my head.

"What's off in these?" he asks.

"Like I said, there was a bit of a clearing on each side of the river. There weren't any rocks or trees right up against the water's edge."

"Okay, let's try one more search," Micah says as he types. He turns his laptop toward me, and I quickly scan again.

I lean forward and point. "That one. It looks almost exactly like it."

Micah carries his laptop to the table.

"How is that helpful?" I ask.

"Give me a couple of minutes. It's more helpful than you know. Let me check a few things first, then I'll explain."

I sink back into Jonas' arms, not really sure how in the world me finding a picture similar to what I saw through Chase's eyes is going to help. There must be thousands of streams in North Carolina alone.

"I'm proud of you, kiddo," Cyle says from the hearth.

"For what? I haven't done anything to help yet."

Cyle laughs. "Ah, some things never change. You don't give yourself enough credit. You're willing to do hard things to help stop this guy. That's not nothing."

"And you never change either," I say. "You always look on the bright side."

"What's going on?" Jonas asks.

"Oh, Cyle just trying to tell me how proud he is of me and that I shouldn't discount what I'm doing to help."

"Smart man. You should listen to him," Jonas says.

"I agree," Chaundra adds.

Cyle laughs. The sound is beautiful. "Ha! Told you!"

"Ugh. Whatever!" I can't help but smile.

"You guys aren't gonna believe this," Micah yells. "I think I found it."

He rushes over and shows me a picture on his laptop.

"Well?" he asks.

I'm suddenly lightheaded and overcome by dizziness as a sweat breaks out across my brow. It looks exactly like where I saw Chase running for his life. I give a slight nod.

A look of satisfaction crosses Micah's face. "It's the Davidson River in Pisgah National Forest."

"Oh my God!" Jonas says.

It's less than fifteen miles from us.

CHAPTER 30

With the new information about Chase, Micah makes us promise to sit on it for now until he has a chance to do some more digging and make a few phone calls. He wants to ensure we don't immerse ourselves further into any investigations involving the missing children, especially since we're already on the police and FBI's radars. We both agree, and the four of them leave with the plan to touch base in the next couple of days.

It's hard for me to not get involved, though, knowing that Chase's remains probably lie within fifteen miles of us. And that he needs to be found. It is essential that his family gets answers, and that justice is served. I made a promise to Jonas that I'd let it all rest for the next couple of days, or at least until we hear more from Micah. So far, I've kept myself occupied enough that I'm not dwelling on Chase and the other missing children. But they're always with me, lingering in the shadows of my mind. Calling out my name. Begging for me to help bring them home.

One of the best ways to stay distracted is by working on Zoe's nursery. We're going with a nature theme since Jonas and I both love the outdoors, and it fits perfectly with our home's aesthetic. Plus, I'm not much into the pink princess themes for most little girls. Our little

Zoe is going to be fierce, and a warrior. I can already tell. Jonas has already painted a base coat on the walls, so while he assembles the furniture for her room, I get to work painting a mural on three of the four walls. I am making our daughter her own little forest, complete with towering trees, woodland creatures, as well as a few mythical elements tucked in. I can picture it perfectly in my mind and hope that I can emulate it on the walls.

Jonas and I both work best to music, so we crank up the volume and get to work. I quickly lose myself in the vision for the mural. My enormous belly makes things a bit difficult, and Jonas insists on stopping whatever he's doing whenever I need to climb even one rung on the ladder. His protectiveness makes me laugh, but it also warms my heart. It's one more item to add to the long list of things I love about him.

We've been at work for about two hours, and I've almost finished one wall when the doorbell chimes.

Jonas stops the music. "I'll go get it as long as you promise to stay off the ladder."

"Okay," I say without stopping.

Jonas clears his throat. "Ahem, Tessa."

I turn toward him, my paintbrush lingering in mid-air. "Yes?"

"I know you too well and, therefore, need you to look in my eyes when you agree to not move or go up on the ladder." He smiles.

I narrow my eyes and with an intense gaze, I say, "I promise you, Mr. McCafferty, that I will not go on or move the ladder without you here to supervise."

He laughs. "Okay, I'll be right back."

As his feet pound down the stairs, I begin painting again. I'm thrilled with how it's turning out so far. Our baby girl is going to love it. After only a few moments, Jonas rushes back up the stairs.

"Tessa," he says from the doorway.

I keep working. "Yeah, hon."

"You need to come downstairs." His tone is clipped.

I turn to him—he's wide-eyed and his face is ashen. "Are you okay? What's wrong?"

He stumbles over his words but finally gets them out. "There are two special agents here… from the FBI."

I stumble back a step or two, almost dropping the palette. "Why? What do they want? What do we do?" The questions pour out of me, but I hold up my hand to tell Jonas I don't expect an answer. I put the palette on top of the ladder. "Dammit. Okay, I'll be down in a second. Let me wash my hands first."

He sucks in a sharp breath. "I'm sure it will all be fine. I'll go put on some coffee. Please hurry."

My mind races as I head to the bathroom to wash my hands. They really think we had something to do with this. What do we need to do to convince them we don't? What if they won't believe us?

Zoe does a somersault inside of me, almost as if she is worried about the same. I rub my belly. "It'll be okay, baby girl."

I'm not sure if I'm trying to soothe her or myself.

I STAND at the top of the stairs for a few minutes, trying to calm my racing heart. The quiet hum of voices fills the air. It sounds like perhaps a man and a woman. Cyle's suddenly beside me.

"C'mon sis. You need to go down."

"Come with me, okay?"

"Of course," he says and steps onto the first step, holding out his hand for mine.

I take a deep, steadying breath and follow him. I was right—a man and a woman stand just inside the front door, while Jonas sits at the table. His hair is tousled, a sure sign that he's been restlessly running his hands through it as he always does when he's stressed.

I quicken my pace forward with my hand extended. "Hi! I'm Tessa McCafferty."

"Special Agent Monroe with the Federal Bureau of Investigation," the man says while he shakes my hand and holds out his badge with the other.

"Special Agent Kempton," the female says while doing the same with the whole handshake, badge thing.

A red flash sweeps through me when our hands connect.

"Please have a seat," I say, surprised my voice doesn't betray me, while pointing to the table.

"I already offered, but they declined." Jonas' voice quavers.

"Oh. Well, how can we help you?"

"We have a few questions for you and Mr. McCafferty," Monroe says.

"Okay, well please have a seat, and we will do our best to answer them," I say, much more politely than I feel. My heart pounds like it's about to explode.

"We need to speak with each of you separately. We can do that here or at the police station," Kempton says.

I whip my head toward Jonas to gauge his reaction. He wipes his hands on his pants and stands.

"I'm sorry. We want to obtain legal counsel before we answer any questions."

"Do you have something to hide, Mr. McCafferty?" Kempton narrows her eyes.

"We have nothing to hide," I practically shout.

"Then how about you answer a few questions. If you still want an attorney, we can stop at any time," Monroe adds.

I look at Jonas, searching for the right answer. "My wife and I need to speak for a moment. We'll be right back."

I grab his hand and follow him to the back bedroom. Cyle comes along too.

"What should we do?" I ask. "I feel like it makes us look guilty if we don't answer questions."

Jonas runs his hand through his hair and clenches a fistful. "I don't know. It is so easy for them to read into any innocent statement and turn it into something nefarious."

"Cyle, what do you think?"

"I think having an attorney present is a good idea. But maybe you could see what type of questions they want to ask, and if you get any bad vibes, then stop the questioning."

I repeat this to Jonas.

"I'd feel better if we could be together," he says.

"Please tell him I'll be with you, and I'll make sure you stop the interview, if need be," Cyle adds.

I share this with Jonas.

He takes a deep breath and then grabs each of my hands in his. "Okay. But you must stop if it goes in a direction you don't like or that makes you uncomfortable in any way."

"And you do the same." I stand on my tiptoes and kiss him.

He grabs my hand, and we walk back to the family room, where the agents still stand at attention. Good God, they could relax a little.

"Tessa and I will answer a few questions, but we reserve the right to stop the interview at any time," Jonas says.

"Of course," Agent Monroe agrees.

"Why don't you and I meet elsewhere in the house, Mrs. McCafferty?" Agent Kempton says. I wish I could talk to Monroe as Kempton is stern and no-nonsense.

"We can meet in my studio if you'd like. It's upstairs." I point and she nods. "Would you like some coffee or water first?"

"No, thank you. Agent Monroe will talk with your husband here." She points to the table.

I nod and walk toward the steps.

"Love you, babe. I'm right here if you need me," Jonas says. His eyes are widened in fear, and his forehead glistens with sweat.

"Same."

I head upstairs, with Cyle by my side and Agent Kempton following behind.

"If I say stop the interview, you stop it whether or not you understand why. Okay?" Cyle whispers.

I give a slight nod, knowing the agent will think I'm completely insane if I answer aloud.

Once in the studio, I sit in the chair and the agent takes a seat across from me on the couch.

"You have a beautiful view up here." It's the first thing she's said that makes her seem human.

"I know. I love this space. It's perfect for my artwork." As soon as this is out of my mouth, I catch sight of the painting from the corner of my eye. I forgot to remove the damn thing from the easel. It's the macabre half boy/half bone creature.

Shit! Shit! Shit!

"Tessa, poker face on and quit staring at the painting," Cyle says sternly.

I force my face to relax by unclenching my jaw and narrowing my eyes into a more normal position, even though I'm still freaking out. She's going to see this painting and think I'm guilty of something. There's no way anyone who's familiar with these missing kids would not think it has something to do with them.

"Move to the chair in the other corner of the room so she doesn't have to see it every time she looks your way." I give a slight nod that hopefully only Cyle notices.

I pull myself up and put my hands on my belly. "I'm going to sit over here where it's more comfortable. I tell you, it's almost impossible with this enormous stomach."

She actually smiles. "I remember those days."

"I enjoy being pregnant but I'm certainly ready to not feel like a bloated whale anymore."

Agent Kempton nods with another smile. "Men cannot understand what it feels like to grow another human inside of you."

I chuckle. "Even when we try to explain it in detail."

The agent reaches into her bag and pulls out a notebook and pen. Obviously, our small talk is over. "I have a few questions for you."

I nod and put my hands underneath my thighs to steady them.

"How long have you and Jonas been married?"

"Three years but we've been together for five." Easy enough of a question.

"When and why did you move to the area?"

"About ten years ago." I pause, trying to figure out how to say why

I chose this area without disclosing anything about dead brothers or special abilities. "I grew up in New York, right outside the city. I needed a change of scenery and to get away from my family. There were a lot of issues."

"Why did you choose this area?"

"When I left, I packed up my car and decided to drive until I found the place for me. I picked my direction—southwest—and took off. I pulled off the highway into Chandlersville for gas, lunch, and a quick stretch. I fell in love with it instantly."

The agent's pen scratches across the paper. While this sound usually calms me in Ophelia's office, now it feels like an assault. "It is a beautiful place. I bet even more so when it's not winter."

I nod. "That's for sure. But usually, the winters are pretty mild here. This year's a bit of an anomaly."

"How did you and Jonas meet?"

My lips curve into a smile as I remember. "We met at the symphony and hit it off immediately."

"In my research, I saw that you and Jonas were part of a search for a missing student from Cardell," she pauses and flips through her note-book, "Hailey Garrison."

Her face wrenched in pain floods my mind. "That was awful."

"And that Jonas was connected to most of the victims?"

"As a professor, yes."

She scans the page in front of her and taps it. "What about Mallory? Weren't they engaged?"

I nod again as confusion swirls. What is she getting at? Why is she bringing all of this up? It was proven through DNA that Matthew was responsible for all the rapes and murders.

Agent Kempton sits back and taps her pen against her lips, deep in thought. The only sound is the ticking of the clock hanging on the wall behind her head. I stare out the window to avoid her gaze.

"I guess I'm a little confused and was hoping you could help me fit some pieces together. Do you know how rare it is to be closely involved to a case involving a serial murderer?"

I shake my head.

"Well, I'm not sure about the exact numbers, but it's *very* rare. Most people don't encounter it in a lifetime." She leans forward with her elbows on her knees. "And yet, you and Jonas have now been involved with two different such cases, supposedly committed by two different serial killers."

I clear my throat. "I'm not sure what you want me to say. It's more than odd. It's horrible, life-altering, disturbing—I could go on and on. Trust me, I wouldn't wish this on anyone."

"Perhaps the gruesomeness of the situations is keeping you from seeing the truth," she says matter-of-factly.

My hands ball into fists as anger courses through my veins. "And what truth would that be?"

"That your husband, the man that you love, is somehow involved in both of the cases," she says flatly, as though she's simply reporting the weather.

I pound my fist onto the arm of the chair. "No, he's not. You don't understand. I know he's not involved."

"You would be surprised by how many women have said the exact same thing only to find out they were wrong." She huffs out a laugh.

"I'm. Not. Wrong," I yell.

"Tess, cut this off. Now." Cyle demands.

I push up from my chair. "I'm done here. If you have more questions, fine, but I want a lawyer present." I march to the door.

She slowly and carefully puts her notebook and pen away, then stands and smooths out her pants. She meanders to the doorway and pauses right as she's about to step over the threshold. She slowly turns around and points at the painting I was hoping she wouldn't notice.

"That's an interesting piece of artwork. When we call you in for more questioning, I have many questions about it." She pulls her phone from her pocket and snaps a few pictures, then smiles. "I wanted to make sure to get some photos of that in case something were to end up happening to it." She makes air quotes when she says happening.

My face is hot with rage, and my breathing is ragged. I've never wanted to slap someone so badly before. How dare she come into our home and accuse my husband of crimes he's been proven to have nothing to do with?

"Thanks for meeting with me today. We'll be in touch."

As she descends the stairs, Cyle walks over and puts his arm around me. I feel no comfort, though. My mind is too focused on what she said. Not *if* we call you in for more questioning, but *when.*

CHAPTER 31

I ease my way down to sit on the top step, trying to hear the discussion from below, but it's impossible.

Cyle sits next to me. "Hey, are you okay?"

A tear of rage slides down my cheek before I respond. "Not really," I whisper.

"Oh, kiddo. I'm sorry you're going through this." Cyle plants a kiss on my temple. "Do you get why I told you to stop the interview?"

I nod. "How can they even think that Jonas or I have anything to do with this?"

"I don't know, but they need to hurry and eliminate you guys as suspects so that they can find the real killer."

Before I can respond, I catch a snippet of Jonas' raised voice. "... need an attorney."

I stand as quickly as my pregnant body will allow and rush down the steps, probably sounding like a stampeding elephant on my way. Jonas is red-faced and his eyes bulge with anger. He stands next to the door, with his hand on the knob, while the two agents remain seated at the kitchen table.

I walk over and grab his hand. "Are you okay?"

"No, not really. These two," he pauses and points at the agents, "think that I had something to do with the murdered kids. And to make it worse, they're once again bringing up the investigation into the women. Of which I've been cleared twice now." I rarely hear Jonas yell, but now he's completely lost his cool.

"We would like you to leave until we can seek legal counsel," I say in a surprisingly steady voice that doesn't give away my anxiety.

To my shock, both agents pack away their notebooks and rise from the table. Jonas mouths the words *thank you* to me as he opens the door to expedite their departure. Agent Kempton steps out first, but Agent Monroe pauses inside the threshold.

"I'm sure that both of you are aware, but we will be in contact for further questioning. Do not leave this area."

I want to tell him to go screw himself, but instead, I point to my stomach. "In case you haven't noticed, sir, I'm very pregnant. We must stay in the area so that I'm close to my doctor when I go into labor."

He smirks and then walks out the door. Jonas slams it shut behind him.

"What the actual hell?" he shouts as he paces. "I totally get how they'd want to talk to us about the missing kids since we were near two of the dead bodies but bringing up Mallory and the other women is completely uncalled for." Jonas sinks to the hearth and buries his head in his hands.

I sit next to him and pull him toward me. His body is rigid. I don't realize he's crying until I hear him sniffle. I'm completely caught off guard, as I've only seen him cry a handful of times and those were usually over happy events, like our wedding.

"Babe, it will be okay," I say while stroking his hair.

"I want to believe you, but I don't see how. They really think we, or at least I, had something to do with this. Do you know how such an allegation could affect my job?" He glances up at me and his despair crushes me. He looks so shattered.

"I know. We've got to trust this will all work out. They have to clear us as soon as possible so they can find the real killer. This is all a huge waste of time."

Jonas puts his hand on my stomach, and Zoe greets him with a kick. "Whoa! That was a strong one!" A smile brightens his tear-soaked face.

"You should try feeling it from the inside."

He leans forward and lays his head on my stomach. "Hi, baby girl. I promise you that Daddy will get this all sorted out before we get to meet you. I love you, little one."

Every time I catch a glimpse of how he will be as a father, my heart melts a little more. Zoe kicks again, and Jonas jerks back with a laugh.

"She kicked me right in the nose!"

I lay my hand on my stomach where she kicked. "Hey, little miss, it's not nice to kick your daddy…"

My words vanish as a green flash consumes me. It takes my breath along with it.

"You okay, Tess?" Jonas asks.

I smile and nod. He's been through enough today. He doesn't need to hear about my flash and what I pictured along with it.

"Yes, just another really hard kick." I tuck the image of Jonas being interrogated by the FBI agents into the recesses of my mind to process later.

"So, what do we do?" Jonas looks to me for the answers, which is new. It's usually me relying on him for such things.

"Well, we need to find attorneys. We need to talk to Micah. And then we need to take a nap. I'm exhausted."

He nods. "Sounds like a plan. Although I say we move nap into first position and take care of the other things later. I'm beat."

I stand and hold out my hand for him. "Let's go, Mr. McCafferty. Our bed is calling us."

CHAPTER 32

I'm so confused when I wake up to darkness. I grab my phone and see that it's 8:30. We slept for four hours. I have fifteen unread texts and six missed calls. I nudge Jonas in the back as I open my messages. All of them are from Chaundra.

> *Call me!*

> *Are you okay?*

> *Worried about you!*

> *Call me ASAP!*

> *IMPORTANT!*

I'd forgotten to un-silence my phone after talking with the agents. It's probably a good thing, seeing as how we wouldn't have gotten any sleep. Since Chaundra was so vague in her messages, I press the call button.

She picks up on the first ring. "Dear God! Are you okay?"

"We were napping. It's been a crazy day with visits from the FBI.

Are you okay? You've texted and called about a million times. And what's up with how vague you were being?" I laugh.

Chaundra sucks in a breath. "This was a conversation we needed to have in person, well, at least through talking. I take it you haven't seen any news?"

My heart leaps in my chest. If it's newsworthy, it must be something big. "No. What happened?"

That question, along with my quivering voice, yanks Jonas from sleep and he bolts upright.

"They found remains in the Davidson River."

I gasp. "Oh my God! Chase? How? Why?" I can't even form a complete sentence. Thankfully, Chaundra understands.

"Chase, probably. How, that requires a longer explanation. Why, also a longer conversation."

"Wow! This is good news, right? Two FBI agents were here earlier, questioning Jonas and me. They really think Jonas has something to do with these murders. They had the audacity to bring up the murdered women too."

"Damn! Let's hope finding these remains is enough to get them off your case. At least once he's identified."

"Not to be selfish, but I hope it's soon. Well, also for his family's sake."

Jonas pokes me in the arm. "Everything okay?" he mouths.

I shrug because I don't know how to answer. Is everything okay? Will finding these bones matter, or will we both still somehow be on the FBI's suspect list?

"Go watch some of the news, and we'll talk later tonight or tomorrow. Do you guys have plans?"

"Jonas has class in the morning, but that's it for the day. I'm trying to get the mural painted in Zoe's room, hopefully before they cart us off to jail." I force a laugh, but it's one of anxiety, not happiness.

"No one is going to jail. Watch the news, then we'll talk later. Love you!"

"Love you, too!"

I hang up and toss the phone on the nightstand.

"What's going on?" Jonas asks.

"They found remains in the Davidson River. Chaundra said to turn on the news."

"That's a relief! Didn't Lily say he was the first? If so, then we're off the hook. Right?"

"I hope that's what it means, but who knows how long it will take for them to identify the body? And then, they'll have to link him to the other missing kids. I wish they'd hurry up and catch this guy. Liam is in danger, and Zoe will be here soon. This all needs to end."

"Me too. We have to trust that it will be," Jonas says as he pulls on a pair of sweats.

"Sis?" Cyle calls from the other side of the partially closed bedroom door. It's still such a pleasant surprise every time I hear his voice.

"Yeah? You can open it. We're decent."

"Everything okay? I heard you guys talking."

"We're okay. Chaundra says we need to turn on the news. I think they've found Chase."

"Okay. I'll head downstairs. See you in a few."

Jonas pulls me into a hug, which is getting more awkward now that my stomach bulges so much. "I feel good about this."

"I wish I could too, but there's still so many more bodies out there, waiting to be found. We're clueless about who the killer is and why he's doing this. I want this all to be over."

He tightens his embrace. "I know. Me too. We've got to remember, we're closer than we were several weeks ago. You know more about the killer now. You've helped get several of the kids back to their families. It will all come together."

I pull away. "You and Cyle are so much alike. You're both so optimistic. Blech!"

"And you love us both for it!"

"Keep telling yourself that! Let's go watch the news but..."

Jonas interrupts. "But first, coffee. I know, I know."

Warmth spreads through my entire body, knowing that coffee is on its way and how loved I am.

∼

I FLIP through news channels trying to find coverage while Jonas gets coffee ready. Finally, I find a report on one of the local stations.

"Police have not shared much information, but we do know a body was recovered this afternoon from the Davidson River in the Pisgah National Forest. Police say they received an anonymous tip that led them to this location. There is speculation that the body could be that of missing thirteen-year-old Chase McMann from Brevard, North Carolina who disappeared on March nineteenth, 2006, on his way to meet friends to go fishing."

Several pictures of Chase flash across the screen. One is his school picture. One is him with what I assume to be his family. The third is right before he left to go fishing, holding his fishing pole and tackle box.

The truth settles in the pit of my stomach. "That's who I saw in my mind running away from the killer."

"Police plan to hold a press conference in the upcoming days about the investigation into these remains, as well as the recent discoveries of several other children in the surrounding area. Back to you, Scott." The channel goes back to the studio, so I press mute and slump back against the couch.

Jonas hands me a mug of coffee. "That's decaf, by the way. You alright?"

Cyle snorts out a laugh. "Hell no, she's not okay with decaf."

I glare at him. "Shut up!"

"What'd I do?" Jonas asks.

"Not you—Cyle. Making a smartass comment about caffeine. Anyway, I don't know how I am. I mean, the child I saw in my mind was definitely Chase. And Micah seemed confident that the place I described was the Davidson River—how he came to that conclusion I'll never understand. So, I have to assume it's Chase. Now, we wait. God, I'm rambling!" I take a sip of my coffee. Caffeine or not, it's delicious.

"The waiting is the worst," Jonas says. "Especially when we have the FBI breathing down our necks."

I watch the steam rise in a curlicue from my cup and replay the events of the last month in my mind.

"Hey, where'd you go?" Jonas asks.

"Oh, sorry. Just thinking of everything that's happened lately. It seems like my flashes have been back forever now but, really, it hasn't even been that long. This has all been a lot to handle, especially while I'm this pregnant."

Jonas nods. "It's been a lot for me too, and I'm not carrying an extra person in my body. I wish I could make this all better."

"It's weird. My flashes are so different now, and I don't really understand it. Like I'm not afraid to touch people this time around because when I have a flash, it doesn't really change me. I mean, sometimes, I'll sense a feeling like happiness or sadness, but it's like I don't absorb it. Does that make any sense?"

Jonas nods. "That's interesting. I haven't asked much about them because I know you hate that they're back. I'm almost afraid to ask this, but have you been getting them when you touch me?"

"Only once and that was a blue flash, which means a good memory, so I didn't mind it. That's what is so weird. I'm not getting them often from you or Chaundra or these investigators. And sometimes, like in the car before my wreck, I don't even have to be touching anyone at all." I laugh. "I'm trying to make sense of something that is completely nonsensical—just like normal."

Jonas grabs my hand. "Hey, don't beat yourself up. Of course, you want to make sense of this. You spent your whole life trying to figure out these flashes. Now that they're back and, especially because they're different, your mind wants to work out what it all means."

"Sorry to intrude on your conversation, but have you tried writing down all the flashes you've had? At least those you remember. That might tell you something," Cyle says.

"I haven't, but that's a great idea."

"What is?" Jonas asks.

"Oh, sorry. Cyle suggested I write down all the flashes I remember having because that might help me figure out why they're back."

"Where is Cyle?"

I point to the chair across from us.

Jonas turns his head in that direction. "Man, I sure wish I could see you and talk with you. You give the best advice and have been such a blessing to Tessa. You kept her safe all those years so that we could find each other and build this beautiful life together."

Cyle clears his throat and looks as though he's trying to hold back tears. "Tell Jonas that he has been an absolute God send for you, and that I know he would do anything in his power to take care of my little sis. I'm so glad you have him."

As I repeat Cyle's statement to Jonas, a lump swells in my throat. I clasp my hands to my chest and rest them directly over my heart. "You both are incredible. I can't believe I'm so lucky to have the two most wonderful men on the planet in my corner, fighting for me, making sure I'm okay."

"You're worth it," Jonas and Cyle say at the exact same time.

Cyle and I laugh. Jonas' brow scrunches in confusion.

"You guys just jinxed each other with the *you're worth it* comment. Dear Lord, I married my brother apparently."

"We really are alike, aren't we?" Jonas chuckles. "Anyway, do you want to watch more news, paint, relax, work on the nursery? I have a little grading to do before tomorrow's class, but that's about it."

"You grade, and I'll work a bit more on the mural."

"Sounds like a plan."

I hoist myself from the couch, filled with gratitude and love.

CHAPTER 33

Jonas leaves for class and, as much as I love him, I'm glad to have some alone time. Well, except for Cyle, but I told him to make himself scarce for a while. I've been so worried about how all of this is affecting Jonas that it's been stifling, like I can't take a deep breath. And I know he's been equally terrified for me, so he must feel the same. Hopefully, he'll be able to get a sense of normalcy being in class today. His students always seem to energize him.

I pull up the calendar to see what's on my schedule for the week. Only two things, an OB appointment on Wednesday and then an appointment with Ophelia on Friday. That will give me plenty of time to finish the mural in Zoe's room and perhaps work on some of the commissioned pieces I need to complete.

But first, I need to make a list of the flashes I've had to see if looking at it on paper makes any difference in my understanding of what's going on. I start with the first one.

Green flash the day of the accident

A rush of flashes the day I found Tatum's remains

Blue flash with Ophelia

Blue flash with Jonas

A rush of flashes with Lily when she spent the night

Green flash in the forest when we found Dominick

Red and yellow flash when I touched Lily to find Cyle
A rush of flashes again touching Lily
Green flash touching my stomach

I sit back and peruse the list. The first thing that strikes me is I've had so few of them that I can remember most of them to make this kind of list. Before, this would have been impossible if I'd been around other people. Back then, it was a constant onslaught and unfeasible to keep track in any way, shape, or form. Perhaps I've forgotten a few, but not enough to make a tremendous difference.

Green. *Where did these come from and why?* I can't make sense of that at all. And it's completely baffling that I've had flashes when I'm not touching another person. Have any of the flashes changed me in any way? Not that I know other than the obvious of helping me find Cyle and information about the missing children.

I toss the pad of paper and pen onto the end table. I'm psychoanalyzing myself like I'm in a session with Ophelia. I'll take the list to her on Friday to discuss. Perhaps she'll see something that I don't. For now, I have painting to do.

I head upstairs, intending to work on some of my commissioned pieces, but instead head into the nursery. I feel a sense of urgency to get this mural done, since I'm due in a little over a month. It's one of the few things I feel like I can control right now, getting ready for our little girl. As soon as that thought passes, another flits through my mind—you only have six weeks to catch the killer before Liam gets hurt. I suck in a sharp breath. How are we going to stop him when we still have no clue who he is?

Instead of letting my thoughts spiral out of control, I tell Alexa to play alternative nineties music and get to work painting a magical forest for my precious angel.

CYLE CLEARS HIS THROAT. "Hey, Tess, sorry to bug you, but your phone's been going off like crazy for about an hour."

"Oh crap! I left it downstairs." I quickly wipe my hands on a rag and race down the steps.

I have many missed calls and texts from Chaundra. I don't bother to read them or listen to voice mails and call her instead.

"Hey, sorry. I was working in the nursery and left my phone downstairs. What's up? Everything okay?"

Chaundra sniffles. "Yeah, but a lot has been going on in my mind. I've been having some visions."

"Of?"

"Nothing that's too clear, other than a few with Liam, but I think things that have to do with the missing kids. It's all pretty hazy."

"What kind of things are you seeing?"

"Different locations. I've tried writing them down to see if they lead anywhere or if Micah can make sense of them."

"Do you need to come over? You sound really upset."

"No, I'm okay. I'm just overwhelmed. These kids, my visions, worrying about Liam, you, and Lily, and then my feelings for Micah. It's all too much."

"Oh hon. How are things with him?"

Chaundra lets out a little sob which makes my heart drop into my stomach. Chaundra never cries. "They're actually wonderful," she says. "But that's what is freaking me out. Like they're too good."

I can't help but laugh. "You're upset because things are too good with Micah. I'm confused."

She half laughs and half cries. "I know I must sound crazy. After everything with Adam, I swore off relationships. Obviously, he left me with tons of trust issues, but more than that, I was so broken after we split up. I never wanted to be that vulnerable again, so, I built all these walls around myself and focused on raising the kids. Those walls are crumbling right now, and it scares the shit out of me."

"Girl, do I understand that feeling. It's scary as hell."

"I know this sounds crazy because we haven't been going out for long, but I think I'm in love with him," she whispers. "And I'm pretty sure he feels the same."

"Hon, that's wonderful. You deserve to feel loved and be happy."

"You don't think it's nuts?"

I laugh. "You're actually asking me if I think something is nuts? But seriously, I think I knew I loved Jonas on our second date. And look how we ended up."

"Yeah but look at how many relationships don't go the way yours and Jonas' have gone. I cannot give my heart away again only to be destroyed."

"Have you asked Lily about this at all? Like, what she sees happening with you and Micah?"

"She's said a few things, but I've been too scared to ask her. She's always right, and I'm terrified that she'll say we don't make it."

"You need to ask her. Today. And then we'll deal with whatever she says together."

"Ugh. I know you're right. Why do I freak out when things are going so well? Why can't I just be happy?"

I laugh. "You're seriously asking me, the queen of freak-outs, that question?"

"True. But you're right. I'll ask Lily later today and let you know what she says."

I debate whether to ask the question I really want the answer to and pause for a moment. "Sorry to change the subject, but how did they find Chase's body?"

Chaundra takes an audibly deep breath. "We need to keep this between us. Well, I mean, Jonas can know, but that's it. Micah called the tip line from a burner phone he picked up with an anonymous tip, indicating he knew Chase's remains were in the Davidson River. He took a wild guess about the approximate area. It looks like he was accurate considering they found a body."

I'm stunned. "Wow! That sounds pretty risky for him to do."

"Uh, yeah. But he knew they needed to find his body to clear you two. Plus, this is all eating away at him so much, knowing the man who murdered his sister is still out there killing more children. And his fear that he won't be stopped in time to save Liam. He wants this guy caught."

"We're all in the same boat on that note, that's for sure. Any word on how long it will take to identify the body? I'm hoping it's before the FBI decides to take Jonas or me into custody."

"Again, between us, I don't think it will take long. I guess there were some identifying markers that will make the process go faster."

Identifying markers? There couldn't have been more than a pile of bones left of him. What could they possibly find that could allow them to quickly identify the body without waiting on DNA results? I want to ask but don't want to put Chaundra in a tougher position.

Chaundra clears her throat. "Earth to Tessa. You still there?"

"Yeah, sorry. Just lost in thought."

"I can probably guess what's going through your mind, but I can't tell you anything more. That's all Micah told me, which he'd be in big trouble for if anyone found out."

"I promise my lips are sealed, other than Jonas, of course."

"Speaking of Jonas, what's his schedule like this week? And yours? We need to plan another meeting of the minds."

"Hold on a second," I say and pull open the calendar on my phone. Mommy brain has already made me forget even though I checked earlier today. "He's got a full schedule on Tuesday and Thursday. We have a baby check-up on Wednesday, and I meet with Ophelia on Friday. Other than that, things are open. What works for you two?"

"Micah was able to go back to work today after his suspension. He's supposed to stop over tonight after he gets off—don't tell, but probably for a sleepover." Chaundra giggles like a young girl in love. "Anyway, I'll talk to him and see if we can come up with a plan."

I chuckle. "Yeah, I'm sure a plan with us will be at the top of your sleepover agenda."

"Definitely not at the top, but I'll make sure to include that conversation at some point during our visit."

"By all means, get your needs met first."

"Oh, honey, you don't have to tell me that twice. That man has me wrapped around his little finger with the miracles he can pull off in that department."

"I am so happy for you, Chaundra. Please talk to Lily and let yourself feel the happiness and joy you deserve. You've got a good thing going here. Get rid of all those crazy thoughts and questions in your head about whether it's too soon, or going to last, or whatever. Just relax and enjoy it."

Chaundra guffaws. "It is hilarious that *you* are saying that to me."

"Yeah, whatever. Anyway, talk to Lily. Work out some of that stress with Micah and let me know what the plan is."

"Alright, I will."

I should hang up now and get back to painting, but I can't stop myself. "I'm worried about Liam. My due date is only six weeks away. Seeing as how sicko's kill date and my due date are the same, I'm scared."

"I'm terrified. And, for the first time ever, Lily is no help. She can't see anything happening with Liam other than what the two of you saw in your visions. Besides school, I'm not letting him leave my side. I hope that's enough. God knows I will kill any asshole who tries to hurt my child," Chaundra says boldly, but I can hear the fear lingering among her strong words.

A vision of Chaundra dressed as Wonder Woman flashes through my mind, and I laugh. "I know you would. Just picturing you kicking someone's ass cracks me up, not that I have any doubt that you could and would." I pause and pick some dried paint off my fingers. "Do you think we'll be able to stop him in time?"

"We don't have a choice."

Despite my doubts, I say the things she needs to hear. "You're right. He's got all of us to get past first. You, Lily, and I are basically superheroes anyway, then we add in the handsome professor, the charming detective, and the ghost of my dead brother—this asshat doesn't stand a chance."

Chaundra bursts into laughter. "My God. We are quite a crew when you put it like that! We need a name for our group."

"And uniforms! Can you picture Micah and Jonas in tights?" Imagining it makes me laugh so hard that I cry, and Chaundra's doing the same.

After several minutes, we finally regain some composure. "I need to get off here before you make me laugh Zoe out."

"That wouldn't be good. Thanks for talking me off the ledge and for the laugh. I needed it."

"As you've done for me so many times through the years. Love you!"

"Love you, too," Chaundra says. "Oh, and I'll pick up some tights for our boys before we get together again."

She hangs up before I have the chance to comment. Still chuckling, I check my phone for the time, only to see my entire morning is gone. It's already one-thirty. Jonas should be home because his class ended at noon. I check my texts and calls, but there are none from him. Perhaps he got stuck talking to a student, which happens often.

I wolf down a sandwich, grab a bottle of water, and head back up to the nursery to work on the mural.

CHAPTER 34

I stand back and inspect my work so far. It's coming together nicely —Zoe's going to love her little woodland creature-themed room. I grab my phone to take a picture of my progress and notice the time. It's five o'clock. Why didn't Jonas poke his head in to say hello when he got home?

I yell out the door. "Jonas! Are you here?"

No response.

I hurry down the hall to our room. It's empty.

I yell over the banister in the loft. "Jonas, hon. You down there?"

"He's not here," Cyle answers from downstairs. "I've been down here all afternoon. He hasn't been home."

"What? He should've been home hours ago." I rush down the stairs as I dial his number. It rings four times and then goes to voice mail. I shoot off a text asking him to call and then dial his desk phone. Again, there's no answer.

"Is it snowy out? Do you think he had an accident?" I ask as I head to the door to look outside. There's no freshly fallen snow and the roads are clear.

I pace back and forth in front of the wall of windows.

"Sis, calm down. I'm sure he's okay. Maybe something came up with work."

"Calm down? If something came up at work, he would've texted or called. He'd never leave me hanging like this. He knows I'd freak out." I take another trip back and forth in front of the windows, not sure what to do.

"Does he have a colleague you can call to see if he's still at work?"

I open my phone and scroll through the contacts. "His TA. I'll call him."

"Hello," the young man on the other end says.

"Hi! Is this Eric?"

"Yes, it is."

"I'm so sorry to bug you. This is Professor McCafferty's wife, Tessa," I say breathlessly. "We met at the picnic last summer."

"Oh, yes, hi Mrs. McCafferty."

"Did you happen to see Jonas today?"

"Yes, I was in his eleven o'clock class and then walked back afterward to his office with him."

I continue pacing. "Did he leave then? I'm worried because he's not home yet."

"I'm not really sure. I was supposed to talk through some assignments that needed grading. But when we got back to his office, there was a man and woman waiting for him, so he told me we'd catch up later in the week."

A man and a woman waiting for him? Who?

My legs are suddenly so shaky that I'm afraid they may give out. I lower myself into the chair. "Oh, could you tell me what they looked like, by chance? I'm sorry for asking but it's very odd that he's not home yet, and he hasn't let me know."

"Um, let me think." Eric is quiet for a moment. "They both had suits on. The woman had short, brownish hair. The man was very tall, kind of gray hair."

Oh no! I know exactly who it was.

I fight against the tightness in my throat to say, "Thank you so much, Eric. This was helpful. Take care."

I hang up and immediately dial Chaundra's number.

"What'd you find out," Cyle asks as it rings.

I hold up a finger to tell him to wait a second.

Chaundra finally answers, completely out of breath. "Hey, Tess, hold on a sec." There's a lot of rustling, and it sounds like she threw the phone down. "Okay, sorry about that. I had to dry off. I was in the shower making sure I'm all clean for Micah tonight." She laughs.

Fear tightens its hold on me, and I'm terrified to utter the words I need to say, as if doing so will make them come true.

"Tess, what's up?"

"I think they've taken Jonas in for questioning," I finally divulge.

"Who? Who's taken him in for questioning?"

"The FBI. The agents that were here the other day showed up after his eleven o'clock class. I haven't heard from him since. I don't know what to do."

"Let me try to get a hold of Micah. Hang tight and I'll call you back."

"Okay," I say and hang up.

"Why do you think that they've taken him in?" Cyle asks.

"His TA said two people were waiting for him after class. A man and a woman, both in suits. He described Agents Monroe and Kempton. It was them, I'm sure of it. What do I do?"

My eyes are on fire from trying to hold back tears, and my thoughts whirl around like a tornado. What do I do? Who do I call? Why did they take him in?

Cyle sits next to me and tries to pull me into a hug.

I jerk away. "Please, not now. I can't be touched right now. I just need to think."

"Okay, but I'm not leaving you alone. I'll just sit here."

"Whatever." It comes out much more harshly than I intend.

I lean back and close my eyes, hoping it will slow down my thoughts enough to figure out what to do. I hate that I put Jonas in this position. And now, I'm going to bring this innocent little girl into the world, into my craziness. How did I ever think that *normal* would last for me? I should've known better.

The ringing of my phone pulls me out of my whirlwind of self-deprecation. It's Chaundra.

"Hey!" She takes a deep, shuddering breath. "Are you sitting down?"

"Yes. Just spit it out."

"I talked to Micah. He did some digging and yes, the FBI took Jonas in for questioning."

My heart drops into my stomach and I suddenly can't breathe.

"What... what do I do?"

"He needs an attorney. Did you guys find someone to represent you?"

Damn! We were supposed to but didn't.

"No. Do you know of anyone?"

"Micah gave me a few names. I'll text them to you. Have whichever one can get there fastest, go to him. They're operating out of the Sheriff's department for now." Chaundra pauses. "Try to calm down. Jonas needs an attorney, but bottom line is they can't hold him without his consent unless they're able to make an arrest. He must've agreed to go with them to answer questions or they couldn't have forced him unless they have some mystery information that we're not aware of."

"Which would be impossible. Okay, send me the names and I'll contact someone." Despite my efforts to maintain calm, my voice quivers.

"Keep me posted, please."

I hang up and thirty seconds later, a text comes through with the names and numbers of five attorneys. I dial the first on the list.

"Hawkins, Ebright, & Luallen Law Offices. How may I direct your call?" A cheery voice on the other end answers.

"I need to speak with Anya Luallen please."

"I'm sorry, she's gone for the day. Can I take a message?"

"Um, yes. My husband..." I clear my throat. The words that need to come out feel unnatural. "My husband has been taken in for questioning by the FBI, and I'm searching for someone who can represent him."

"Oh, dear. Let me get a few details from you."

She asks me his name, when he was taken in, and where he's being questioned. I stumble through answering her questions.

"Okay, let me call Ms. Luallen, as I'm sure she'll want to be of service. I'll have her call you shortly."

"Okay, thank you."

I hang up and don't know whether I should wait to hear back or keep working my way down the list.

"Is she going to represent him?" Cyle asks.

I clutch my hair in my hands and want to scream. "I don't know. The assistant took down my information and says the attorney will call me. Do I wait on her? Do I keep calling? What do I do?"

"Give her a couple of minutes. Go get some water or a sandwich or something."

I nod and walk to the kitchen with phone in hand. I open the fridge, but I'm too anxious to eat. I grab a bottle of water as my phone rings.

"Hello," I say.

"Hello, Mrs. McCafferty. This is Anya Luallen. My assistant relayed your information to me. I wanted to touch base and let you know that I'm headed to the Sheriff's department now."

I almost fall to my knees in gratitude. "Thank you so much. What do you need from me? A payment? Me to meet you there?"

"You sit tight. Let me get there first, and we'll go from there."

"Okay. Just so you know, he's not guilty of what they're accusing him of. He had nothing to do with these murdered children. I'm sure you hear that all the time, but I promise you, it's true." The words tumble out of my mouth.

"Please take some deep breaths. My job as an attorney is to make sure he is represented, so his guilt or innocence is not a factor to me."

Her statement catches me a bit off guard, even though it makes sense. "Okay. Thank you."

"I'm only a few minutes away, so I'm sure you'll hear something soon. Bye."

I throw my phone onto the counter. I'm filled with rage. At the FBI. At the killer. At these damn flashes. At myself.

"Sis, what can I do to help?"

"Nothing. Absolutely nothing," I snarl.

"Hey, I'm on your side. I just want to make this better for you."

"I know, and I'm sorry. I need to distract myself from this situation and all these damn feelings. I'm going to go paint."

"Okay. Do you want me to come sit with you?"

I shake my head. "Thank you, but I need to be alone."

He nods. "I'll be here if you need me."

I know I'm being nasty and don't mean to take it out on him. I throw my arms around him in a hug. "I'm sorry I'm being hateful. It's all too much."

Cyle doesn't say anything while he holds me close, which is exactly what I need. I finally pull away.

"Off to lose myself in colors."

I head up to the nursery and grab a paintbrush. I blast heavy metal through the speakers as it fits my mood the best right now.

CHAPTER 35

I nstead of completely losing track of time as I usually do when I'm painting, I glance at my phone every couple of seconds to make sure I haven't missed a text or call from Jonas.

"Hey," Jonas says from behind me.

Without even wiping my hands, I lunge into his arms. Neither of us speaks for several moments. Finally, I pull back to see tears streaming down his face.

"Oh, hon! Let's sit, okay?" I grab his hand and lead him into the studio.

He sits on the couch and buries his face in his hands. I caress his back and rub his neck. This is the most upset I've ever seen him.

"Hey, talk to me. I'm worried about you," I whisper.

He finally relaxes into the couch and grabs a tissue. "I'm sorry. I didn't mean to break down."

"You have nothing to be sorry about. Nothing at all," I say. "What happened?"

"God, what a nightmare! After my second class, Agents Twee-dledee and Tweedledum were waiting outside of my office. They asked me to come to the Sheriff's department for questioning. Stupid me, I thought, why the heck not? I have nothing to hide."

Jonas grabs another tissue and blows his nose. "Sorry I didn't text or call but I really felt like it would go quickly, and I didn't want to stress you out."

"Don't worry about me. Please."

Jonas lets out a chuckle full of misery. "Like that's possible. Anyway, I get there, and they put me in a room where I had no phone reception. Like I couldn't text or call. Otherwise…"

"Stop. Please. I understand."

Jonas sucks in a shuddering breath. "So, I get there, and they start hounding me hard. I answered all their questions honestly, but of course, that wasn't good enough for them. Then, they brought out the pictures. The dead women. The murdered kids. Mallory…" A sob overtakes him.

I wrap my arms around him and let him cry into my embrace, wishing I could take away his pain.

"That was so awful of them," I say, enraged that they would hurt him like this.

"Of course, I got visibly upset by seeing all of that, as any normal person would have. Seeing Mallory's dead body. Which only fueled them to press harder because apparently having emotions means I'm guilty of these awful crimes."

"Why the hell are they even bringing Mallory and the murdered women into this? That's over and done with."

"I guess they're grasping at straws, but I get their point. It is weird that we've been involved with both of these cases."

I hear the words he's not saying. Because of my *gift*, we're in this situation. He's on the FBI's radar. Without me, he'd have a normal, happy life that most people crave. Like everything else, my gift returning has screwed up that possibility for him. For us. I shove these thoughts aside to examine later. Right now, Jonas needs me.

"They don't understand me, what my gift is like. I wish we could make them understand." The doubts and guilt linger, gnawing at my soul.

"These people think in black and white, good and bad. There's no making them understand, so it's pointless to try."

I know he is right. But how I wish he wasn't.

"Anyway, thank you for calling Ms. Luallen. She came in and shut it down immediately. I didn't understand my rights, thought I had to talk to them since this was a more official interview, being at the Sheriff's Department and all. I didn't realize I could end the interview at any time. I feel so damn stupid."

"You're not stupid. How were you supposed to know? It's not like we've had tons of experience with this sort of thing."

"I've had enough, trust me."

Another stab of guilt plunges through me. "I know. Me too. I'm sorry I put you in this position."

Jonas pounds his fist on the arm of the sofa. "Dammit, you didn't do a thing to put me in this position. It's not your fault, so don't accept any of the blame."

I wish I could believe him. "Hey, it's not about me. Let's get back to you and what happened. So, Anya came in and shut it down. Now what?"

"Well, I owe her a retainer of five thousand dollars, which sucks, and I have no idea how we're going to afford it. And if they keep up this investigation into me, we're gonna blow through that money quickly."

My mind instantly starts racing, trying to figure out what I can do to get the money. I have several paintings that I could try to sell—ones I've held back because they're the most personal to me. That might take a while, though.

"We will figure it out," I say, even though I do not know how we can do that quickly.

"This is not the best time for all this to happen, with Zoe about to be born."

"I know, hon. I'm sorry."

"Quit apologizing. Please. It's not your fault." Jonas raises his voice, which catches me off guard.

I nod and whisper, "Okay."

"Sorry for yelling. I'm hungry and tired. I'm going to eat and then go to bed."

"I can heat some leftovers for you real quick."

Jonas shakes his head. "Really, I just need some time alone to process all of this. No offense."

He squeezes my hand before getting up and heading downstairs. My mind races. He says he's not angry with me, but rarely has he pushed me away for the sake of alone time. And, really, it doesn't much matter if he's mad at me because I am enraged at myself. I can try positive self-talk all I want about this not being my fault. About not asking for this gift or causing my flashes to come back. Bottom line is it's all bullshit because, without me, Jonas wouldn't be going through this. No amount of positive thinking or self-talk can change that fact. As I spiral down the comfortable rabbit hole of self-deprecation, I know I need to stop it, but I'm incapable. Apparently, I need to get in to see Ophelia before Friday.

My phone buzzes. It's a text from Chaundra asking about Jonas. I fire back an answer that he's home and we'll talk later. I've got too much to figure out, like how are we going to pay the attorney. How can I protect Jonas? And most importantly, how am I going to take care of a baby when our lives seem to be falling apart?

Cyle pokes his head in the door. "Hey! You need to talk?"

"Thanks, Cyle, but no, not right now. I have some things to figure out. I'm sorry about being so bitchy earlier."

"You were stressed. It's okay. What do you need to figure out? Maybe I can help."

I let out a hollow laugh. "That's a long list, but the first thing I need to figure out is how to come up with five thousand dollars to pay the retainer for the attorney for Jonas. And that's only a starting number. If they keep up this investigation, it could cost much more."

Cyle sits in the chair across from me, lost in thought, with his hands steepled in front of his mouth.

"I know where you can get the money," he finally says, with one eyebrow raised.

I throw my hands up in the air. "Do tell. Please."

"Mom and Dad."

I feel like I'm going to puke. "No way. I'm not taking anything more from them."

"I don't really think you have a choice. Sure, you could sell some paintings to come up with five thousand, but you and I both know that money may not last long. Then what?"

He's right. I know he is, and I hate it. I haven't talked to my parents in months, since I called to let them know I was pregnant. They acted surprised and happy but, of course, their true colors have shown through in the fact that they have had no other contact with me since then to see how I'm doing, my due date. Nothing but radio silence.

"Tessa?" Cyle's voice snaps me back into the room.

I nod. "I'll call them tomorrow."

"You know they'll say yes, without a second thought."

I clasp my hands together and stare at the ceiling. I know they will say yes, but after I go through the whole explanation. I've been able to keep the details of my life relatively private from them. How do I explain this one without going into the flashes being back, the murdered children?

"Tomorrow, I promise."

Cyle nods and stands. "Okay, I'll give you some space. Yell if you need me."

I give a thumbs up and sink back against the couch. Zoe squirms inside of me. I know this stress isn't good for her. She must feel every single one of my emotions. She's not even in the world yet, and I'm already not protecting her. I have failed her before she's even been born.

I close my eyes and try to pretend that I'm somewhere different. Someone different. Someone better. Someone normal.

CHAPTER 36

I wake up to a blanket covering me and complete darkness, except for the sliver of moon shining through the windows. I grab my phone to check the time. It's two in the morning. My heart sinks at realizing Jonas left me here to sleep instead of waking me to come to bed with him. He has every right to be upset with me, though. I am the reason he's in this nightmare. If I were a normal person, he could work, come home, get ready for our baby, and enjoy life. But I'm not normal —the past five years made me forget that somehow.

Stop it! I shout in my mind. I flip on the lamp and pull up the site to try to reschedule my appointment with Ophelia before Friday. I don't think I can last that long, considering my current spiral of self-pity. Thankfully, she has an opening after my doctor's appointment on Wednesday. Once that's set, I scroll through my phone for a few minutes. I should head to bed, but now that my mind has started, I know it will be pointless to try to go back to sleep. I head downstairs to grab a water bottle and my laptop. I might as well try to find out more about these missing children if I'm going to sit and obsess about them and our situation, anyway.

I type in the words, *Missing Children Tennessee North Carolina March,* and hit enter. A wave of nausea washes over me as I realize the FBI is probably tracking us and can see all the internet searches we've done. I have no doubt it adds to their case, makes us look guiltier. But I also know that the key to proving our innocence is by finding out more about the missing kids. Or, better yet, finding the actual killer.

This is the first time I've narrowed it down to searching only in these two specific areas. From what we know so far, all the murdered children have been found in one of these two places. Page upon page of results comes back, so it will take time to read through them to see which ones apply to the children from my flashes. I need a faster way to get this information.

It hits me like a ton of bricks. I go back up to the search bar, leaving all the same words and adding the name Sam. I hit refresh. There are only a few articles, but none of them are about the Sam I am looking for. I replace the name with AJ, wishing I knew what the initials stood for, as that would be quite helpful. Several pages of search results appear. I quickly scroll through the first page but see nothing helpful. At the top of page two, though, I find an article that takes my breath away. The thumbnail picture is definitely the child from my memories. I click on the article.

Twelve-year-old Andrew Josiah, also known as AJ, went missing from the Great Smoky Mountains National Park, where he was on a camping trip with his family. He'd gone to the bathroom by himself to get ready for bed and never returned. Searchers were called in and his body was located two days later down a ravine less than a mile from the bathrooms. His right leg had been removed. His cause of death was blunt force trauma to the head.

There are many more articles about the investigation and search for his killer, including pictures of the crime scene. I scroll through article after article, skimming each one and studying the pictures. They break my heart, especially the ones showing his family. AJ had three siblings, two older sisters and a younger brother. I can't imagine the guilt his parents must carry every single day and the questions that must plague them. They have to wonder if their son would still be alive if someone else had gone with him to the restroom, if he wouldn't have been alone.

I scroll to the next article, which has many pictures of the campground and surrounding area, including those of the search team that eventually found AJ's body. I zoom in on one of the pictures when another green flash courses through me. As I catch my breath, a sense of understanding engulfs me. This picture must have some details I need to see. I zoom in as close as the computer will allow and feel like a hammer hit me upside the head when I realize what I'm seeing. Who I'm seeing. Ezekiel, the killer, dressed in his ranger's uniform, standing at the edge of the crowd. I can't see his face clearly, but it's him, without a doubt.

I read through the article to see if there's any mention of the searcher's names, the ranger's names, anything that can help identify him other than the blurry photo. There's nothing in this article, so I read through every single one I can find hoping that there's a mention of the park ranger or rangers who worked in the national forest or who were on duty when AJ went missing. No matter how many articles I peruse, there is no information about the mysterious man lingering in the crowd.

My mind wanders as I continue digging. Why hasn't the FBI been called in before now? Why haven't the police been able to link all these murdered children together? Most of them, if not all, happened in two states. I open a word document to type up a timeline of what we know so far about the missing kids.

2006–Chase: Right upper arm removed, recently found

2007–Anna: Micah's sister, right lower arm removed, body found near time of disappearance

2008–No information

2009–AJ: Right Leg missing, body found near time of disap-pearance

2010–Tatum: Lower left leg missing, body recently found

2011–2015 No information

2016–Dominick: Left arm missing, body recently found

2017–present day: No information

I tap my finger against my lips as I look over the list. Some bodies were found relatively soon. Others not until recently. Is there a reason for this? Did the killer want them to be found quickly? And so far, we only know of five of his victims and the details of how they died. We need to find the others.

I make a list of what I know of the others from Lily and my visions.

Leah–right foot missing

David–right skull taken

Stephanie–auburn hair, left foot removed

Scott–lower right leg removed

Sam—? (Was he his father's first victim?)

In my heart, I really don't believe Ezekiel killed Sam. I think it was some sort of accident that made him lose his mind and start this killing spree. I look at the clock in the corner of the computer screen to see if it's late enough to call or text Chaundra. I need to talk to her and Lily to see if we can fill in the blanks with the missing kids and the years where no murders took place on the calendar. They fit in there somewhere. I'm just not sure where or when. Also, I need to tell Chaundra about the picture I found so that she can share it with Micah. He may be able to get that information to the right people to figure out who the man in the picture is. It's only five-thirty, but I decide to send a text for Chaundra to see when she wakes up.

> *Hey! Sorry so early. Call or text when you're awake.*

I put the phone down and lay my head on the table. I'm so tired and should go back to sleep, but my thoughts are whirling around like a hurricane, trying to make sense of everything we know and filling in the pieces of the things we don't yet understand. I force my jaw to relax from the anger pumping through me that no one has put all of this together before now. This shouldn't be something we, random people, are trying to piece together like a puzzle with essential pieces missing. How the hell have they not found a connection between the missing kids?

"Hey, sis. Why you up so early?" Cyle says with a yawn and stretch.

"Oh, you know. The usual. My brain working on overdrive."

Cyle points to the laptop. "Have you found anything?"

I nod. "A picture of the killer and information about AJ, one of his victims. I need to tell Chaundra about all of it to see if Micah can figure out who this guy is. And quickly, before my husband is arrested for something he didn't do."

Cyle clears his throat. "Not to be a pest, but have you called Mom and Dad yet about the money?"

"Ugh. No. I'll call later today."

Cyle leans down and looks at my laptop. "You know they're probably up by now seeing as how they don't understand the words retirement and sleeping in."

"I'll text Mom and ask her to call when she can." I grab my phone and shoot off a quick text to her.

"Chicken!" Cyle taunts and sits down next to me.

I slap him on the arm with my notebook. "Easy for the dead guy to say."

Cyle clutches his chest. "What a low blow! Making fun of me for being dead? The nerve."

My ringing phone interrupts. Ugh—it's Mom.

"Hi, Mom!" I try to sound happy to talk to her when inside I'm dying.

"Is everything okay? I saw your text. Is the baby alright?" Her words rush out as if she's afraid I won't give her the chance to ask any more questions. Which, to be fair, may be a valid point on her part.

"The baby is fine. It's a girl, by the way. Zoe Cylia is the name we've picked out."

Mom sniffles. "Oh, my goodness, how exciting! There's nothing quite like a daughter."

Yeah, especially when your daughter turns out to be a freak with special abilities.

I bite my tongue to keep from sharing my real thoughts. "We're both excited. How are you and Dad?"

Mom sighs, and I know I'm in for a long, dramatic explanation. "Old. We're both falling apart, it seems. I don't think we'll be around much longer, to be honest. We'd love to see you more while we still have time."

God, this woman is good at piling on the guilt and at taking zero responsibility for why we don't see each other more often.

Again, I bite my tongue, afraid that if this conversation lasts much longer, I may chew the damn thing off. "I know, Mom. After Zoe's born, maybe we can come for a visit, or you can come here. We would love for you to see our home."

"We'd love that if we can make it there. I just don't know. It's hard to tell what condition we'll be in by then."

"My due date is next month, so hopefully you're not deteriorating that rapidly, or you should both really get in to see a doctor," I say, letting a bit of my sarcasm shine through.

Cyle glares at me, attempting to shoot daggers out his eyeballs, which is his way of saying I need to be nice. I flip him off.

"I'm assuming you need something since we don't hear from you otherwise," she says with a sniffle.

I hate that she's right about this. "I... We actually do need something. We need to know if we can borrow fifty thousand dollars."

Mom gasps. "Oh, no! What in the world do you need that kind of money for? Did Jonas get fired?"

I chuckle at her dramatics—I can't help myself. "No, Mom. Jonas did not get fired. It's a long story that I really don't want to go into over the phone, but there have been some things going on, and we need to get an attorney. The retainer is a big chunk of change that we don't have right now. And we don't know how long or how expensive it will end up being."

Other than a few sniffles, I'm met with silence. I know she's tearing up a tissue or two.

"I promise we'll pay you back. We can agree to whatever terms you'd like."

"You're our daughter. Of course, you don't need to pay us back," Mom says. "But what kind of trouble have you gotten into? Does this have anything to do with your special, um, talents?" She says the word *talents* like it's a curse word, which I suppose it is to her.

I don't know how to answer this. "Hold on a second, Mom." I mute the phone and turn to Cyle. "What do I tell her? She wants to know what kind of trouble I have gotten us into with my freakish abilities."

"Tell her the truth. A short version of it at least."

"Seriously? She won't understand. She'll chalk this up as another example of me being a lunatic."

Cyle grabs my hand. "You have to tell her the truth. What if fifty thousand isn't enough? What if this somehow ends up on the news with Jonas being named as a suspect?"

My stomach drops and I feel like I'm going to throw up. As if I needed more *what ifs* to consider. But, as always, he's right.

I unmute the call. "As I said, it's a long story, but we found some bones of a missing child on our property. It turns out there are many missing children from this area." I pause to clear my throat, hoping it will make my voice stronger. "Anyway, because of this, the FBI is involved, and they've questioned both Jonas and me. Which is why we need attorneys."

Mom half cries, half shrieks. "Oh, my lord. How do you get yourself in these situations? Let me guess, you had some sort of... what do you call them? A burst of color. And that got you into this. Tessa, are you still seeing your lovely counselor?"

I grit my teeth. "Yes, Mom. I'm still seeing Ophelia."

Cyle rests his hand on my back in the attempt to calm me down.

"So, was it one of your *visions* or something that got you into this mess?"

"Does it really matter at this point what got us here? We're in a situation and we need help," I say through gritted teeth, fighting the urge to yell. "If you don't want to help, just say no. We'll figure it out. But I really don't need the added stress of you insinuating this is my fault or that I'm crazy."

"Now, Tessa. Calm down. I said no such thing. I only asked how you got into this situation."

I take a deep breath. "I'm sorry for losing my temper. Like I said, there were bones found in the stream on our property which makes us suspects, I guess. That's really all I can share right now."

Again, Mom sniffles and stifles a sob. "I worry about you. I hate how hard things are for you and wish it didn't have to be this way."

"I know, Mom. Me too. I don't mean to stress you out." Can she just freaking tell me whether she will loan us the money and not put me through this rollercoaster ride of emotions? I feel like I'm about to snap.

"Well, I will need to talk with your father and let you know. He may have some more questions for you. We'll get back with you later today."

"Okay, I have some appointments today, so if I don't answer, please leave a message or send a text," I lie. I do not want to talk to either of them again today, or really anytime soon. "And also ask what he thinks about coming to visit to meet Zoe and see our house."

"As I said, I'm not sure we're strong enough for that trip, but I will mention it to him, along with everything else. One of us will be in touch later today."

"I love you, Mom. If you can't come visit, we'll come see you when Zoe is old enough."

"Assuming we live that long," she says.

Instead of screaming, like I want to, I say, "I hope and pray you do."

As soon as she hangs up, I lightly pound my head on the table. "God, she drives me insane."

"I know. But you did well," Cyle says. "Mostly."

"She's so damn dramatic and finds a way to get her jabs in, no matter what. I already feel guilty, and she doesn't help that one bit."

"She never has, and probably never will, as much as I hate to say it." Cyle squeezes me into a hug. "Well, did she say yes about the money?"

I puff up my cheeks and blow air out. "Really? You know better. She'll talk to Dad, and they'll call me later today. Are they really falling apart physically? She acts like they're both on their deathbeds."

Cyle shrugs. "They're not on their deathbeds, but they are old. You really need to make some kind of peace with them while you still can."

I pull away from him. "Make peace with them? Are you seriously putting this on me?"

"Calm down. You know I'm not."

"Well, it sure as hell sounded that way. What do you mean, if not that?"

"Seeing as how I'm dead and all, trust me when I say you want to be able to live with yourself once they're gone. All I'm saying is clean up your side of the street and do whatever you need to do to be at peace with yourself once they pass away. I'm not saying forget all you've been through but try to extend some forgiveness. They're flawed people, just like the rest of us."

Again, he's correct. But I can't find the words to say anything. If I speak, the tears will fall and, given everything that's going on, once they start, they may never stop.

"We'll talk later," I say and rush off to the bathroom. Cyle calls my name, but I can't talk to him about this right now without crying.

I shut the door and splash cold water on my face. I do need to figure out how to extend some grace and forgiveness to them. I know that, even though they didn't handle most things in my life correctly, they love me. I rub my stomach and know that despite my best efforts, I will end up failing Zoe in some ways, too. I hope and pray that she will forgive me for my faults and understand my humanity. I need to do the same with my parents before it's too late.

The problem is—I have no idea how in the world to do that.

CHAPTER 37

J onas comes downstairs as I'm finishing cooking him a breakfast of bacon, eggs, hash browns, and toast. And, of course, coffee. I need it today more than ever because I'm exhausted from the emotional rollercoaster of the past twenty-four hours.

"Hey," Jonas says as he pours a cup of coffee. "Sorry for last night and my attitude. Leaving you on the couch."

He doesn't make eye contact with me as he talks. Rather than his usual morning greeting of a hug and kiss, he sits at the island, staring into his mug. My heart clenches, realizing he must be really pissed at me.

"It's okay. I understand. You had one hell of a day yesterday," I say and lean forward on my elbows to force him to look at me. "Were you able to sleep last night?" It's kind of a pointless question since he has bags and dark circles under his eyes.

He gives me a sheepish smile. "My guess is you know the answer to that by looking at me."

"You do look rough around the edges."

"I was up most of the night thinking about everything and now have a full day of classes ahead of me." He chuckles sadly. "Unless, of course, the FBI shows up and decides to question me or worse yet, arrest me."

I reach across the island and grab his hand. "Hey, that's not going to happen, okay?"

He says nothing, just gently pulls his hand from mine. "Breakfast smells great, but I don't have much time. We can talk about all of this later."

I nod and fill a plate for him. He scrolls through his phone the entire time we eat. I have no idea what to do or say to make this better.

As he carries his plate to the sink, I blurt out, "Don't worry about the money for the attorney. I talked to my mom this morning and asked her for a loan."

He whips around, his face flaming with rage. "Dammit! That's something we should have talked about first. You can't make all these decisions on your own. We're married. It's a *we* decision."

He stomps to the front door and puts on his coat, then grabs his laptop case.

"I'm sorry. I didn't think. I wanted to make it all better and ease at least one of your worries. Cyle thought…"

He holds up his hand. "Please. Stop. I don't have the time or energy for this right now. I'm your husband. Cyle is your dead brother."

I flinch at the cruelty of his words. "I'm sorry," I whisper.

"I'll check in later today." He walks out and slams the door behind him.

What the hell? I've never seen him this upset about anything before. I truly thought he'd be relieved about getting the money from my parents, not more pissed off. And his anger about Cyle? Where was that from?

My phone rings and pulls me from the questions. It's Chaundra.

"Hey," I answer.

"Hey right back. I got the text you sent at an ungodly hour this morning. Is everything okay?"

I bite the inside of my cheek as I answer. "Not really, no."

"What's up? Did something else happen with the FBI?"

"So much. I don't even know where to start." The metallic taste of blood forces me to unclench my jaw and stop biting my cheek.

"Lily and Liam have the day off school for parent-teacher conferences. How about we come over in a little while?"

"I don't know. I need time to think through everything and figure some things out."

"Stop right now. You and I both know the *last* thing you need when you're upset is more time alone in your head. So, let me re-phrase. Lily, Liam and I *will* be over soon."

I laugh despite my stress. She totally gets me. "Okay, I'll be here, wallowing in my self-made sea of misery."

"Oh, lord. Stop it. We'll see you soon."

"Okay," I say and disconnect the call.

I'm suddenly mentally, emotionally, and physically exhausted. I head upstairs, intent on burying myself in sleep until Chaundra and the kids arrive. Maybe in my dreams I can forget all this real-world madness involving angry husbands, murdered children, and returning flashes. Maybe sleep will allow me to return to the land of normal, if only for a while.

LAUGHTER FROM DOWNSTAIRS AWAKENS ME. My chest tightens in panic until I realize I hear Chaundra, Lily, Aiden, and Cyle. I grab my phone. I've been out for two hours and could easily stay in bed the rest of the day. Instead, I get up, pull on a sweater, and head down.

Lily, Aiden, and Cyle are engaged in a deep discussion about elephants. Lily excitedly shares details with them about some of the things she's been learning in school.

"Hi, sleepyhead!" Chaundra says.

I wave and flop down onto the sofa.

"We didn't want to wake you, so we've been hanging out for a bit."

I yawn. "You could have gotten me up. I just needed a little nap."

Chaundra laughs. "It looks like you need about three days straight of sleep."

I run my fingers through my hair, trying to calm it down a little. "That's not about to happen considering life and this." I point to my stomach, which seems to have grown even larger in the last several hours.

"I'm telling you, sleep all you can now because soon sleep will be a thing of the past."

"I wish. But given these flashes, missing and murdered children, being pursued by the FBI, and an angry husband, sleep isn't in the cards right now." I look around. "Where's Liam?"

Chaundra sits next to me.

"He's upstairs playing video games. I didn't think you'd mind."

"That's totally fine."

She grabs my hand. "Listen, you're going through a lot right now. I wish I could help with some of it. Why is Jonas mad?"

I relay to her the events of last night and our spat this morning. Despite my best efforts, I'm an emotional freaking wreck.

"Oh, hon. He's stressed out. He loves you more than anything in the world. Men are fixers, and he doesn't know how to make this better. You both need a break from all of this."

I know she's right. He does love me, but every relationship has a breaking point. What if this is ours?

Chaundra grips my hand. "No. Stop it."

"What?" I ask.

"You forget I'm psychic. Even though my abilities aren't constant, I can still read your mind sometimes. So, to answer your questions, no, this is not the breaking point for you and Jonas. This is a temporary setback. That's it. Nothing more."

"Are you sure?"

"One hundred percent positive."

My phone rings, and I see it's my dad calling. I toss it onto the coffee table. Chaundra raises her eyebrows in question. "I can't deal with him right now. I told my mom I had appointments today and to leave a message."

"Why were you up so early? And what did you need?"

Damn! I had almost forgotten everything I found in my research. I hold up my finger and go grab my laptop and notebook. I pull up the searches and thrust the computer toward Chaundra.

I sit back and close my eyes while she reads, relishing in the sound of chit-chat between Cyle and the kids. Cyle's moved on to telling Lily and Aiden about his safari trip and all the interesting things he learned about elephants. They've always been his favorite. It fills me with sorrow that he hasn't been able to share all these stories and memories with his own children in the same way he's doing with Lily and Aiden right now. I need to remember to tell them about his adventures.

Chaundra exhales loudly. "Wow! You found some good information. We now know who AJ is and how he died."

I nod. "There's more." I lean over and open the tab with the photo of 'Ezekiel.' "There he is."

"Who?"

"Ezekiel, or whatever the hell his real name is. The killer."

Chaundra zooms in and squints to get a better look. "You sure?"

"One hundred percent. I got a green flash when looking at the picture and suddenly knew that he was there."

"Could you find out any information about him?"

I shake my head. "Couldn't find anything about him anywhere."

"It looks like he was a ranger at the Great Smoky Mountains National Park in 2009. I wonder if he's still there."

"Yeah, me too. How do we find out? Could Micah help?"

"Possibly. Let me send him a message and the link real quick."

Chaundra grabs her phone and shoots off a text to him. Despite the grimness of the situation, a smile pulls up the corners of her mouth.

"What's the grin about?"

She laughs. "Oh, you know, just love."

"Girl, did you really just say the l word?"

"Don't worry, I haven't said it to him… yet. But I definitely feel it."

At least one good thing has come out of this entire insane nightmare we're trapped in. Despite my mood, I smile.

"I'm thrilled for you."

Chaundra leans close and whispers. "We had a lovely little sleepover last night so, this smile you see," she pauses and grins from ear to ear, "is left over from a wonderful and fulfilling adventure."

"I'm jealous."

"Oh, stop it. Like you haven't been having the best sex ever for the past four years."

"You're right. I'm ecstatic for you. It's nice to see you so happy and relaxed. All along you just needed a good romp in the hay to chill you out."

"I guess so."

Chaundra's phone rings and she answers. "Hey, Tess, I'm gonna go upstairs for this call because that child of mine is noisy." She points at Lily.

I grab my phone to see if I've missed any texts or calls from Jonas. There's nothing from him, but Dad left a voice mail. I dial the number to listen, holding my breath that he says yes about the money.

"Hello, Tessa. It's your father. Your mother shared your predicament with me. I'm arranging a deposit of fifty thousand dollars into your account. It should be available by two this afternoon. Please call and let me know you received it. I also have a few questions." He says his phone number as what I assume is a jab of some sort to indicate that I never call him.

Despite his back-handed comment, relief sweeps through me. We need that money. Now, regardless of what the FBI wants to try to pin on us, we can at least afford good legal counsel. I start to text Jonas the news, but this morning's conversation makes me reconsider. It will be better to have this one face to face, or at least via phone if he decides to call. I know he blames me for everything—this morning's discussion and his coldness made that abundantly clear.

An ear-piercing shriek comes from upstairs. Cyle and I both bolt up the steps to see what's happening. Chaundra is on the floor of the nursery with her head buried in her hands, sobbing in obvious distress.

I stoop down and put my hand on her back, unsure of what is going on. "Chaundra, are you okay?"

She flinches at my touch, and her entire body quakes. Without lifting her head, she lifts her finger to point in front of her at the wall in Zoe's nursery.

Before I see what she's pointing at, Cyle says, "Oh shit!"

"What?" I ask, my eyes rapidly scanning the wall. And then I see it. Liam lying among the trees in the serene scene I've painted, with his head bloodied and half of his skull missing.

Instantly, the killer's voice fills my mind. *I am so sorry. I didn't want to hurt you, but you are a vital piece of the puzzle. You will bring my boy back to me.*

"Mom," Liam says from the doorway. "Are you okay?"

His voice is enough to pull me away from the killer's thoughts. I rush over to the door and step into the hallway. "She's okay. You can't come in right now." There's no way he can see the horrific image I've painted on the wall of my baby's nursery.

"But..." he says.

I cut him off. "She's upset with me about something. I'm going to talk to her. Go play video games, okay?" My voice quivers as I reach out to tousle his hair.

Again, the killer's thoughts take over as my hand touches Liam's head. *This piece will fit perfectly. I need to get him away from here, somewhere quiet where we can be alone, and I can prepare my sacrifice. God, I hear you. I know he's the one.*

Liam wrenches away from my grasp. "Aunt Tessa, you're scaring me."

The door opens, and Chaundra screams, "Get away from him! Don't touch my son!" She pushes past me and grabs Liam by the arm, rushing him into Jonas' office and slamming the door behind her.

Cyle squeezes past me into the nursery. "Tessa, what the hell?"

I rush in, open a paint can, and dip the brush in. I slap paint on the wall to cover the gruesome portrait I did of Liam on the forest floor. Tears pour from my eyes as two distinct thoughts battle within my mind. *I need him to bring my boy back,* and *I cannot let this madman hurt Liam.*

After I have layered on enough paint to cover the mangled portrait of Liam, I rush to Jonas' office and knock on the door. "Chaundra? Liam?"

After a few moments, Chaundra opens the door. Her eyes are swollen, and her face is flushed. Liam walks toward me with a look of terror on his face but refuses to come close to me. He glances up at Chaundra.

"Can you move to let him pass? He doesn't want to touch you." Her voice comes out bitter and strained.

I step out of the way and Liam bounds down the stairs, away from the monster inside of me.

"Can we talk?" I ask.

She takes a few steps backward. "Do I have a choice?"

"Yes, you do. I'm so sorry. I didn't know I painted Liam. Please don't be angry with me. I painted over it. It's gone now."

Chaundra slumps into a chair, and sobs quake through her entire body. I move to Jonas' desk chair and let her cry without interrupting, even though I desperately want to comfort her.

Finally, her cries quiet, and she looks up at me. "It's not just what you painted that upset me. I was sucked into another place and saw it happen. I saw him cutting into my son's head. No, actually I didn't see *him* doing it—I saw you."

Hearing her say those words, along with the thoughts that invaded my mind while touching Liam, a knot of shame settles in my stomach. I bury my face in my hands. "I would never hurt him," I say, but don't fully believe myself. It felt like I was quite capable of harming him.

"I know you wouldn't. But it felt and looked like you. I know you couldn't see it, but the look of fear on Liam's face when you were touching him sliced through my soul."

I glance through my fingers at her. "I'm so, so sorry."

Another sob escapes Chaundra. "I know you are. I'm terrified. With the vision I just had, I don't think we're going to be able to stop him. I think he's going to kill my son." Her entire body convulses with grief and fear.

Even though she's upset with me, I can't stop myself. I walk to her and wrap her in my arms. "We will not let that happen. I promise you. I don't know how, but we will stop him. He will not get Liam."

"I wish I could believe you, but what I saw…" she hiccups back a sob. "I don't think there's any stopping him."

"We don't have a choice. We *will*," I say as a green flash sweeps through me. Chaundra violently shudders in my arms.

She sits back and stares at the wall for a few moments. Her posture goes rigid, and a sense of determination settles across her face. She swipes the tears from her cheeks. "You're right. There's no way in hell he's hurting my child."

CHAPTER 38

I don't know why or how Chaundra's entire perspective changed in an instant, but she is once again the best friend that I know and love. The one who trusts me implicitly. She and Lily spend some time talking with Liam behind the closed doors of Jonas' office, convincing him I would never hurt him, and calming him down.

While they are upstairs, I try to sort out everything in my mind and convince myself of the same. But Ezekiel's need to kill Liam and remove his skull is still strong within me. His desire courses through my veins. Cyle tries to console me, but I can't talk about all of this right now. It's too scary to say these words out loud.

After what feels like hours, Chaundra and the kids bound downstairs. I'm afraid to meet Liam's gaze, so I sit at the table and stare at my hands. I'm prepared for Chaundra to announce that she no longer wants to be around me because her son is terrified of me.

Instead, small arms wrap around me from behind. "I love you, Aunt Tessa," Liam says.

I turn and pull him into my embrace as a green flash envelops me. Truth settles in my spirit. I don't care what craziness was trying to invade me because I would never hurt this child. I love him.

"I love you too, buddy. I'm so sorry I scared you."

"I know. Mom and Lily told me what happened. You just weren't yourself for a minute. It's okay." He looks at me innocently, his fear now completely erased.

I suddenly feel like a thousand-pound weight has been lifted from my chest, and every muscle in my body relaxes.

Chaundra wraps her arms around both of us and after a moment says, "Okay, enough of all this. We've got a crazy dude to catch."

Liam, Lily, and Aiden rush back upstairs to play video games.

I sigh. "Again, I'm sorry. I would never…"

Chaundra raises her hand to cut me off. "Enough of that. I know. No more talking about it. We've got work to do." She smiles, and I can't help but match her grin.

"I filled Micah in about the link I sent and the things you figured out. He's going to see if he can get more information, off the radar of course." Chaundra pauses and pulls at the hem of her shirt. "So, I was thinking something that may sound crazy."

I raise my eyebrows. "Crazier than everything we've already been through today? Care to fill me in?"

She points outside. "Well, it's a sunny, semi-warmish day. How about you, me, and the kids—oh, Cyle too if he wants—head to Great Smoky Mountains National Park and stop by the Visitors Center? Maybe we'll meet the man himself or at least be able to get some more information. We may be able to work faster on our own without all the red tape that Micah is sure to encounter."

I tap my fingers against my lips, deep in consideration. Part of me wants to say no way in hell because I know I need to stay away from this investigation as much as possible to keep Jonas and me out of trouble. Also, the thought of taking Liam anywhere near this guy scares the shit out of me, especially now that I've been inside of the killer's mind. The other part of me knows Chaundra is right about us being able to perhaps find some things out quicker. And that getting some answers means we can put this all behind us much faster. At least I hope that's what it means.

"Well?" she asks with an almost excited grin.

"Why do you look so damn happy about this prospect?"

She forces her smile into a frown. "Oh, sorry. Is this better? I want this whole thing to be over for all of us and for these families to get justice." She clears her throat. "Plus, after the visions I had today and the fact that we're on a short timeline, we need to stop this bastard before he gets to my son."

"You're leaving something out." I laugh. "You love these kinds of investigative adventures. You missed your calling in life."

"Well," she says and shrugs. "You're not entirely wrong."

I wonder if I should call Jonas and get his opinion, but I don't think I can deal with his iciness. "Sure, let's do it."

"Yes!" Chaundra hollers. "I mean, okay."

I shake my head. "I'm going to go change and will be ready in a few."

I rush upstairs and dig through the closet to find a warmer sweat-shirt that still fits over my swollen stomach. I end up grabbing one of Jonas' oversized hoodies from his college days, which is a bit snug, but it'll do. I grab my hiking boots and start lacing them up, which is no easy feat with this bulging belly, when Cyle peeks in.

"Come in," I say.

Cyle sits on the bed next to me. "Hey, kiddo. I heard you and Chaundra talking. I'm not going to come along today but I'm glad everything is okay with the two of you."

"That's fine, but why won't you come with us?"

Cyle takes a deep breath. "Well, I wanted to talk to you sooner, but, with the whole fiasco from earlier…" his voice trails off as he waves his hand in the air. "I overheard you and Jonas this morning. I think it's best if I disappear for a little while. I don't want to come between the two of you."

Panic swells in my chest at the thought of him going away again. "No, please stay. Jonas didn't mean any of it, he's just scared and over-whelmed. How can you come between us? He can't see or hear you."

He clutches my hand in his. "Yet, somehow, I am coming between you. He said it and I honestly believe he meant it. I'm not going away forever, just for a while. Maybe I'll check in on the parents or Tasha and the kids."

Tears fill my eyes. I can't handle this on top of everything else going on right now. "I need you here with me. This is all so much, and I just got you back."

He nods. "I know. But this is a special time for you and your husband, welcoming your first child into the world. And with everything going on, it's too much. I want to give you both the time you need and deserve to fix whatever is going on before little Zoe gets here." He places a hand on my stomach and Zoe responds with a kick.

I smile. "Did you feel that?"

"She was telling me hello. Or maybe she was agreeing with Uncle Cyle."

I shake my head and let the tears fall. I don't know what to do. I need my brother here so badly. But there is truth to what he's saying—I know this deep in my soul even though I'd much rather deny it.

"Tess, I'm not asking for permission. I'm telling you that this is what I'm going to do. You both need this from me. I will come back. I promise."

"How can you promise that? It's not like you went away on purpose before. You vanished from my life in an instant. What if, while you're away, that happens again?"

Cyle wraps his arms around me and lets me cry against his chest for a few moments. "I promise to do everything in my power to not vanish again without saying goodbye. But you're right, I can't guarantee with one hundred percent certainty." He squeezes me tighter, and I wrap my arms around him, afraid to let go.

What if this is goodbye forever?

"Chaundra is waiting. Go do what you need to do today. Enjoy this last little bit of time with your husband. I'll come back to meet my niece."

I try to hold back my sob, but it comes out anyway.

"I love you, sis."

"I love you too, Cyle. Please come back."

He holds up his pinky, and we connect fingers just like the old days. "Pinkie promise."

~

As soon as Cyle leaves the room, the weight of our whole situation crashes down on me, and I fall apart. I'm unable to breathe. Unable to move beneath the weight of my grief, shame, and fear. He says he'll be back, but how can he guarantee that I'll be able to see him, touch him, or hear him once he does? And what does he mean about getting in the way of my marriage? Jonas was just upset and didn't mean it. Right? The questions swirl around in my brain.

"Tess, are you ready?" Chaundra pokes her head in the door. I'd totally forgotten that she and the kids were waiting for me and our planned trip.

"Oh, sorry. I… Cyle…"

Chaundra sits on the edge of the bed. She reaches out and puts her arm around my shoulders. "Yeah, I know. He told Lily he was leaving for a bit, but promised he'd be back. I gave you some time, but if we want to make it to the ranger's station today, we really need to head out. Unless you're not up to it…"

I shake my head and wipe my cheeks. "No, I'm fine. We need to do this."

"You sure? You don't look fine." She smiles, but I can see in her eyes that she feels my sadness.

"Let me splash some water on my face. I'll be ready in five minutes. Getting out of the house and away from my thoughts will help. Plus, let's hope we can get some answers."

"Okay, if you're sure. I'll pack some drinks and snacks. We'll be ready whenever you are."

I hoist myself off the bed and go into the bathroom. Chaundra's right—I look like hell. I run a brush through my hair and pull it into a messy bun. I splash water on my face and blow my nose. Each time my sadness threatens to pull me back under, I re-direct my thoughts to finding this killer and being done with the madness that's threatening to destroy my family. Dammit! Family. I need to tell Jonas what we're doing. My stomach sinks, knowing he will not approve. I grab my phone and shoot off a vague text that's not exactly a lie, but certainly far from the whole truth.

Hey, babe. Spending the day out and about with Chaundra and the kids. Sorry about our fight this morning. Dad did deposit money into our account, so go ahead and pay the retainer for your attorney. We'll talk later. I love you.

I feel a stab of guilt about my evasiveness but, given the way our morning went, I really can't deal with another argument right now. Jonas has enough to worry about without me adding this to his list. I look at the phone screen as I head downstairs and see the three dots appear as if Jonas is typing a reply. But by the time I reach the bottom, the three dots are gone, and no reply came. He must be really pissed at me. Maybe I should suggest that we both meet with Ophelia on Friday.

"Okay, ready!" I plaster a smile on my face as I grab my coat and gloves.

We head off in search of a killer.

CHAPTER 39

On the trip, I do some internet searching to figure out exactly where the ranger's station is located. It's about two hours away and attached to the visitor's center, which is good. Maybe we can do some looking around, without drawing suspicion, before talking with anyone official. Chaundra and I both recall being at other ranger stations in the past and seeing photos of the park rangers either as a group or individually with nameplates hanging on the wall. That's what we're both hoping for.

Lily and Liam are engrossed in watching YouTube videos on his phone. I check my phone many times on our drive, but so far there's been no response from Jonas. I admit my omission to Chaundra, and she says she's glad I brought her up to speed because she told Micah exactly where we are headed. That revelation is like a stab of guilt straight through my heart.

After several hours full of chit-chat and Chaundra giving me more details about her and Micah, we arrive outside the Visitor's Center and head inside. There are a few other people milling about and looking at pictures and exhibits. With a quick scan of the walls, our hopes are dashed. There are no pictures of staff hanging around, other than that of the Chief Ranger, who is definitely not our guy. He's much younger than the man in my visions, with dark brown hair and eyes and chiseled cheekbones. Definitely not the overweight, middle-aged, blue-eyed man that's been living rent-free in my head this past month.

"Do we talk to someone?" Chaundra whispers.

"It looks like we're going to have to. Let's wander around a bit first. Maybe there are pictures somewhere that we haven't spotted yet."

She nods in agreement. Lily and Liam are fascinated by all the interactive displays. I try to force myself to slow down to enjoy them, but I can't stop my racing heart. We could find an important piece of the puzzle here—to find the killer and stop my marriage from imploding.

"May I help y'all with anything?" A man's voice booms out from behind us, thick with a southern drawl.

Chaundra and I lock eyes for a second and I take a deep breath before turning around, afraid I'll be looking into the face of the man that's invaded my mind.

I let out a huge sigh of relief at the realization that it's not him.

"Actually, there is something we need to ask about if you have a moment," Chaundra says.

"Certainly."

Chaundra pulls out her phone and types something in, then holds it out to the man. "We need to know who this man is."

I peek at the screen as she hands it over to the ranger—it's zoomed in on the face in the crowd.

He studies it for a moment and then hands the phone back to Chaundra. "Are ya'll reporters or something?"

"No. We're looking into the murder of AJ Williams for a friend of ours. Any help you could give us would be greatly appreciated."

Damn, Chaundra's good at thinking on her feet. The gentleman looks us both up and down and then nods.

"Follow me, please," he finally says and heads toward a closed door.

We all follow behind and take seats once inside his office. He leans back and puts his arms behind his head.

"So, you're friends of the family?"

"Kind of. It's complicated," Chaundra says.

He grabs a toothpick from the desk drawer and puts it between his teeth. "I'm Ranger Ferguson, and you are?"

We each introduce ourselves and shake his hand. I brace myself for a flash, but thankfully none comes.

"What can I do to help you?"

Finally, I muster up the courage to speak. "We really need a list of all the park rangers that assisted in the search if possible. It would be great if you could identify the one in the picture, but I know it's not that clear."

"I, for one, was involved in the search efforts. That poor family. I'll never forget the sound of that momma's wail when she found out that her son's body had been found. It keeps me awake at night sometimes." He takes a deep breath and then shakes his head as if to clear the memory. "This isn't information I can comfortably share with you though."

A green flash envelops me, steals my breath. He has to share this information because without it, we're left floundering. I lean forward and place my hand on top of his. "Please, we really need to know."

A tremor passes through him, and he pulls his hand away. He looks stunned, as if his thoughts are no longer his own. After a moment that feels like an eternity, he collects himself and my breath returns.

"Okay, let me pull up a list of employees at that time. Let's see, that was 2009."

Relief swells in me as he types something into the computer and then studies whatever document he's pulled up. "Y'all sure you're not reporters? That family has been through enough. I don't want to put them through any more pain."

"Neither do we," I say. "We swear we're not reporters. As she said, we're personally connected to this case in a variety of ways. This information is only for us."

Still chewing on his toothpick, he nods again as he presses a button. The printer behind him whirs to life and spits out two pages. He studies them a moment and then hands them to me. My hands are so jittery that I almost drop them. Chaundra leans over, and we peruse the list together. I'm hoping for the name Ezekiel to jump off the page, but somewhere deep inside, I know that's not the real name of our guy.

"Is there any way you could look at this list and mark the employees that are no longer with this office? And, if it's not too much to ask, maybe tell us where they are now, if they're still a ranger that is?" Chaundra asks and holds out the list to him.

He grabs it and squints at us. "Why are you all so interested in our staff?"

I have no idea how to answer this. I avert my gaze to Chaundra, who stares at her hands in her lap.

"Because one of them killed AJ," Lily bursts out.

Ranger Ferguson laughs until he realizes Lily is dead serious. "What makes you say that, little lady?"

She sits up straight in her chair and looks straight into his eyes. "I'm psychic, and I know."

I wish I had half the balls of this little eight-year-old warrior. I hold my breath, waiting for his reaction.

"Well, I'm a firm believer that there are things in this world I don't understand. Psychic powers would be one of those things. But I can tell by looking at you, that you aren't joking. I'll help how I can, but I really don't think that's the case. At least I hope it's not."

He grabs a pen and starts going down the list. He marks about eight names with a star and circles three. He hands the list back to me. "The ones with the star are no longer employed here. The ones with the circles are deceased."

I skim the list of names. Of the eight, two are women, so those can be eliminated. "The six men. Can you tell me if they're still employed by the National Park Service?"

"Oh, sorry about that." He reaches his hand forward and makes notes on the list.

Out of the six, five are still employed by the park service and one is retired. I read the names, but none of them grab hold of me automatically. I hand it to Chaundra, and she and Lily do the same. Both shake their heads, which I know means nothing jumped out at them either.

"Thank you so much for your help, Ranger Ferguson. We really appreciate your time." I say and hold out my hand.

This time, a red flash consumes me. Along with it, a woman's heart-shattering scream fills my mind. Without a doubt, it's AJ's mother and the scream that haunts Mr. Ferguson. It's full of loss, despair, and grief. A pain I hope to never know.

CHAPTER 40

O nce we're in the car, we decide a pit stop to eat is needed on the way home because we're all famished. A quick Google search brings up a place I've always wanted to try—Locals, which is about a half-hour away from home. I've still not heard from Jonas, which is not like him at all. I re-trace our conversations over the past two days to try to figure out what I've done that's made him so angry. Or if it's just me—who I am, my powers, the whole package. I don't come up with any specifics, so it must be all of me. My appointment with Ophelia can't come quickly enough.

As we get out of the car to walk into the restaurant, Chaundra freezes, clutching my arm for support.

"Chaundra, what's going on?"

Her eyes go wide, and she whips her head from side to side, scanning the parking lot. "Liam! Lily! Come here, please."

They both bound back to us from the door.

"Do not leave my side," she says firmly while still perusing the parking lot. "Lily, do you feel anything?"

Lily stands still for a moment and then replies, "Nope."

Chaundra sucks in a deep breath.

"What is happening, Chaundra?"

"I don't know for sure. I feel like he's here somewhere. The killer.

But I can't tell where." A shudder works its way through her entire body.

I look around the parking lot but feel none of whatever it is Chaundra is sensing. "Maybe he's inside the restaurant, which would be quite coincidental. Do you want to just head back to my house?"

She clenches her jaw as her hands ball into fists. "Hell no. I hope he's here. Knowing what that bastard has planned, I'd love to meet him face to face."

Uneasiness fills me, wondering if Chaundra's intuition is correct and that Ezekiel is near. If he is, I don't want him anywhere near Liam. I wrap my arm around his shoulders. "Okay, if you're sure."

In response, she marches toward the front door. I grab each of the kids' hands and follow behind.

Chaundra and I continue to study every person we come across once we're inside. There's a gift shop attached to the restaurant full of crafts by local artists, which is one reason I've always wanted to visit. While we wait to be seated, we peruse the selection. My paintings would be a great addition to their collection. While Chaundra and the kids look around, I proceed to the counter and ask if I can speak with someone about my artwork. The salesclerk goes to get the manager. I try on several bracelets as I wait. Finally, a woman in her mid-fifties greets me with her hand outstretched.

"Hi! Thanks for meeting with me. I'm Tessa McCafferty," I say as I shake her hand.

"Nice to meet you. I'm the store manager, Cora. How can I help you?"

I talk with her about my paintings, including some of the awards I've won, types of work I can do, and sizes. Cora says she's very interested and that we can schedule an appointment for me to bring in some pieces in the next couple of weeks. She asks if she can call me in the next day or two to set something up. I grab a business card from my bag and hand it to her.

"Thanks so much for your time," I say, extending my hand.

"My pleasure."

The moment she grasps my hand, red and orange flashes consume me. They're so powerful, they take my breath away, and I pull away, swaying a bit on my feet.

"Ms. McCafferty, are you okay? Let's get you a chair." She places her hand on my back to steady me. Her touch again brings on an onslaught of flashes—blue, green, red, orange. I can't see anything but the images zipping through my mind.

A casket with a young boy. Her sobbing on the floor next to an empty bed. Flowers, so many flowers. A funeral home. Her anguished cries full of pain and grief. A man's comforting embrace, saying *I'm sorry*. Her fists pummeling the man's chest, screaming, *How could you? Why did you let it happen? Why didn't you stop it?* His arms try to reach for her again, but she pulls away. Her heart fragments into a million tiny pieces as she clutches a stuffed dog on her son's bed. She cries out for her lost child—a name I know. Sam!

"Tess, are you okay?" Chaundra stoops down to look in my eyes. I'm somehow now sitting in a chair. "Is he here?"

I force my eyes open, but I can't focus on anything. My eyes dart around the room, and I shake my head, unable to speak.

"We were talking, and she started swaying a bit. Do you need me to call an ambulance?" Cora asks.

Chaundra again scans the room before looking back at me.

"No ambulance," I say.

"Maybe she could sit here for a few minutes. The pregnancy hasn't been easy on her," Chaundra lies. She knows my reaction has nothing to do with pregnancy.

Lily and Liam stand next to the chair, each with three toys in hand. Lily takes one look at me, hands her toys to Chaundra, and then turns to Cora. She reaches out her hand and touches Cora on the arm. Lily's gaze goes blank as she stares off into the distance. Then she gasps and removes her hand. She's seen it, too. Or she's sensed something, I'm sure of that.

Cora's eyes widen, and she looks flabbergasted at Lily latching onto her arm. She clears her throat a few times before asking Chaundra if she should take the toys to the register to ring them up. Chaundra looks back and forth between Lily and me, knowing there's so much more going on beneath the surface.

"Yes, please. And I think we'll need to remove our names from the list to eat, if you could take care of that."

As soon as Cora walks away, Chaundra whispers. "What is going on with you two? Is the killer here?"

"Not the killer. Sam," is all I can say.

Chaundra's face scrunches in confusion. "She has something to do with Sam? She knows him?"

"It's his mommy," Lily says as a tear falls down her cheek.

"Oh, shit. Wow!" Chaundra says and then rushes over to the counter where Cora is ringing up the toys.

I can't hear anything past my shock, horror, and grief. Lily sits on my lap and lets me cradle her as she weeps.

Only a few minutes later, Chaundra returns. "Let's go," she says and ushers us to the car in silence.

Once the doors are closed, she says, "You guys are going to have to give me the full scoop when you can, but I think I've filled in some of the blanks. So maybe the weird feeling I had when we arrived was because of whatever happened in there with the two of you. I got her business card so that we'd have her full name, and my gut says we'll need to talk with her again soon."

I try to respond but can't. I'm suddenly exhausted. I lean my head against the headrest and shut my eyes, thankful that Chaundra was smart enough to ask for her card.

I OPEN my eyes when the car comes to a stop, and I wake up disoriented because it's now dark outside. A quick look around tells me we're home.

"I hope your nap helped. Whatever happened knocked you and Lily out."

I turn and Lily is conked out in the backseat, her neck bent at a very uncomfortable angle, with her arm around a sleeping Aiden. When did Aiden join us? It still catches me off guard each time I see him. Liam looks up from his phone and gives me a grin before glimpsing back at his game. I'm so relieved that he no longer looks like he's terrified of me. Before responding, I pull out my phone to see if Jonas has texted or called. There's still nothing from him and the cabin is dark, which means he's not home.

"Thank you. Do you want to come in for a while? It looks like I have the place to myself."

"I think I need to. We need to talk about what happened with you guys today and decide on next steps."

"We can heat up some leftovers. I'd say that Jonas could bring us some food home, but it seems he's not speaking to me."

Chaundra grabs my hand. "I'm sorry. He's trying to process this all in his own way. He loves you and everything will be okay. Just give him some time and space."

I rub my temples, trying to make this all fit together in my mind. Jonas has never needed or wanted time or space from me. It's a foreign feeling.

I point to the back seat. "Should we wake her?"

Chaundra nods. "You and Liam go on in, and I'll get her. She's got to be starving."

I get out and press the button to call Jonas on the way in the house. It goes to voice mail after four rings. This is so unlike him that I can't help but wonder if something's wrong or if perhaps the FBI has again taken him in for questioning. He has never acted this way with me before, and, God knows, this isn't the first time he's encountered my craziness. It's not as though this is all new to him.

I flip on the lights and begin to pull leftovers out of the fridge, but suddenly I'm hit with the strong craving for Chinese food. We'll order that instead if it's okay with Chaundra—which, knowing her, Chinese food is always okay. With the stress of everything going on lately, comfort food is a must.

"Aunt Tess, can I go play with Jonas' VR?" Liam asks.

"Of course." Before I can get the two words out, Liam bounds upstairs with Aiden on his heels.

When Chaundra and Lily walk in, Lily is rubbing the sleep out of her eyes. I share my plan about dinner, which evokes smiles from both of them. I place our order and then join them in the living room.

"So, what happened today, ladies?" Chaundra asks.

Lily and I make eye contact, and she tips her head toward me to tell me to explain.

"I think Cora is Sam's mom. When I touched her, I got bombarded with flashes and memories. Of Sam's funeral and all the flowers. Her sobs. Her soul-crushing grief. Snippets of her yelling at someone, asking why and how they could've let that happen." Saying all this aloud brings the feelings right back to the surface, threatening to crush me beneath their weight.

"Wow! That has to be why I had such a powerful reaction in the parking lot," Chaundra says and turns to Lily. "Anything else that you saw?"

"I could see some of that, but mostly I saw Sam, like through her eyes. Memories of him up until his funeral. I could see him in the casket." Lily stares at the ground while she shares.

"Did either of you see Sam's dad or get any information about him?"

We both shake our heads. I wish we could've gotten some details about him. But we do have a name to start with, Cora.

"Chaundra, what is Cora's last name? Let's start with looking for information about her."

Chaundra pulls the card from her purse. "Cora Davis."

I grab my laptop and type her name into the Facebook search bar. A profile comes up and has some pictures that aren't set to private. The first several are of her alone or with groups of friends. After scrolling for a bit, I come across a picture of her with a man, saying that it's their anniversary. It is not the man I've seen from my flashes.

"Lily, is this who you've seen as the killer?" I ask and turn the laptop toward her to get a better look.

She shakes her head.

"Yeah, me neither. So, either she and Sam's dad weren't married or are now divorced. The caption of this anniversary picture says that they are celebrating their tenth anniversary, which means they would've gotten married around 2010."

I scroll back further when a picture shows up that takes my breath away. It's a memory from March nineteenth, 2012, with a picture of a smiling Sam. The message reads: *My life forever changed eight years ago today, when my precious son left this world. He left a hole in my heart that can never be filled. No matter what's going on in your life, please hug your babies and tell them how much you love them every single day. You never know when it will be their last.*

"Sam died in 2004. March nineteenth, as we suspected," I say.

Chaundra and Lily both say something, but I tune them out and type Sam Davis into the search bar. Nothing comes up. I search online for Cora Davis, but the only thing that comes up is the restaurant and gift shop website and white pages search databases.

"Nothing on Google for a Sam or Cora Davis. So, what next?" I ask.

Chaundra grabs a notebook off the table. "Let's make a list."

"We need to search for the park rangers from the list we got today. See if we can find any information about any of them, or pictures at least." I say and Chaundra scratches it down.

"Do even more searching for the other missing kids we know about and children who disappeared on or around March nineteenth from 2004 on," Chaundra says as she writes.

"We need to somehow find information about Sam and how he died," I add.

Chaundra nods. "I don't feel great about this suggestion, but we may need to try to talk to Cora about her son's death."

Butterflies of anxiety fill my gut. I cannot imagine dredging up so many painful memories for a woman who's already lost so much.

"Like I said, not a great option but one we might need to look into if we can't come up with anything else."

"I sure as hell hope it doesn't come to that."

Headlights from the road bounce off the family room walls. I slip my shoes back on and head to the porch to meet the delivery driver. I don't realize that it's not our food until Jonas exits the back seat and stumbles toward the house. Why the hell did he get an Uber instead of driving himself home? My answer comes quickly as he sways so badly on his feet, he almost falls over.

"Hey, babe," he says, his words slurring together.

I can smell the alcohol from two feet away. Adrenaline surges through me as my hands clench into fists. This drunken man is nothing like the Jonas I know. He trips over his feet and stumbles toward me with his arms outstretched. Thankfully, I'm there to break his fall.

"Where have you been?"

He laughs. "I needed a few drinks."

I bite my tongue to keep myself from screaming at him. It would be pointless at this minute. "I've been worried about you. Why didn't you text or call me?"

Jonas smiles and points his finger at me. "I'm very mad at you. I didn't want to talk to you." He boops me on the nose between each word like it's all a funny joke. "But I'm better now."

"No, you're drunk now. That's not the same thing."

"It feels better. I figure I could end up in prison tomorrow so I might as well enjoy today." He laughs maniacally.

"Let's get you inside. Chaundra and the kids are here, so why don't you just go to bed?"

He turns and rushes toward the door, throwing it open. "Chaundra. Lily! Two of my favorite gals."

Chaundra's eyebrows shoot up in surprise. I mouth the word *drunk,* and she nods in understanding.

"Okay, Jonas, say goodnight. Let's get you to bed."

He stomps his feet like a petulant toddler. "But I don't wanna. I want to stay and visit with all of you."

Inside, I'm boiling with rage. We have serious things to take care of, and I don't have the time or energy to deal with a drunk ass husband right now.

"No! Bed." I snarl and grab his arm, dragging him toward the stairs.

He sticks out his lower lip in a pout. "Fine. Goodnight girls. My mean wife is making me go to bed."

I yank him by the arm up the stairs, and as soon as he's in the room, he plops down on the bed. "Let's make love." He reaches up and grabs my breast.

I slap his hand away. "You need to go to sleep." I slip off his shoes and pull the covers over him.

"I want you with me," he says. "Or do you need to spend time with your brother? You always choose him over me."

I fight the urge to slap him. "Enough!" I shout and flip off the lights. "We will talk in the morning."

I slam the door behind me and take some deep breaths. I did not need a drunk, obnoxious husband tonight after everything else.

WHEN I GET DOWNSTAIRS, the entire table is covered with cartons of Chinese food, as it always is when Chaundra and I order it. We can never decide on just one or two items. Instead, we sample a bit of everything.

Chaundra looks up from setting the table. "Is everything alright?"

I let out a whoosh of air. "I'll be better after we eat."

"Then, eat we shall! Liam, food!" Chaundra yells upstairs.

Liam and Aiden fly down the steps so fast I can't help but laugh. The word food is definitely the way to a growing boy's heart.

With our plates piled high, we dig in and quietly savor each bite.

"Do you want to talk about Jonas?"

"I'm so pissed at him. How dare he go out and get so wasted without letting me know where he was? I get that this is all stressful, but what the hell? I don't want this anymore than he does. And then, as I'm forcing him into bed, he makes a jab about me choosing Cyle over him." I slam my water glass down on the table.

"Oof. Bad move especially after today."

"No kidding! But, of course, he doesn't know about today because he was being a big baby and refusing to talk to me. And tonight, he's too drunk to have a sensible conversation."

Chaundra covers her mouth with her hand, but I can see that she's laughing. I glare at her.

She holds her hands up in the air and lets her guffaws break free. "I'm sorry. I know it's not funny, but this is the first fight I've ever seen you guys have. In all honesty, I'm kind of scared for his life with how pissed off you are."

"You should be," I say while trying to keep a straight face, but Chaundra's laugh is infectious. I can't help but join in.

Lily and Liam look back and forth between the two of us like we've lost our minds, which perhaps we have. By the time we get ourselves under control and bring our giggle fit to a close, we both have tears streaming down our cheeks.

"I'm gonna make a suggestion. Please hear me out before you veto it, okay?"

I cross my arms and shoot daggers at her.

"You are very pregnant and emotional. You've had a helluva couple of months. Let me take the list with me because my guess is Micah can get information much quicker than we can. Then, I'll check in with you tomorrow after your doctor's appointments to make sure Jonas is alive," she laughs, "and then we can make plans to get together sometime this week to go over everything."

"We all need this to end before Zoe arrives and before Liam..." I let my voice trail off, unable to finish.

Chaundra reaches across the table, grabs my hand, and squeezes. "You're tired. You've had an emotional day between everything with Liam this morning, Cyle leaving, the FBI, and Jonas. Take tonight off. Sleep, paint, read, watch TV. Just relax. Nothing is going to happen between tonight and tomorrow."

I lean forward and rest my chin on my hands. "I wish you could promise that. It seems like I'm trapped in a tornado and everything's spinning out of control. Who the hell knows what else can happen in the next twenty-four hours?"

She squeezes my hand again. "Listen to me. Things will be okay for the next twenty-four hours. Lily, will they?"

Lily closes her eyes for a moment. "I think so."

I take a deep breath. "Okay, fine. Have Micah try to find more information about Cora, too. She may be our best lead so far."

"I will. Now, let's get this cleaned up and we'll get out of your hair so you can *relax*."

We clean up the table and I send most of the leftovers home with her. Even though I'm still pissed at him, I save a bit of the cashew chicken and shrimp lo-mein for Jonas since they're his favorites.

I hand the list of rangers over to Chaundra, tempted to take a peek at a few of the names to look up once she's gone. Instead, I force myself not to. She's right—I need to relax. I hug Chaundra and the kids. A blue flash whirls through me when Lily and I embrace. Along with it, an image floods my mind—a giggling young boy who looks so happy. In my heart, I know it's Sam.

CHAPTER 41

After Chaundra and the kids leave, I need to distract myself for a while, so I finish the mural in Zoe's room, including covering the spot where Liam's bloodied body was this morning with several woodland nymphs hoping that by placing them there, it will ensure no harm comes to him. Utterly exhausted, I finally crash into bed at midnight.

My alarm goes off at eight to give me plenty of time to get ready for my doctor's appointment today. Jonas isn't in bed, and I wonder if he remembered the appointment or if he's choosing not to go because he's still pissed at me. I head downstairs for a cup of coffee before showering and find Jonas with his head buried in his hands at the kitchen island. He peeks out at me from between his fingers as I pour myself a cup of coffee.

"Sorry about yesterday," he says with a raspy voice.

"Which part exactly? For your vicious comments in the morning? For ignoring me all day? Or for coming home like a drunken idiot last night?"

He sighs and shrugs. "All of it."

I don't really have a response because I'm going to need a bit more than a blanket apology to get over it. I move to the couch to savor my coffee. If he wants to talk, he can come to me. I scroll through the newsfeed on my phone, and within minutes, Jonas comes over to sit next to me. I don't bother looking up. He finally reaches forward and grabs my phone, laying it on the coffee table. He then links his fingers with mine. I jerk my hand away.

"I am really sorry about how I acted yesterday. I'm sorry for treating you awful."

I peek out at him from beneath my hair. He looks like he genuinely feels bad, but I really don't feel like being nice today, at least not yet. "What was up with you?"

He slumps back into the couch. "I don't know. I'm so mad, and I took it out on you."

"You seem pretty angry with me, especially given some of the hurtful things you said."

"I'm not angry with you, just this whole situation. The flashes taking over our lives. Feeling helpless to do a single thing to help our predicament or to make sure you and Zoe are safe. The FBI questioning me and dredging all these painful memories back up. I want to demand that you stop trying to catch this guy, but I know you won't listen to me. I'm trying so hard to be your rock, but it seems like now that Cyle's back…" He doesn't finish the sentence.

"Well, about that. He overheard your rant yesterday and left for a while. Hopefully, not for good." Saying that out loud pulses a fresh wave of anger through me. And fear that I'll never see him again.

"Shit! Hon, I'm so sorry. That's not what I wanted at all." He rakes his fingers through his hair. "I hate how insecure and jealous I've been feeling. It's not his fault. It's on me, entirely."

"Yeah, it is on you," I bark, then take a few calming breaths. Biting his head off will not get us anywhere. "It's not like you, which is probably why it caught us completely off guard."

Jonas nods. "I feel like I'm going to explode with all the pressure to make everything okay for you and Zoe. It's all too much." He covers his face with his hands.

I lean into him and let my head fall back against his chest. "I'm feeling all that, too. But we're a team. You can't turn against me. And getting so drunk last night! What the hell?" I look up at him.

He hangs his head in embarrassment. "I know that wasn't okay. If it makes you feel any better, I feel like absolute hell today. I'm afraid I'm losing my mind."

His words hit like a punch. I've never known him to feel this way. He is my rock, my strength. I'm the one that falls apart, not Jonas. He sounds so broken and defeated. I raise my face and kiss him because I don't know what else to say or do.

He pulls away after a second. "My breath is terrible, and my mouth is full of cotton. I love you with my whole heart, Tessa. Tell me this is all going to be okay."

A million doubts flutter through my mind. "It will all be okay. We'll get through this." I hope I'm not lying to him.

He leans his head against mine. "I hope so. I'd do anything for you and Zoe. Absolutely anything. I just don't know what it is I need to do right now to take care of you guys or myself."

"As Ophelia has told me thousands of times through the years, we only need to keep taking one baby step forward at a time, even if we don't have all the answers. Speaking of Ophelia, I have an appointment with her today after the doctor's appointment. Maybe we should go together."

His head bobs in agreement against mine.

"First, though, we have to meet with the OB about little one," I place my hand on my baby bump. Jonas does the same.

"She'll be here soon," he says. His voice is full of sorrow, though, instead of its usual joy. "We need to get our act together quickly."

"We do, and we will. I'll fill you in on everything that happened yesterday. I think we're getting close to finding some answers."

Jonas blows out a huge breath of air. "That would be a relief."

"I'll tell you all about it on the way to our appointment. I need to shower first. You go pull yourself together a bit."

He gasps in mock horror. "You're right, and I need to take some aspirin for this headache. I'd forgotten how much hangovers suck."

I stop halfway up the stairs, and without turning around, say, "I love you, but you deserve a hell of a headache for the way you acted yesterday."

I don't give him a chance to respond before bounding up the stairs.

∼

BY THE TIME we reach Dr. Weyman's office, the tension has dissipated between the two of us. He made the call to Ms. Luallen to put down the retainer and officially secure her legal representation. He agreed that, while he's not happy to be indebted to my parents, it was the right call since we couldn't have come up with the money otherwise. Hopefully, being under the watchful eye of the FBI will soon come to an end, but it's nice to know we're taken care of, if not.

Dr. Weyman does my examination and then sits back with her arms crossed. "Have you been having any contractions?"

"Maybe a few Braxton Hicks, but nothing that lasts long."

"Well, you are dilated to a one right now, so you could go into labor at any time. The baby is in the right position."

"Isn't it too soon?" Jonas asks, his voice laced with concern.

Dr. Weyman opens my chart on her tablet and scrolls through it. "We'd like to be able to hold off as long as possible. Tessa is now at thirty-six weeks, so at this point it would be considered a late pre-term delivery. There are risks of complications at this stage, so the longer we can keep the baby in utero, the better."

"Complications? What type of complications?" I ask as Jonas grips my hand so tightly that the circulation cuts off.

"Complications could include RDS, Respiratory Distress Syndrome, sepsis, low birth weight, difficulty regulating temperature, and sometimes we see developmental delays or worse."

Jonas and I lock eyes, the question of what worse could mean lingering between us. He shakes his head as if to tell me not to ask.

Dr. Weyman clears her throat. "I see your concern. From your latest ultrasound and my examination today, your baby is exactly where she's supposed to be growth wise. I really don't suspect we'll have any complications even if you deliver in the next week. But to make sure, I am recommending partial bedrest and lowering your stress level as much as possible."

"What exactly does partial bed rest mean?" Jonas asks, finally letting go of my hand.

"Minimal walking, moving around, standing, and sitting. You don't have to lie in bed all day but minimize movement as much as possible. We want to slow down the process as much as we can. And eliminate stress. That's equally important."

A cynical laugh bubbles out of me. If only she knew the amount of stress we've been under, she would know better than to even suggest this. How in God's name do we eliminate stress?

Dr. Weyman puts her elbows on her knees and leans toward me. "I know getting rid of stress altogether is impossible, but do your best."

I rub my belly, silently begging Zoe to stay put a while longer.

"We'll need to see you weekly from this point on. If your water breaks, get to the hospital immediately. Since we're worried about a pre-term birth, please also go in if you have contractions six minutes apart that last for about a minute for over an hour."

Jonas and I both nod.

We schedule our next appointment and then head out to the car in silence. Once the doors close, Jonas turns to me with a dead serious look on his face.

"From this moment on, I need you to do exactly what she said. No more painting, talking about missing kids or the FBI, and you need to lie down as much as possible."

I know what he's saying makes sense, but I also know it's impossible. We are so close to figuring out who killed these children that I can't stop now. And, with Liam's life being in danger, how do I not worry?

"Tessa?"

I take a deep breath. "Hear me out, okay? I will lie down as much as possible—no painting, no housework, nothing strenuous. But I can't agree to stop trying to find the killer. We are so close."

Jonas slams his hand against the steering wheel. "Dammit Tess. You and Zoe are more important than finding this killer."

I reach over and grab his hand. "Look at me, please." After a moment, he turns toward me, red-faced and with his jaw clenched.

"Chaundra, the kids, and Micah are supposed to come over tomorrow evening. Let's see what they have to say and what Micah has figured out. I know it's all so much, but we have to figure this out now, before he kills Liam. Chaundra has already lost one child. She cannot go through that again. I couldn't live through that either, knowing we could have potentially stopped it from happening. And we need him to be caught to get you off the list of suspects before Zoe is born."

"You don't need this stress. It could be putting our child's life at risk," he says, resting his head against the steering wheel. "But I'm also worried about Liam. I don't know what to do!"

I rub his back, trying to ease his tension. I know he wants what's best for all of us. This whole situation is impossible.

"Let's talk with Ophelia today and then ask Lily if she can see whether Zoe will have any problems and go from there. Okay? And trust me, I don't want this stress any more than you do, but it's where we are. I hate it, but for whatever reason, it's the hand we've been dealt right now. I know we are supposed to stop this guy, like I did with Matthew."

Jonas sighs and starts the car. "Is it even okay for you to do the appointment with Ophelia today since you're supposed to be laying down?"

I shrug. "I don't know, but we both need this appointment. I know I do anyway, and it certainly seems like you're in the same boat."

"I don't even know what choices are right and wrong anymore. Let me think on the drive to Ophelia's. I need time to process everything."

I nod.

We drive the rest of the way to our appointment in silence.

CHAPTER 42

Jonas drops me off at the front door of Ophelia's office to minimize how far I have to walk. I sink into one of the couches in the waiting room while he parks the car. I shut my eyes and try to force my shoulders to relax. I hear Jonas enter but keep my eyes closed, hoping that he too can allow the calm to wash over him while we wait.

I open my eyes when Ophelia's office door opens. "Hi Tessa. Oh, and Jonas. I didn't realize you were coming today."

"It was a last-minute decision," I say as Jonas holds out a hand to pull me to my feet. "I hope it's okay."

She scoots out of the doorway to give us room to enter. "Of course, it is."

Instead of my usual chair, I sit next to Jonas on the sofa and grab his hand.

"Would either of you like water, coffee, or tea?" Ophelia asks, grabbing a notebook and pen off her desk.

"I'd love a water even though it may make me have to pee about ten times in the next hour." I force a smile.

"Yes, me too, please," Jonas says.

Ophelia hands us each a bottle and then settles into her chair. "You look like you're about to pop, Tessa." She points at my bulging stomach.

"Yes, I'm huge. We actually just got done at the doctor and it seems I'm dilating already. So now, I'm on partial bedrest for the duration of my pregnancy."

"How have things been? How are both of you doing?"

Jonas releases a forceful breath. "Things have been insane and not going so well."

"Can you tell me more about that?" she asks, pen poised above the paper, ready to take notes.

With only that question, the floodgates open and Jonas fills her in on everything that's been going on with the murdered children, the FBI, the pregnancy, and us. As the words pour out of him, I can finally see the full picture of how hard this has been on him. Stress is etched across his face and laced in every word.

"That's a heavy load you both have been carrying. Tessa, do you have anything to add?"

"Jonas did a great job of summarizing our current nightmare, but he left a few things out. Cyle was back briefly but then left again yesterday, supposedly only for a while, because he felt like he was coming between us. We're both under an incredible amount of stress, and instead of coming together, it feels like it's tearing us apart. We're both trying to deal with everything in our own way and not doing so well with that."

Ophelia looks from me to Jonas. "With the amount of stress you both have been under, it's important that you communicate and approach this as a team rather than as individuals. Which one of you would like to talk first about that?" She raises her eyebrows, waiting for a response.

I hold out my hand to indicate that Jonas should talk first, and he gives a curt nod before he begins.

"My main concern is that Tessa and Zoe are okay. I feel like it's my job to protect them. Tessa, however, seems to think she's some kind of wonder woman and can hunt down a killer, stop Liam from getting hurt, and have a healthy, normal pregnancy. I feel like she's listening to everyone but me even though I have her best interests at heart."

I pull my hand from his grasp and cross my arms over my chest.

"Tessa, tell me what's going through your head right now, please." Ophelia says.

"I know Jonas loves me and wants to make sure the baby and I are okay, but I also know my gift is back for a reason. Part of that reason is to keep Liam from getting hurt. I feel like Jonas just expects me to cut off that part of myself, the flashes, and I can't. I wish I could, trust me." I clear my throat. "I feel so guilty for putting Jonas in this position. I've been beating myself up, feeling like, without me, none of this would be happening and he could have the life he deserves." A tear escapes down my cheek and I quickly wipe it away.

Jonas wraps his arm around me and pulls me to him. "It's not your fault. You didn't ask for this. I wouldn't want a normal life if it meant not having you as my wife."

I close my eyes to keep more tears from falling.

"There's a lot to unpack here. Let's go back a minute to one thing you said, Jonas, and that is," Ophelia pauses and scans her notes, "Tessa is listening to everyone but you. Can you tell me more about that?"

"It seems like she was turning to Cyle more than me, which is where that anger came from. I understand that he's her brother, and she's missed him, but I'm her husband. I don't get why she can't talk to me openly and honestly about everything that's going on with the flashes."

Ophelia nods. "Tessa, do you feel like you've been open and honest with Jonas about things?"

I take a moment to think through the past several months before responding. "Honestly, no. I haven't."

Jonas' grip tightens around me.

"And why do you think that is?" Ophelia asks.

I take a deep breath and grab a tissue, preparing for an onslaught of tears. "I don't think I understood it until right this second. I've lived with these flashes for my entire life, other than the past five years. Cyle is the only person I had for most of that time who believed me or understood the hell I went through because of them. Since the flashes went away, I've found a new support system in Jonas and Chaundra. I feel like Chaundra totally understands the confusion that comes with having a special ability like mine because of her own gift, and she's been inside of my mind." I take a drink of water to give myself time to figure out how to further explain.

"Jonas and I met when I was still having flashes, but our relationship didn't really start until after they were gone. He's never known me on an intimate level with them. Part of me wants to protect him from that side of me and the ugliness that comes with it. The other part of me is terrified that his opinion of me will change if he knows how crazy things get inside of my mind." I wipe the tears away and grab a second tissue.

"Hon, I love you no matter what. Nothing will change that, ever. I can't help if I don't know what's going on inside of you," Jonas says and tucks strands of my hair behind my ear.

"Tessa, can you tell me what you just heard Jonas say?" Ophelia asks.

"That he loves me and wants to understand and help."

Ophelia nods. "I think on some level you already knew that, so what keeps you from turning to him in an open and honest fashion, rather than Cyle?"

I pick at the skin along my thumb nail as I respond. "I don't think I realized I was doing that until now." I look up at Jonas. "I'm sorry. I didn't mean to shut you out. I just feel so guilty that you have to go through all of this."

Jonas kisses me on top of the head. "Again, it's not your fault. I'm willing to go through hell with you."

Ophelia taps her pencil against her notepad. "Tess, I want to go deeper. Without thinking, I want you to answer this question for me— why have you turned to Cyle instead of Jonas?"

"Because Cyle loves me no matter what, and he understands. What if Jonas sees how crazy these flashes can make me and decides he can't deal with it? Or that he doesn't want to. I hate myself when I'm having these flashes. I can't imagine anyone other than Cyle loving me through this madness." I slump against Jonas and cover my face with my hands. "I've been spiraling into a pit of self-loathing and pity lately, beating myself up for this whole situation."

"I would never leave you," Jonas says.

I try to believe him.

"Jonas, what Tessa is saying makes sense to me. She has a PTSD-like response to these flashes. With them returning, it brings back all the thoughts, feelings, and self-loathing that she lived with for most of her life. The only way she knew to comfort herself before was by turning to the one person she had, Cyle. I'd venture to say she's not shutting you out on purpose or to hurt you, rather it's a self-protection mechanism. Everyone else in her life, prior to the past five years, has abandoned her. When PTSD is triggered, our actions go into auto-pilot mode, which for Tessa means turning to self-deprecation and to her brother."

Hearing her say it this way makes it all click together in my mind. I finally understand what I've been doing and why.

"That makes sense. So, how do we fix it or do it differently?" Jonas asks, quietly.

"As I've said to Tessa many times throughout the years, you are only responsible for your side of the street. You cannot fix this for Tessa. She needs to figure out new ways to cope, and you both need to work on communicating openly and honestly with each other even when it's uncomfortable."

I want to scream. I have no idea how to do this differently. "I'm lost. My normal coping mechanisms are failing or causing more problems."

Ophelia nods. "Yes, they probably are because you're not the same person you were five years ago. You have a strong and solid support system now with Jonas and Chaundra. Instead of shutting them out and reverting to only relying on Cyle, you need to lean into them. The only way you're going to learn that other people can and will stick by you, besides your brother, is to give them a chance by letting them in."

All the breath gets sucked out of me. By holding things back from

Jonas, I haven't given him the chance to fully love and support me. I've not given him enough credit that he will stay even if he sees the scary parts of me.

"You're right. I finally understand your anger, Jonas. I've been beating myself up and convincing myself that you were pissed at me because of the flashes. When really, your anger and frustration are coming from me shutting you out."

His head bobs against mine in agreement. "I'm never going to get angry with you for being who you are. I went into this knowing about your flashes and with no guarantees that they'd never return. I hate what the flashes do to you and the situation we're in. However, I love you. I want to know all of you—the good, the bad, and the ugly. If these flashes are here to stay, so be it. We can work through it together as long as you let me in."

I gaze up into his eyes and see nothing there but love and concern. There's none of the judgement or hatred that I've projected onto him and assumed he was feeling. How quickly I returned to my old thinking when thrown back into a life with flashes.

"I'm sorry for shutting you out. I will work hard to handle things differently."

Ophelia sets down her notebook and pen on the side table. "We've made some progress here today, but I think it's best if we plan on having more sessions after Zoe is born. Marriage is hard work, especially when there's extra stress like both of you have been under. Assignments for both of you. Tessa, instead of getting caught up in your own thoughts, assuming what Jonas is thinking or feeling, you need to talk to *him* about it. Not Cyle, not Chaundra, your husband. Allow him in."

I nod in agreement, knowing this is what I need to do.

"Jonas, you also need to share your honest thoughts and feelings with Tessa as they occur rather than letting them build up to the point where you explode in anger or get drunk to deal with it."

"Agreed."

Ophelia stands. "Please be in touch to let me know when you have the baby, and we'll set up appointments at that time. In the meantime,

I'm a phone call away if you need to talk through anything or need me to come to you for a session."

Jonas stands and holds out his hands to me. I hoist myself up and wrap my arms around him, filled with a new understanding of myself and appreciation for him.

"We'll get through this, hon. I love you," he says.

And for the first time, I believe he fully understands what loving me truly means and that he's committed to being by my side through it all.

CHAPTER 43

The walls that have been erected between Jonas and me seem to have crumbled since our counseling session. We both talk late into the night, sharing our fears, our hopes, and our anxieties about the case, Zoe, and our marriage. As ordered by the doctor, I spend the rest of the day and entire night lying down after the appointments. Jonas reluctantly agrees to allow Chaundra, Micah, and the kids to come over tonight as long as I vow to lie on the couch other than eating. Chaundra offers to bring dinner plus some meals for us to freeze for later. Jonas repeats several times that he wishes he knew how to get in touch with Cyle to have him come back. My guess is that he mostly wants him to return so he can babysit me. Although I'm not too thrilled to think my husband wants me to have a babysitter, I'm hoping that wherever Cyle is, he hears this and returns.

I'm lying on the couch when everyone arrives, and Jonas has a fire roaring in the fireplace. They all come in with arms loaded with casserole dishes, Tupperware containers, even a few pans.

I start to sit up, but Chaundra immediately turns to me. "No. You stay there until dinner is ready. I'll tell Jonas what everything is, and I've put notes on each dish on how to warm it up."

I laugh and lay my head back on the pillow.

As soon as Lily has put her arm loads down, she skips over and gives me a hug. I brace for a flash, but none comes.

"Hey, sit down here a sec, please." I scoot to make room for her. "I need to ask you something, and I need an honest answer."

"Okay," she says.

"Can you see any problems with Zoe? Like, is she okay when she's born?"

"Can I touch your belly?"

I grab her hand and rest it on my stomach. Zoe starts to kick and stir as a green flash whooshes through me. Lily stiffens, so I know she feels it too. Once my vision returns, I study Lily's face. She removes her hand.

"I can't...," she says, stumbling over her words. "I can't tell. I don't know. I can't even tell you anymore when her birthday is. It's all gone blank." Lily bites her bottom lip.

I reach out and grab her hand. "Hey, Lil, it's okay. You don't have to always know." While I say the words she needs to hear, dread fills me. Why can't she see what's going to happen with Zoe? I hate how much I've come to rely on the comfort of her visions. She's only a little girl. "Go help your mom with the food. Thank you for trying." I force a smile.

I throw my arm over my eyes and try to wrap my head around what Lily said. What's changed? Why has Lily been able to see everything so clearly until this moment? Have I done something to change the outcome with Zoe? Have I put her in danger?

"Hey," Jonas says, pulling my arm off my face. "I saw you and Lily talking. Is everything okay?"

I wrestle with whether to tell him the truth. Ophelia's assignment, to be more open and honest with our communication, sits like a brick on my chest because we need to stop this killer. If I share what Lily said, there's no way in hell he'll let me continue trying to figure this out.

Doing the right thing wins. "Lily said she doesn't know. She can't see anything. It's all blank for her now."

Jonas' eyes widen in horror. "That's not good. She usually can see what's going to happen. Why can't she now?"

"I wish I knew, but I don't. Maybe it's for the best because all of this has been a lot for her, too."

Jonas rakes his hands through his hair. "You're right, but damn. That worries me sick."

I can barely get my response out past the lump in my throat. "Yeah, me too."

He leans down and kisses my belly. "Zoe, you stay put in there where it's safe." He rises and looks into my eyes. "You just need to do everything in your power to keep both of you protected, which means obeying doctor's orders, okay?"

I grab his hand. "I will. I promise."

After a curt nod, Jonas goes back to the kitchen to help Chaundra.

Worry wraps its tendrils around my throat, choking me. What has changed that Lily can no longer see the outcome with Zoe? From day one, she knew the date of her birth. Fear nestles itself right next to the worry, nauseating me. I don't think I can survive something being wrong with Zoe. Maybe I should stop all this madness now, with trying to find this killer. But what if it's too late? Liam's laughter fills the air, and guilt clutches my heart that I'd even consider such a thing. Despite the risk to our baby and myself, I cannot and will not give up on trying to keep Liam safe. I love him like my own child, and Chaundra... she's already lost too much.

I place a hand on my stomach and gently caress it. *Zoe, please be okay. We have to keep Liam safe. God, please don't let anything happen to either of them.*

"Dinner!" Chaundra yells.

As I pull myself up, I bury all my fears and questions in the recesses of my mind where they belong. I don't have a choice but to continue what we've started.

∼

WE TRY to keep the conversation light through dinner. Chaundra made stuffed shells, salad, and garlic bread, which is delicious. She cooked enough for a small army so that we can freeze some for later. This huge food delivery is a true act of love and friendship, since Chaundra detests cooking. I don't know what I did to deserve such an amazing friend, but I'm filled with gratitude. She's the sister I never had.

As soon as we finish eating, I'm ordered back to lie on the couch while the five of them work together to clear the table and load the dishwasher. It's amazing how quickly the process goes with all the extra sets of hands.

Once the clean-up is complete, they all join me in the living room. Jonas hands me a bottle of water while he, Chaundra, and Micah each enjoy a beer. I cannot wait to have a glass of wine or a beer again. It sounds like that may be sooner rather than later, other than the whole breastfeeding issue.

"Are you sure you're up for this, Tessa?" Micah asks as he opens his laptop.

Jonas snaps his gaze in my direction, seemingly trying to will me to say no.

"Yes. We all need this nightmare to end."

Lily plops down on the floor in front of me and I weave my fingers through her hair to braid it.

"Uncle Jonas, can I go up and play video games?" Liam asks with his foot already on the first step.

"Of course you can." Jonas hasn't even gotten the final word out when Liam pounds up the stairs with Aiden trailing behind.

"I swear these kids act like they were raised in a barn or something," Chaundra laughs.

Micah types something on his computer and then sits back in the chair. "Okay, I was able to get some information. I started with the list of rangers who have left Smoky Mountain National Park in the past ten years, which was," he pauses and scrolls down the page on his laptop, "a total of five. I then narrowed that down to the ones who are early forties to late fifties since that's what you and Lily both saw, which eliminated one. So, out of the four names left, one was a black man, which doesn't fit with the visions you both have had. The three left are Gabriel Hockman, Roger Diley, and Logan Henry. I've got pictures pulled up of each of them for you guys to take a look."

Chaundra grabs his laptop and carries it over to us. We take a few minutes to study the images and then we both shake our heads at the same time.

"Damn. I was hoping this would be simple," Chaundra says.

"Really? You think anything is simple when it comes to this case?" I laugh.

"True, true." She carries the laptop back over to Micah.

"Okay, well, in case that didn't work, I have a plan B. Not including Ferguson, who you guys spoke to yesterday, there are twelve other male Rangers on staff. Give me a sec and I'll pull up their names and pictures."

As his fingers clack against the keyboard, mine continue to weave through Lily's hair, which is so comforting.

"Okay, here we go. Take a look at these guys."

This time, Micah walks the laptop over and slowly scrolls through each face.

I make eye contact with Lily before speaking to ensure we're on the same page. "He's not there."

"Dammit. I was afraid of that," Micah says and walks back to the chair.

I shut my eyes and rub my head, trying to bring up the image from my mind. "Maybe I got it wrong. Maybe he wasn't wearing a ranger uniform."

"No, you didn't. I saw it too," Lily says. "He's a park ranger."

Shit!

"So, what now?" Jonas asks and rubs my swollen feet.

Chaundra sighs. "Well, I tried to look into Cora Davis. There's not much I can find that's relevant. All her social media is about her life now, with her new husband, Eli, other than that one Facebook memory that popped up about Sam's death. I, of course, searched for Sam Davis' death but couldn't find anything because he must have a different last name. Micah may be able to find out more, but he's got his hands full right now and it may be a few days."

"We don't have a few days. This needs to end now," I say. I don't know why, but in my heart and soul, I know we don't have much time. "Have they positively identified AJ's body yet?"

Micah shakes his head. "I can't share much but I think we'll have an ID in the next couple of days, which is super quick, but there were some distinguishing characteristics that should make him easier to identify."

Distinguishing characteristics on a pile of bones? I can't imagine what those could be. I pinch the bridge of my nose to clear away the thoughts.

"I have an idea," Chaundra says. "Jonas, you're not going to like it but please hear me out."

Jonas' hand tightens around my foot. "Okay..."

"When Tessa and I were at the restaurant, we mentioned possibly having some of her paintings on commission in the attached gift store. Cora seemed quite interested. I was thinking maybe Cora would be willing to come here to look at some of the paintings to pick the ones she wants for the store. We've got the perfect excuse with Tessa now being on bed rest."

"No, absolutely not," Jonas states firmly.

While it doesn't sound pleasant, I think Chaundra's idea is brilliant. That would be the quickest way to get some answers—from Cora herself.

"Hon, I think it's a great idea." I nudge him with my foot.

He crosses his arms and shakes his head.

"Well, see, here's the thing and I'm sorry. Please don't hate me," Chaundra says, her face crinkled in concern. "I already called her and asked if she could come over on her next day off in case we hit a wall tonight."

"Dammit, Chaundra!" Jonas stands and stomps to the kitchen to grab another beer.

Chaundra's eyes fill with tears. "I'm sorry, but we're running out of time. We need to stop him before he hurts my boy. If you could've seen my visions, perhaps you'd feel the same."

Jonas stops mid-stride and covers his face with his hand. "I'm so sorry, Chaundra. I'm being a selfish ass and have only been thinking about Tess and the baby."

I'm relieved to hear him say this because it seems he's forgotten what's at risk here. I understand his worry about me and Zoe, but the threat to Liam is just as real and imminent.

After a moment of silence, Jonas finally speaks. "I'm worried all this stress is going to send Tess into labor, especially since Lily can't see what's going to happen with Zoe anymore."

Chaundra whips her head around to look at Lily and me, her face full of questions.

"I asked Lily a little while ago, and she can no longer see what's going to happen with Zoe." I feel Lily tense beneath my hands, so I squeeze her shoulder. "It's okay, Lily. Everything is going to be fine."

I wish I could believe that.

"Cora said her next day off isn't until Monday, so three days from now. I know you have class, but I promise to stay here with Tessa the entire time. I can stay afterwards until you get home, if you'd like."

"Tess, do you feel okay about this?" he finally asks.

I push my fear and anxiety to the side. "Yes, I have to be. One, March nineteenth is rapidly approaching. Two, I really want to get my paintings into the store. I don't know when little Zoe's coming, but it could be any day now. I want this all resolved as quickly as possible." I reach out and grab his arm as he walks past, forcing him to stop. "Hey, look at me."

Once his eyes meet mine, I continue. "I promise I'll be okay. This really is the best way to go about this. If there was something we could easily find online, one of us would've found it by now. This is our last resort. Because of his job, Micah has a mile of red tape to work through to get anything done. No offense to you, Micah, but this will be faster."

Finally, Jonas sits down by my feet again. "I don't like it. At all. But I know you two ladies are two of the most stubborn people on this planet, so there's really no stopping you. Plus, we need to make sure Liam's safe."

Liam yells from the loft. "Do you guys need me? I keep hearing my name."

"No, hon. You're fine," Chaundra yells, and he stomps back towards Jonas' office.

"Does he know everything?" I whisper.

Chaundra shrugs. "He knows some of it. Besides everything that happened with you the other day, he knows that we've seen something, but I didn't want to scare him too badly. Just enough that he understands my over-protectiveness."

"That's smart. If we could find this guy's picture, we could at least show him so that he knows to scream and run if he comes across him," I say.

"And that's why you both need to meet with Cora later this week," Jonas says as he finally relaxes, sinking back into the couch. "Okay, so let's set some ground rules."

CHAPTER 44

Some of Jonas' conditions to make him more comfortable about our meeting with Cora today were that Chaundra has to come over first thing in the morning, before he leaves for work, and she must stay with me all day to make sure I'm okay. It's annoyingly sweet how much he worries about me. But I understand—I don't want to put Zoe at risk either, at least not any more than I already have. Wanting to save Liam and needing to keep Zoe safe are constantly warring in my mind. The two notions are in opposition to each other, but what choice do I have? I don't know how to best protect everyone.

Lily begged to come with Chaundra today, and she gave in, thinking it could be helpful for her to be with us. Liam has an away soccer game after school and will ride the bus with the team. Thankfully, his dad agreed to go to the game without too much fuss. Chaundra drilled it into Liam's head that he isn't to wander off alone anywhere, and she also shared her concerns with Adam.

Cora is due at the house at eleven, so I run a brush through my hair and put on a few splashes of perfume before heading back to the couch where Chaundra and Lily serve me everything I need. Each time Chaundra brings me something, she refers to me as Queen Tessa or Your Majesty. I do feel ridiculous making her wait on me hand and foot, but I really don't have a choice. Chaundra and Lily lug down the paintings from my studio that I would like to have featured in the shop. I have ten to present for Cora's consideration but will be thrilled if she chooses even a few.

Chaundra and I develop a game plan for how we're going to go from looking at paintings and discussing them being in the store to more personal information, like her dead son. We're both quite nervous about how this is going to play out. We set Lily up at the kitchen table with a coloring book and markers, and Chaundra brews a fresh pot of coffee.

Cora arrives at five minutes before eleven. Apprehension fills me as she walks up to the porch. I hate how we're planning to ambush her with painful memories from her past and a loss so deep that she probably never gets a moment's break from it.

Chaundra opens the door and lets her in, offering her a cup of coffee, which she gladly accepts. I coax Chaundra into allowing me to have one extra cup today. She should know I can't smell coffee brewing without needing one.

"Cora, while Chaundra gets our coffee, please come have a seat."

She chooses the chair closest to the fireplace. "Ooh, this feels wonderful. It's chilly out there today, even with the sunshine."

"Thank you for coming all the way out here. As Chaundra told you, I'm on partial bedrest for the rest of my pregnancy, unfortunately." I rub my stomach. "I was eager to talk to you about getting some of my work in the store before our little one arrives."

Cora smiles as she takes a mug from Chaundra. "No worries at all. I have today off work and was headed this way to drop off some things to a former employee who just had surgery. So, the timing was perfect. I will admit, I looked up your work online after we spoke yesterday, and I'd be thrilled to have some in the store. When is your due date?"

I blow out a breath. "Well, it seems it could be anytime now. The longer she stays in here though, the better."

Cora and Chaundra both laugh. "Oh, Cora, I know you guys kind of met the other day, but the little gal at the table is my daughter, Lily."

Lily glances up from her coloring book and gives a smile along with a wave.

"Do you have any children, Cora?" Chaundra asks.

Cora stares into her coffee mug as if she's trying to find the answer to the question in there before finally shaking her head. "Yes. I mean, I did. My son died almost sixteen years ago." Her eyes brim with tears. "That's one of the hardest questions to answer. Am I still a mom if my child is dead?"

"You absolutely are. I also lost a child—a son, in fact—many years ago. It still hurts like it happened yesterday. I'll never get over his loss, but Aiden is still my son. Just as—what did you say your son's name is?"

"Oh, I don't think I did. His name is Sam. Or, rather, it was…" Cora's voice trails off as she takes a drink of coffee. "I'm so sorry about your loss. Can I ask what happened?"

Her asking this question puts my mind at ease, as it will make the transition a bit easier into the conversation we need to have.

"We lost him a little over six years ago. He was riding his bike and was hit by a car. He died in my arms before the ambulance arrived. They tried to revive him, but it was too late." Chaundra wipes away a tear. "What about your son?"

Chaundra is a master at hiding her loss and pain most of the time, but now I see how heavily the anguish weighs on her every moment of every day. A new determination settles over me and quiets my internal debate about whether I am making the right choice by continuing this quest. It would undoubtedly destroy Chaundra if anything happened to Liam.

Cora grabs a tissue from the end table as I brace myself for the story she's about to tell, trying to force my mind to remember every single word she says.

"We lived out west, in Arizona, at the time. He was hiking with his father at the Grand Canyon and fell off a ridge. I still beat myself up to this day about not going on that trip with them."

A green flash envelops me as she finishes her sentence. I'm transported to Sam's father's body, trying to reach for my son's arm as he plummets over the edge but missing by just a tiny bit. His horror and pain rips through me, tearing apart my soul. His howls echo in my mind at realizing his boy is gone. Stones cut into my knees as he crumples to the ground, unable to hold himself up. My heart splinters into tiny shards of grief and guilt along with his.

Chaundra's voice pulls me back to now. "Tessa, are you okay?" She stands next to me and reaches down to touch my arm.

I shake my head to clear away the memories. "Oh, sorry. Yeah. A contraction, I think. I'm so sorry about your son, Cora. I can't imagine how painful that was, and still is, for you."

Chaundra mouths the word *flash* to me, and I nod. She squeezes my hand before heading back to her chair.

"I'm sorry if this is prying too much, but did you and your husband stay together after losing your son? I know a loss like that can destroy even the best of marriages. My husband and I had split up prior to losing Aiden—I know we wouldn't have made it through his death if we had still been together."

Cora sighs and stares into the fire. "We tried to make it work. We even moved across the country to get away from the place that stole our son from us. But I blamed him for letting Sam fall. I was never able to get past it."

"Was it his fault?" I ask.

"Technically, no. But, to me, absolutely. He was a park ranger at the Grand Canyon and had taken our son to work with him that day. He got distracted by visitors and wasn't watching Sam. If he had been, he would've noticed he was too close to the edge." She coughs to clear the sob caught in her throat. "It was his job to keep visitors safe, and he failed with the most important person on the face of the earth. Our son."

Chaundra reaches over and grabs Cora's hand, while Cora dabs her eyes with a tissue. "How terrible for both of you. It's easy to blame yourself or whoever's close to you in a situation like this. Placing blame helps us make sense of the unexplainable."

Cora nods. "He never really recovered from it. Never remarried or had any relationship after ours, as far as I know. I got remarried but never wanted to have another child. I felt like if I did, I would only be trying to replace Sam. And the thought of even a remote possibility of losing another child was unimaginable." Cora leans back and takes another drink of her coffee. "Okay, well, enough of the heavy talk. I'd love to see your paintings, but could I use the restroom first?"

"Absolutely. It's the second door on the right." I point back into the hallway.

Once Cora has left the room, Chaundra bolts up to look out the windows.

"What's going on?" I ask her.

"I'm not really sure, but I'm getting the same feeling I had outside of the restaurant the other day. Like the killer is here," she says. "But I don't see anyone out here. Lily?"

Lily looks up from her coloring book. "What?"

"Do you sense anything strange right now? About the killer?" Chaundra asks, her voice shaking.

Lily goes rigid and shuts her eyes. "Nope, not at all." She begins to hum and turns her attention back to her coloring.

Chaundra finally pulls herself away from the windows and plops back in the chair. "It's so weird. Why do I keep getting this feeling?"

"I'm not sure, but it must have something to do with Cora, and being around her," I say as I hear the bathroom door open.

Chaundra shrugs and nods, forcing the concern from her face.

"I can't wait to see your paintings," Cora says, walking to those lined up against the wall.

As she peruses them, I go into the details about each, the title, the price, and any significance to the local area or me personally. Cora seems mesmerized by them and ends up selecting five to display in the store, agreeing to a twenty percent consignment fee for those that sell. She also asks me to consider placing more in the store as these sell out, which, of course, I agree to.

At about one, Chaundra asks Cora if she'd like to stay for lunch, but she declines, saying she has some errands to run since it's her day off. She stands to leave, and I realize our opportunity to get more information is coming to a close.

"Can I ask you a couple of questions before you leave?" I ask.

"Sure," Cora replies.

"I'm not trying to be nosy, but I was wondering if your ex-husband is still a park ranger."

Cora nods.

"Here locally?" Chaundra asks.

"We're not really in contact anymore but, the last I heard, he was kind of a fill-in ranger for whichever National Park or Forest in North Carolina and Tennessee needed him. Kind of like a traveling park ranger."

Aha! This makes the puzzle in my mind fit together perfectly. How he kills in different areas—always in the two states she mentioned, at least as far as we know.

"My husband, Jonas, is from Arizona, and I'm wondering if he knew your husband or his family. What is his name?" I ask and then hold my breath while waiting for her answer.

"Bryan Benson. What part of Arizona is your husband's family in?"

"Phoenix," I manage to say, even though the name Bryan Benson is playing on repeat in my mind.

"Yeah, we were up near the canyon so there's probably no connection." Cora slips her coat on. "Anyway, ladies. Thank you so much. I'll be in touch when any of your pieces sell and good luck with your baby. Enjoy every single second."

She walks over and shakes my hand. "Not to be weird, but can I touch the baby?" She points to my stomach.

"Feel free," I say.

Before she can do so, Lily interrupts. "Miss Davis?"

Cora turns toward Lily. "Yes, sweetheart?"

"I hope you don't think this is weird, but Sam is here. He says he loves you and wants you to be happy. He also said he's okay."

Cora gasps as her hand flies to her chest.

Chaundra rushes to her side and grips her arm to help steady her. "My daughter and I are both psychic. Her powers are much stronger than mine. She also sees my son, Aiden, all the time."

"Aiden is standing next to you right now, Mommy," Lily says with a smile. "And Sam has his arm around you, Miss Davis."

A few tears race down Cora's face as she whips her head around, trying to see her son.

"Where is he, Lily?" Chaundra asks.

Lily points to the left of Cora. "His head is on your shoulder."

In a bittersweet and beautiful moment, Cora caresses where Sam's head would be if she could see him. "I love you, my beautiful son. I miss you so, so much."

This tender interaction sends shocks of grief through me. We all watch in silence as this broken-hearted mother is given a small chance to interact with her son after sixteen long years.

A shudder works its way through her body, and she covers her mouth in surprise. "I felt him here. I couldn't see him, but I felt him." A smile breaks out across her face, despite her tears. "Wow! Thank you for that, Lily!"

"I can sometimes feel my Aiden, too. It helps that Lily can see him and reminds me often that he's with us. I know what a relief it is to feel his presence." Chaundra opens her arms to Cora, and they hug—two mothers who share a bond over the most powerful loss on the planet.

Cora wipes the tears from her cheeks. "Again, thank you. I have to go now though." She points to my stomach and raises her eyebrows.

I nod.

As soon as her hand touches my stomach, flashes consume me—red, orange, yellow, green—so rapid fire I can barely breathe.

"Ooh, she's feisty. I can feel her kicking." I hear Cora say, but I can't respond. I'm lost in a sea of color—Cora's life and loss seeping into my own heart and soul.

SOMEONE'S SHAKING MY ARM. "Tess, open up!" It's Chaundra.

I open my eyes and squint against the bright, sunny day. "What happened? Did I fall asleep?" My voice is raspy.

Chaundra shakes her head. "I was hoping you could tell me. Cora was touching your stomach, and you started thrashing around. You were saying things, but it was all unintelligible."

Cora must think I'm insane. "So many flashes." I lean forward for my water but can't quite reach it. As I try to hoist myself up, Chaundra hands it to me and I gulp it down. "What did you tell her?"

Chaundra waves her hand in the air dismissively. I raise my eyebrows in question. Instead of answering, she walks away.

"Chaundra, tell me what you said."

"I told her you'd been having lots of difficulties with your pregnancy and sometimes you kind of zone out."

"Was she freaked out?" I ask.

Chaundra shrugs. "I don't think so, especially after the whole experience with Sam. I think she was still riding high on cloud nine from that. I told her I needed to call your doctor, so she left in a hurry."

"Have I been out of it long? Did I fall asleep or pass out, or what?"

"You kinda came back enough to tell us you had flashes and then went to sleep. It's been about an hour since all that happened. I figured I should wake you up to make sure you were okay. Plus, we have lots to talk about."

I take another drink and the name Bryan Benson pops into my mind. "Did you look up her husband?"

Chaundra nods. "And I called Micah to tell him about the conversation. He's doing some searching now. I found a few pictures of Bryan and Sam." She grabs her laptop. "Are you okay to look at these?"

I nod, but I'm not really sure if I am. I feel like I've been hit by a truck. Chaundra hands me the laptop and I rest it on my stomach—the one good thing about being so huge is I have a built-in table. I'm going to kind of miss it once I have Zoe.

"I've got the tabs open at the top with some of the articles and pictures I found. Let me know if it's too much, please."

I take a deep breath and click open the first tab where I'm greeted with a smiling picture of Sam, who is precisely the boy from my visions. My eyes brim with tears as I study the young man who was supposed to have so much life ahead of him and my heart aches for Cora's loss. And Bryan's too, I suppose, even though he turned into a monster with his grief. The article goes into the details and specifics about his death, expanding on everything that Cora told us. They ruled his death an accident, with many eyewitness reports on what happened. Sam and his father, Bryan, were at Mather Point when the boy fell over four hundred feet to his death. According to onlookers, Mr. Benson was assisting a group of visitors and had his back turned to his son, who was standing near the edge. One second he was there, the next there was a scream, and he was gone. Mr. Benson lunged forward to try to stop his son's fall when he almost tumbled over the edge himself. One of the visitors he was assisting was able to grab his arm at the last moment to save him. As awful as it is to think, perhaps the visitor should have let him fall. It would have saved many children's lives. I read the rest of the first article and then click on the next tab.

Zoe kicks me as the screen fills with a picture of Bryan in his park ranger uniform and a school picture of Sam next to it. I catch only a glimpse before a green flash consumes me. Bryan's voice fills my head.

This time, I will protect you. I am so sorry, Sam. I should have never taken my eyes off you. This time, it will be different. I won't ever let you out of my sight. I will keep you safe. I won't lose you again. You will be resurrected. Bigger and stronger than ever. God himself will pour life into you where there now is none. He will bring you back to me. His Word promises He will restore what has been lost. You are my reason for existing, for continuing on. To make sure you have the chance to live the life you were meant to have.

I pinch the bridge of my nose, trying to clear his voice from my mind. I want to scream at him and tell him it's too late. There is nothing he can do to bring his son back. He's been gone for sixteen years. A part of me wants to wrap my arms around Bryan to provide comfort because sorrow and despair crush me along with him. The burden of his guilt tightens like a noose around my neck, choking me. The other part of me wants to strangle him for hurting innocent children. For trying to use them to assuage his own culpability.

Another green flash whooshes through me and, with it, come images of the children right before their deaths, each of them with eyes widened in fear. But I'm seeing them through Bryan's eyes, with his thoughts overpowering my own. *I'm sorry. I don't want to do this. I don't have a choice. I must get my son back. My Sam. I have to fix what I've broken. God led me to you. You are a vital piece. I'm sorry. I'm sorry. I'm sorry.* In my heart, I know he is truly repentant and remorseful as he kills each child. Each murder piles more guilt upon his already enormous load. It's crushing him. Erasing the person who used to be.

An understanding sweeps through me. I try to speak but can't get the words out before Cora fills my mind. I'm seeing and hearing her through Bryan's eyes and ears. She falls to the ground, her entire body trembling. She looks up at him—me—and screams. *How could you let this happen? It was your job to keep him safe. Why didn't you protect him? You killed him. It is your fault. I can't even look at you without seeing my son's broken body. You disgust me.*

I feel her sorrow and anguish as well as Bryan's. I'm inside both of them at once. Or they're inside me. Perhaps it's a bit of both. I'm still Tessa, but I'm also Bryan, Sam, and Cora. I'm Chase and Anna and AJ. Tatum, Leah, and David. Stephanie, Dominick, and Scott. I'm all of them and none of them. I'm fracturing inside my mind. Breaking apart just like they all were. I am scattered bones waiting to be found. I am crying out for my mommy and daddy. I am screaming for my lost son.

I am whole. I am broken. I am found. I am lost.

They are me. I am them. I am nothing. I am everything.

CHAPTER 45

My heart pounds violently and a loud, steady beeping noise has taken over the visions and voices in my mind. I feel trapped.

"Hey, sis. It's okay."

I jerk my eyes open. Cyle's here—wherever here is.

"You're here." I choke back a sob.

He smiles and nods. "I told you I would be."

My eyes dart around the room, taking in the pale green walls. I'm definitely not at home. I jerk my head to the side and see an IV pole and finally, I'm able to place the beeping noise to monitors next to the bed. *Zoe!* My hand flies to my stomach.

"She's fine. You're okay." Cyle smooths my hair back from my forehead.

"Why am I here? What happened?"

I didn't even notice Jonas sitting on the other side of the bed until I hear him yawn as he grabs my hand.

"Hey, you're awake!"

"What's going on? Why am I in the hospital? Is the baby okay?"

"Take some deep breaths. You can't get too worked up." Jonas does some deep breathing along with me. The breaths calm my racing heart, but my thoughts still spiral out of control. "First, Zoe is fine. They had to give you medicine to try to stop your contractions, which seems to have helped for now."

"Contractions? Am I in labor?" How can I not know I've been having contractions? The pain should've been an indicator of that, but I have no memory of feeling them.

Jonas points to one of the machines next to the bed. "That one is monitoring contractions. You were having them every seven minutes when you first got here. The medicine has slowed them down to every ten minutes so far. They've also given you a type of steroid to help speed up Zoe's lung development in case you do go into labor."

I caress my stomach, relieved that Zoe's still safely inside of me and seems to be okay, for now. "I don't remember being in labor and coming here. What happened?"

"What's the last thing you remember?"

I sort through my memories like a file cabinet. Visit with Cora. Bryan Benson. Flashes when Cora touched me. Looking at the computer. Seeing Sam and reading about his death. Then Bryan's face and thoughts taking over my mind.

"Flashes. Losing control." I'm only able to blurt out these three words.

Jonas caresses my arm and rests his chin on the bed rail. "Chaundra said you were looking at articles about Sam and his father. One minute you were fine. The next, you were talking nonsensically and moving around, ranting and raving. She tried to get you to lie back down, but you refused. She called me and I rushed home. By the time I got there, you were frantic… and having contractions."

Why don't I remember any of this? It's a complete blank in my memory. I've continued to put Zoe at risk despite Lily's revelations. Jonas was right—I should've never met with Cora today. Why didn't I listen to him? Sobs escape me.

"I'm so sorry. I should've listened to you. How could I…"

Cyle grabs my other hand. "Stop it, sis. Don't beat yourself up. You didn't do this on purpose."

"It doesn't matter if it was on purpose. I still put my baby's life at risk!" I shout.

"Is Cyle here?" Jonas asks quietly, and fear courses through me. Is he going to be mad that Cyle's back? Is this going to be yet another argument or disappointment for him?

I nod.

"Where is he?" Jonas asks.

"Holding my other hand. Standing by the bed."

Jonas takes a deep breath and, for a second, I worry he's upset and going to try to punch a ghost. But, instead, he looks to the side of the bed where Cyle is sitting.

Unbeknownst to Jonas, he stares directly into Cyle's eyes. "I'm sorry about overreacting earlier and for the things you overheard me say. I didn't mean any of it—I was just overwhelmed. Thank you for coming back. Tessa needs you." Jonas' eyes brim with tears, a physical sign he means every word.

I turn to Cyle. "Tell him it's okay and that I completely understand. You both have been under a tremendous amount of stress."

I repeat this to Jonas and he exhales loudly, followed by a smile. "Thanks! It won't happen again. You stay as long as you want."

I can't help but smile. I want my brother here with me for as long as he possibly can be.

"So, what's happening with the information about Bryan Benson?" I ask.

Jonas holds up his hand. "No! We're not talking about it. Micah has everything under control, so put it out of your mind. You need to focus on keeping Zoe in there as long as possible." He points to my stomach.

It's completely a fair point, but I still can't help but wonder. I know Jonas wants what's best for Zoe and me, so I won't bring it up again. I can't make any promises about whether or not I'll obsess about it all, though.

Someone knocks softly on the door.

"Come in," Jonas yells.

Dr. Weyman enters, concern crinkling her face. "I'm glad to see you're awake," she says as she walks toward the monitor tracking my contractions.

"Jonas said the medicine seems to be working at slowing down my contractions, so that's good news, right?"

"Ideally, yes. However, we've seen some things on your monitors that are a bit concerning. I need to check your cervix."

"Okay, I'm out for a bit," Cyle says and bolts toward the door. I hide my laughter behind my hand.

Jonas stands by the side of the bed and grips my hand while the doctor does my examination. She pushes back on her stool and tells me to remove my feet from the stirrups once she's done.

"Well, this is what I expected. You're dilated to a two—which you were only at one when you were admitted. So, it seems the medicine is working partially at slowing down your contractions, but my best guess is that it's only temporary."

Jonas swallows so loudly that I can hear it and squeezes my hand. "Will the baby be okay?"

"The longer we can keep her inside, the better. With the medicines we have you on, Tessa, and with how far along you are, I think she'll be okay. But there's always risk when we're talking about pre-term birth."

Jonas nods but doesn't say anything.

"I want to go over a few final details for when you are in labor. You indicated you want an epidural. Is that still the case?"

"Absolutely," I say without hesitation.

Dr. Weyman nods and types something into her tablet. "We can give you one when you're at four centimeters. I always recommend doing it when you reach that point, so we don't miss the window of opportunity. But you also need to be in active labor, thus having regular contractions."

I nod and look at Jonas, who's now white as a ghost.

"Anything else we need to know or do?" I ask.

"Try to relax and stay as calm as possible. Do you have everything ready to go at home?"

I'm relieved I finished the mural already.

"I have a few things left to do but nothing that needs addressed immediately," Jonas says.

"We'll be checking in on you, Tessa. Daddy, you need to also get some rest. It could be a long few days."

Jonas nods.

As soon as the doctor closes the door behind her, I turn toward Jonas. "Did you hear that?"

"That you're close to being in active labor? Yes, I heard it and am scared to death."

I squeeze his hand. "No, not that. She called you Daddy."

Something akin to terror crosses his face. "Are you sure we're ready? Our whole lives are about to change."

"Hon, we don't really have a choice. Zoe's ready whether or not we are. We're going to do just fine." I hope I am not lying to him. "But, as doc said, you need to get some rest."

Jonas runs his hands through his hair. "Like that's possible. I'm wound up tight right now."

"Pull out the bed and sleep. I promise to wake you if anything changes or happens. This may be your last good rest for a while."

Jonas' eyes widen as big as saucers. I stifle a laugh because he's been so calm through all of this when I've been the one to panic. Now that the time is close, Jonas looks like he's about to faint.

"Okay, I'll try." He leans down and kisses me. "I love you—both of you."

"And we both love you, Daddy!"

CHAPTER 46

Surprisingly, Jonas falls asleep quickly in the chair next to my bed, and somehow manages to sleep through the nurse coming in to check on me. I'm dilated to a three now, so I'll be able to get an epidural soon. I wish Zoe would stay put for a while longer, but it seems she's ready to make her grand entrance into the world. I have no choice but to trust and pray she's physically ready and all will be okay.

Since Jonas is sleeping soundly, I sneak off to the bathroom to call Chaundra. During my latest flashes, all the pieces of this gruesome puzzle finally fit together. I've been trying to keep it locked up in my mind, but I have to get it out. She needs to understand what I now know deep in my soul—the why behind Bryan's actions.

She answers breathlessly. "Is Zoe here already?"

I chuckle. "Um, no. That would be a fast delivery, which I wouldn't mind except they're trying to keep her inside me as long as possible."

"Whew! The kids and I are headed to the hospital shortly. We can't wait to meet her. Why in the world are you calling me while you're in labor, then?"

"Jonas is asleep, and I needed to sneak off to tell you I understand why Bryan is doing this. It finally all fits together thanks to my latest flashes."

"I've been trying to make sense of everything you said during your latest episode, but none of it came together in my mind," Chaundra says.

"Bryan is killing these kids and collecting their bones, trying to rebuild his son. He thinks that building him a new body will bring Sam back."

Chaundra loudly exhales. "That's seriously screwed up. But it makes sense from all the things you and Lily have picked up on."

"And it fits with the scriptures that were running through my mind." Despite trying to keep it in, a moan escapes me as a contraction begins. I try to speak but can only pant breaths instead.

"I'm hanging up now. Go back to bed. Love you!"

I stay in the bathroom and try to muffle my groans as the contraction passes. As soon as I'm able, I pad back to bed, hoping to not wake Jonas. I feel much better now that I've told Chaundra why he's killing the kids. Maybe this will help the police or FBI in some way. Now, one hundred percent of my focus is on Zoe and labor, as it should be.

"Hey sis!" Cyle says through the crack in the door. "Can I come in?"

"Yeah," I say in a loud whisper, hoping not to rouse Jonas.

Cyle sits on the bed next to me. "How you doing, kiddo?" He grabs my hand and squeezes.

"Oh, you know. Overwhelmed. Scared. Anxious. But so excited to meet Zoe. I just wish she wasn't coming so early."

Cyle nods. "It's always scary when they don't follow our plans or the correct timeline. But remember that Harper was born around this time, and she was perfectly healthy. In fact, it was a good thing she came so early, or Tara would have had to get a c-section, which she really didn't want."

I take a deep, calming breath. I had forgotten this about Harper. Even though she was born so early, she weighed over seven pounds. Despite my relief, the question still looms over me—if Zoe is going to be okay, why couldn't Lily see it?

"Thank you for reminding me. I just want everything to be okay."

Cyle smiles. "I'm sure it will be. I know it in here." He places a hand over his heart.

I squeeze his other hand. "Are you okay?" He looks sad and tired.

He stares off into the distance and nods. "I'm okay. I just wanted to come in and talk to you while I could. Soon enough, you're going to be quite distracted, and it will be busy in here."

I punch him softly on the arm. "You don't want to be anywhere near when I'm in the throes of labor. Admit it."

He laughs. "Well, that too. I can only imagine the string of curses that are going to spew out of you." We both laugh and then his smile fades, becoming serious. "I wanted to say that I love you, sis. And I'm so proud of the woman you've become and the mom you're going to be. You and Jonas have made a beautiful life, and you're going to make awesome parents."

Tears fill my eyes.

"Hey, don't cry. This isn't supposed to upset you." Cyle points to the box of tissues, and I grab one to dab my eyes. "What's wrong?"

I hiccup a sob. "I don't know. It kind of feels like you're saying goodbye. Are you?"

Cyle shakes his head, but his eyes are full of uncertainty. "No, not at all. I'll be right here the whole time. I can't wait to meet my niece. Can I?" He points at my stomach.

I nod, and he rests his hand on my belly. A green, red, and yellow flash zoom through me. I gasp because I haven't gotten a flash from Cyle since he died.

"Contraction?" he asks.

"A flash! That was weird. I didn't know I could still get them from you."

"Hmm. That is strange. I'm sorry. Good colors I hope."

I smile and nod even though they weren't good colors at all.

"Anyway, bye for now, little one. I'll see you on the flip side," he says and lifts his hand from my belly. He leans forward and kisses me on the forehead. "You stay strong. You'll do a great job. Just remember through all the pain that it will be one hundred percent worth it."

He stands and I reach forward to grab his arm. "You don't have to go yet. We still have time."

"Sorry, sis. I need to go. I'll see you again before you know it. I love you."

I let my hand drop from his arm as he turns to walk away. "I love you too, Cyle. Thank you for being the best big brother a girl could ever want."

He blows a kiss and exits the room. I close my eyes to stop the tears from falling. A sense of dread clutches my heart because it feels like this is the last time I'll see my brother. I don't have time to dwell on it though because the strongest contraction yet rips through me. I do my best to breathe through it without screaming because I don't want to wake Jonas, but I fail. A howl slices through the air.

Jonas jerks awake and stands, gripping my hand immediately. "Contraction?"

I try to say yes, but I can't speak. All I can focus on is the pain.

"It looks like you're past the worst of this one. It shouldn't be much longer. Keep breathing, hon." Jonas mimics the breathing techniques we watched on YouTube.

I try to breathe along with him, but it seems pointless. Who ever thought that breathing would erase the pain of a child trying to push its way out of your body?

Finally, the pain starts to subside, little by little, and I fall back against the pillows. Jonas grabs a wet cloth and wipes my forehead.

"You alright?"

I nod. "This isn't gonna be fun. I forgot how much I detest physical pain. Not that I've ever felt anything quite like this."

"You're doing great. Do you think she's really coming soon?"

"Oh, yes. I forgot to tell you the nurse came in and I'm still dilating. The meds may have slowed things down, but I think we'll get to meet our baby girl today or tomorrow. When I'm at a four, I can get the epidural, which I am more than ready for."

He pulls my hand to his lips and kisses it. "I'm sorry it hurts but it will be worth it."

I laugh. "Do me a favor and don't say that when I'm having a contraction, or I might punch you."

"Fair enough. Thanks for the warning."

The fear and worry on Jonas' face is palpable, even though he's smiling. "How are you doing? Really?"

"Scared that she's coming too soon. I want her to be healthy." He reaches down and puts his hand on my stomach.

"I know. Me too. Although, Cyle visited while you were asleep and reminded me that Harper came earlier than this and she was completely fine. So maybe it's a genetic thing for us to have babies early."

A moment of relief floods his face. "That's good to hear. Come to think of it, I was born several weeks early too, so maybe it's on both sides of the family. And look at me, I'm almost perfect."

"Wrong. You are perfect in every single way. I'm sorry the past few months have been insane. This all couldn't have come at a worse time, but we've made it through so far."

Jonas taps his fingers against the bed railing. "Let's hope that while we're in here doing important things like having a baby, the FBI are out there finding Bryan Benson and linking him to all these murdered children."

I run my hand up his arm. "No matter what happens, I know in my heart that it will all be okay as long as we have each other."

There's a soft knock on the door before the nurse enters. "Let's do a quick check and see where you are with everything. I saw you had a pretty strong contraction. They seem to be picking up a bit."

She lifts the stirrups and guides my feet to them. She quickly performs the exam and removes her gloves.

"Well, you're at a four, which means you can get that epidural if you still want it."

"There's no *if* about it. I definitely want it."

She laughs. "A woman after my own heart. I will run it by your doctor first because sometimes the epidural allows your body to relax enough to speed up the whole process. I want to make sure she thinks we're good to go in case that happens."

Fear bubbles in my chest. I've wanted an epidural from the beginning. There's no way I can make it through this with nothing to ease the pain.

The nurse must see this on my face. "Hon, you'll be fine either way. I promise you. We will be here to get you through it. My guess is your doctor will give the go ahead, but I need to check to make sure."

I nod and try to convince myself that what she's saying is true. Millions of women have had babies without epidurals and lived through it.

"I'll be back. Rest while you can, but it looks like another contraction is starting." She points to the machine next to the bed and sure enough, a peak is forming on the monitor.

Jonas clutches my hand as the nurse walks out of the room. "Squeeze as tight as you need to."

"It's only been a few minutes. I'm not ready again." I barely get the words out before the pain crescendos.

I yank to a sitting position and try to brace myself while Jonas rubs my back. "How much longer?" I scream.

"I don't know. I can't tell."

"That's not the right answer," I say through gritted teeth. I try to turn my head to look at the monitor, but the pain won't allow it.

"Okay, it looks like you've reached the peak and it should start to lessen now. Keep breathing. You're almost there."

I've never wanted to hit someone so badly as I want to punch Jonas right now. Instead, I squeeze his hand as tightly as I can until slowly the pain subsides.

Once it's almost gone, I slump back against the pillows again, a sweaty mess. "Ice chips."

Jonas scoops some into my mouth.

Once I am less parched, I say, "Go get that nurse and tell her I want an epidural, now."

"I don't want to leave you alone. She said she'd be…"

"Now!" I yell through gritted teeth.

Without hesitation, Jonas scampers toward the door. He turns once to look at me before exiting. I grimace and point which sends the message loud and clear—him going to get the nurse is not up for debate.

CHAPTER 47

Thankfully, Doctor Weyman gave the go ahead for my epidural. Once it kicked in, I was able to drift off to sleep, but not until after Jonas told me that Chaundra and the kids were in the waiting room, eager to meet little Zoe. I hope Chaundra passes my message along to Micah and that it proves helpful in piecing this all together.

I briefly awaken during the nurse's exams, and each time I am a bit more dilated. I am grateful to be feeling no pain and actually be able to get some sleep. I'm relieved that Jonas dozes off because the poor guy is going to need his rest.

I don't know how long I've been in and out since my sleep keeps getting interrupted, but the nurse is back again. I don't even open my eyes as she lifts my legs into the stirrups and does the exam.

"Tessa, you need to wake up. You're at a nine so I'm going to call the doctor. You'll be pushing soon."

That jerks me right awake and utter panic floods through me. Pushing soon?

I turn to Jonas. "I'm not ready. It hasn't been that long, has it? How can it be time already?"

Jonas looks at his watch. "You had the epidural about five hours ago, so I think it's time. I know it's scary, but we will get through this. We'll meet Zoe soon."

Again, his use of the word *we* makes me want to scream because I don't see a baby trying to push its way out of *his* body, but I bite my tongue to stop myself. He doesn't deserve my anger—well, come to think of it, maybe he does. I wouldn't have gotten pregnant without his help.

"I'm scared. What if I can't do this? What if she's not okay? What if…"

Jonas leans down and kisses me before I can finish the sentence. "Stop. You are one of the most badass women I've ever met in my life. If anyone can do it, you absolutely can. And we have to trust she will be fine."

I exhale a loud breath and nod. "Yes, we have to believe that. I don't know about all that badass stuff, though."

"I'm right here with you. If I could do this for you, and take the pain away, I would. You can yell, scream, punch, whatever you need to do. Okay?"

I laugh. "Well, I have actually thought about punching you a few times today."

He holds his hand to his chest and opens his mouth in mock surprise. "You wanted to punch me, huh?"

"Oh, so badly. You have no idea."

We both laugh as Jonas turns to look at the monitor. "Did you feel that one? That was a huge, long contraction."

I turn to look, amazed that I didn't feel it. "Miracles of modern medicine, eh?"

"Indeed."

The door opens and Dr. Weyman comes in all suited up with a team of people to assist. "So, are we ready to meet Zoe?"

Jonas and I look at each other, smile, and say yes at the same time.

Dr. Weyman lifts my legs into the stirrups. "Good, because she's ready to meet you."

CHAPTER 48

M y heart races. *Am I ready? Are we ready? What if I can't do this? What if she's not okay? What if Lily could no longer see the outcome because I interfered with fate somehow?*

Jonas must be able to tell my mind is spiraling out of control. As the doctor sets everything up, he leans forward and kisses me on the forehead.

"It will be okay. We are ready, and you are doing great so far." He pauses and smiles. "We get to meet our baby girl soon!"

He knows me too well because all of that is exactly what I needed to hear. I smile back as the doctor tells me she's going to lower the bottom part of the bed and that I need to scoot down.

"We've cut back on your epidural some, but you still may have trouble knowing when to push. We'll be watching the monitor so the next time a contraction starts, we'll have you push through it."

Jonas grips my hand. "Squeeze as tight as you need to. I don't care if you break my fingers."

"And push!" the doctor orders.

I bear down, and the pressure feels like it's splitting me in two. Flashes consume me, coming so quickly that they all blend together. The room around me fades, other than the tremendous pain of my body being torn apart. Sam's face appears in my mind. He's smiling and looks happy. He yells out, *Hey, Dad! Look at me!* Then I'm tumbling with him off the edge of the canyon wall. Falling, falling, falling. He fades away before he lands. Then Bryan's horror at realizing his son fell rushes through me. His loss pulses through every fiber of my being. I scream a guttural wail, a mixture of his heartbreak and the pain of labor. They both feel equally real to me.

Slowly, the room around me starts to come back into focus—the beeping of the monitors, the glare of the overhead lights, the chatter of the doctor and nurses. Jonas tells me what a great job I'm doing. The doctor instructs me to lie back and relax. I'm back here in this hospital bed instead of tumbling over the side of the Grand Canyon.

"It's important for you to relax as much as you can between contractions, so you don't tire out," the nurse says and hands Jonas a wet washcloth for my head.

I want to tell him all the things I saw while pushing, but I don't want to steal this moment of joy from him. Plus, I doubt I can speak. Only one push, and I'm already exhausted. While he wipes my forehead, I close my eyes and try to catch my breath.

It feels like I've only been resting for a few seconds when the doctor announces it's time to push again. I bear down with all my might, pushing with everything I have in me, and, again, flashes take over. This time I'm Bryan, chasing down AJ. His jumbled thoughts run through my head. *I need to fix my boy. I need to bring him back. I'm sorry. I'm sorry. God will restore him once I've collected all the right pieces and parts. God will bind him back together and make him new.*

I'm whipped away from Bryan's mind and body and am now being chased. It's on our property, back before our cabin was built. Tatum runs as fast as he can, darting behind trees to hide, trying to evade the man chasing him. He thinks he's lost him and peeks out from behind the tree, but slips and falls on the muddy bank of the stream. The bad man is there waiting with a large rock in his hand. Tatum calls out for his mom as the man kneels, plummeting the rock toward his skull. I wail in pain and grab my head. But slowly, the pain fades, and the room once again materializes.

"Lay back, hon. Rest while you can." Jonas again wipes my head with a cool cloth. "Are you okay? Is your head hurting?"

I try to answer but I have no words to explain the immense torture of being trapped in these other people's minds while I should be fully present experiencing the day my daughter comes into the world.

"Okay, here we go," Doctor Weyman says. "Give it all you got!"

I want to scream that I'm not ready yet. That I can't do this. I need a longer time to rest, but the pressure in my pelvis assures me I'm not going to get any additional time. I suck in a deep breath and push.

More colors consume me—all swirled together, indistinguishable from the others. A whirlwind of color and pain. This time I'm in a boy's body, whistling as I traipse through the woods, a fishing pole in one hand and a tackle box in the other. This looks like the picture Micah showed me of the Davidson River. I'm in or with Chase. I don't know which. Maybe both—it sure feels that way. He whips his head to the side, looking for the source of the crunching twigs. He sees a park ranger and relief fills him that it's not a bear. He waves and smiles at the ranger. His joy turns to fear once he registers the scowl on the ranger's face as he barrels toward him, a large knife protruding from his left hand. Chase and I scream together as the blade plunges into him.

I'm carried to a new person and place. This time, it's Anna. Micah's little sister. I'm with her the moment she notices the large man blocking her path, when she sees his grimace and knows he's not friendly. She tries to turn and walk the other direction, but he snatches her by the arm. She and I scream together as his grip tightens. As she struggles to get free, she prays that her parents or brothers or sister will come right now and save her from this crazy man. She knows he's going to hurt her. Her mind is frantic, trying to figure out how to get away when something hits her in the head. Her last thought as she falls is, *help me. Someone, help me.*

Those words come out of my mouth as the doctor says to rest, and I fall back against the bed.

"Are you okay? You yelled for help." Jonas says.

I try to nod but don't think I manage to.

"Tessa, you're doing wonderful. I can see her hair. Daddy, do you want to see the crown of her head?"

Jonas rushes to the foot of the bed. The nurse points to the mirror above me.

"You can see too if you look in the mirror."

I try to see Zoe's little head of hair, but I'm so tired. I need this to be over with. Although, I'm not really sure what *this* I'm referring to—labor, the flashes, or both. I need my baby girl to be okay.

Jonas returns to the head of the bed, smiling from ear to ear. "Oh my God, honey! She has so much brown hair. Did you see?"

I don't have time to do anything other than attempt a smile before the doctor is telling me that again, it's time to push. If they can see her hair, does that mean I'm close? I have to believe it does.

This time the nurse instructs Jonas to grab one of my knees as she grabs the other. They tell me to push against them. I bear down, praying this time I only feel the pain of childbirth, rather than that of death. My prayers are not answered when a kaleidoscope of color again takes over.

This time I'm back in Bryan's body, cutting and sawing on a boy's lower leg. One I've only seen in my mind. The names play through my mind on a loop. It's Scott. Bryan mutters as he cuts through flesh and into the bone. *Thank you for your sacrifice. The Lord will bless you richly. You have fulfilled your purpose and will be part of a new, beautiful whole. My boy. My Sam. You will be resurrected. These bones will walk again. They will rise up from the earth.* The noise of the sawing nauseates me. I want to scream at Bryan and tell him that murdering these children will not bring his son back. There's no way to do that. He's gone. But this has already happened even though I'm living through it for the first time. There's no going back and stopping it. These children are dead. Bryan gathers up the lower left leg once he's removed it. He wraps it in plastic and puts it in a container. Then he carefully covers the boy's body with leaves and wipes the mud-streaked tears from his cheeks before covering his face. *I'm sorry for the pain I caused you.* I try to shout, to tell him he's a sick bastard, but the only sound that comes out is a howl.

I'm back in the room, gripping Jonas' hand. I try to meet his eyes but plop back against the head of the bed, now that this contraction is finally over.

"You're doing so well. I think she'll be here with a few more pushes," the doctor says.

I want to smile. I should be happy. I'm filled with trepidation about her entering this world. Inside of me, she's safe and protected. What if she's not once she's born? Also, a few more pushes means being transported to another place and time, yet again, before she's finally here. She doesn't have that far to go and I'm pushing as hard as I can. How long can it take for a baby to travel two inches? Now that I'm back in this room, the pain of labor crushes me. The pressure is unlike anything I've felt before in my life. How does anyone go through this without medication?

"Time to go. Grab her legs again. Tessa, give it all you got this time."

I want to scream or throw something. I've been giving it all I've got this entire time. I have no more to give. *Please Zoe, come soon, and be okay.* I pray as I push. I pull myself up to bear down as a nurse opens the door to my room. In the split second the door is cracked, I see him lingering outside my room. Bryan is here at the hospital, but that's impossible. These flashes and labor are making me see things that aren't real. I shake my head as flashes meld together in my mind.

This time I know where I am and who I'm with since we were recently in this exact place. I'm with Dominick. He's lumbering along the side of the road, feeling so woozy and tired. He just wants to get home and lie down for a while. He's relieved that he's almost there, but his head throbs with each step he takes. He's angry at his mom because she knew he didn't feel well, but she still made him walk home rather than leave the church for only a few minutes to drive him home. He doesn't hear the car until it pulls to a stop right next to him. He turns to look, and the driver is already out of the car with the trunk popped open. Dominick tries to scream, but the man clasps his hand tightly over his mouth, muffling the sound. Something squeezes his neck tighter and tighter. As he loses consciousness, he thinks, *I can't breathe* over and over again.

I'm whooshed away back into Bryan's body as he carefully strips the bone of its skin. The sight and smell gag me. I try to turn away, but I'm forced to watch as he soaks the bone in some liquid, caressing it as you would a newborn baby before lying it down.

"Lay back, honey," Jonas' voice snaps me back to this room. His hand helps guide me toward the head of the bed. "Are you doing okay?"

My head goes in a circle, shaking and nodding at the same time. I don't know how I'm doing. I need some assurance that this nightmarish loop I'm stuck in will go away as soon as she's born.

"Am I almost there?" My voice comes out in a raspy whisper.

Jonas wipes my head with a cool cloth. "I think so. You're doing such…"

He's interrupted by the doctor announcing it is time again. I want to cry. I don't think I can do this. What if I can't push her out? Do babies ever get stuck inside? Despite my thoughts and worries, I hoist myself up and bear down yet again. The pressure between my legs is in battle with the mounting pressure in my head.

A flash rips through me like lightning, exactly as it happened with Matthew. My entire body feels electrified as images pour through my mind. Children's faces—Dominick, David, Leah, Tatum, AJ, Anna, Chase, Sam, David, Stephanie. First laughing. Then their dead eyes stare up at me. Among them is a baby's face. In my gut, I know it's Zoe. Why is Zoe in the midst of all these dead children? Then Bryan's thoughts again take over my mind. His deep sorrow washes through me, as does his obsession with recreating his son's body. It's a mixture of sadness, guilt, remorse, and need. All of this echoes through my mind on repeat. And then the images in my head transform to bones of different shapes and sizes. I'm tumbling in a sea of bones, lost in this land of horror.

The doctor's voice calls out to me from this dreadful place. "Her vitals are off. Tessa, you need to keep pushing even though your contraction is over. Do you hear me?" I try to nod, but my head lolls to the side. "Dad, we're going to do a vacuum extraction."

Jonas' voice sounds so distant, like he's speaking from somewhere far, far away. I want to tell them not to do the vacuum extraction, that I can keep pushing. I don't want to have her sucked out of me—there are too many risks. I can't say or do anything though because I'm somewhere else surrounded by bones taunting me along with the voices and faces of dead children. I try to reach for Jonas' hand, hoping he can pull me back from this dreadful place, but I am drowning in a sea of death and murder.

And then, it all fades away right as the pressure in my pelvis abruptly ends, followed by a faint cry—a glorious sound. I try to pull myself upright to see my baby girl, but the nurse tells me to lie back. Within seconds, Zoe is swaddled and placed on my chest. One look at her and I'm in love. She's okay. Thank God, she's okay!

"Oh my God, Tessa. She's beautiful. Hi, baby girl. Daddy's little Zoe." Jonas leans down and kisses her on the forehead and then me.

All is right with my world.

CHAPTER 49

The next hour is filled with a flurry of activity. Zoe is one hundred percent healthy, even though she came so early. She weighs six pounds, three ounces, and is seventeen inches long. She has a full head of the silkiest brown hair and has no problems latching on to breastfeed. Jonas is completely smitten with both her and me. He keeps looking at me in awe, like I've performed a miracle, which, in a way, I suppose I have.

The doctor explains that she had to give me an episiotomy which will take some time to heal, and the vacuum extraction was necessary because my blood pressure and pulse were spiking dangerously high. I have no doubt that this happened because of the flashes and the mental torture, but now that I'm holding Zoe, that nightmare all seems like a distant memory.

Once Zoe and I are cleaned up, Doctor Weyman says her goodbyes and tells me I can have visitors in to meet the baby, but only a few at a time. Jonas briefly leaves the room and comes back with Chaundra and the kids. I expect to see Cyle walk through the door with them, but he doesn't come.

"Oh my goodness, look at that little bundle of perfection," Chaundra says, holding out her arms to take Zoe. I hesitantly hand her over.

"You can only have her for a minute. My arms already feel empty without her," I say with a laugh.

Chaundra smiles. "I remember how hard it is to let anyone hold your baby at first."

Chaundra studies her face and lifts the tiny hat from her head, feeling her silky hair. "She has so much hair. Isn't she cute, guys?"

Liam glances at the baby, thoroughly unimpressed, before pulling his phone from his pocket. Lily nods and smiles but keeps her distance. She's probably never been around a baby before and doesn't know what to think.

"She's perfect, right?" Jonas says, beaming with a smile.

"Absolutely. Good job, Tess. How are you feeling?"

"Elated. So happy that's over with. I don't think I ever want to go through that again." I laugh but mean every word. How do women have more than one child?

Lily sits and bites her lip, refusing to get close to the baby. Maybe she's feeling neglected. "Hey, Lily. Come give Aunt Tessa a hug."

She leaps up and leans down where I tighten my grip around her. For the first time in a long time, I don't get any flashes from her. She rests her head on my shoulder.

"Hey, where's Cyle?" I whisper.

She points to Chaundra. "Looking at the baby."

My heart drops. Why can't I see him? What's going on?

"Cyle?" I yell out and then wait.

I whip my head from side to side, but he's not here. "Lily, why can't I see him?"

She shrugs. "Now, he's next to your bed, holding your hand." I flex my fingers but feel nothing.

A tear falls down my cheek. "Cyle, I can't see or hear you. Why?"

"He says he doesn't know, but that Zoe is perfect and he's so proud of you."

A sob escapes me, and Lily pulls away, returning to the chair next to Liam. Jonas comes to take her place.

"It's okay," he says, smoothing the hair away from my forehead.

I shake my head. "No, it's not. Why can't I see him if he's here? I've lost him again."

Jonas pulls me into his arms, and I cry against his chest. "I don't know, babe. I'm so sorry."

Chaundra walks over and hands Zoe to Jonas. "Can I talk to her a second?"

Jonas raises his eyebrows, and Chaundra gives a slight nod, before he steps away with Zoe.

Chaundra sits on the bed next to me and takes my hand. "I don't know how to say this or if this is the right time."

"Do you know what's going on?"

Again, she smiles, but it's full of regret. "Lily, come over here, please."

Lily slowly makes her way to the bed. Chaundra pats the spot next to her and Lily sits. They look at each other without a word.

"One of you needs to tell me what's going on." My voice is louder than I intended, verging on a shout.

"Okay," Chaundra says and takes a deep breath. "Please don't freak out. The flashes, and all the things you were seeing with them? They weren't from you."

My mind tries to comprehend what she's saying. What in the world does she mean they weren't from me? Who else would they have been from?

She must see the confusion on my face. "They're from Zoe. She has your gift. Your flashes never came back."

As her words wrap their way through my mind, a thousand-pound weight drops on my chest, crushing me. I can't breathe. I can't speak. I can't think. Zoe has my gift?

Finally, my voice escapes into a soul-crushing, guttural wail, "No!"

My mind slips into overdrive. Moments of my life whirl through me—those I've now passed onto my precious baby girl. Being called a freak. No one ever believing me or understanding me. Always feeling like an outcast. Visions of things as a child that I should have never been subjected to. Being terrified of touching anyone for fear of how it would change me. Images of people being hurt, abused, murdered. The loss. The pain. The heartbreak. This cannot be my daughter's future. Her destiny.

"Aunt Tessa," Lily says from a million miles away. I can't break the loop in my mind enough to find her or respond. "Aunt Tessa!" she yells and grips my hand.

I snap my head toward her, my eyes wild with panic.

"Cyle said to tell you that Zoe's life will be nothing like yours because she has you. You will understand her and make sure she doesn't go through the same things you did."

I try to absorb what she's saying, or rather, what Cyle's telling her to say. But am I strong enough to protect her? Will I really be able to prevent the same things from happening to her?

"Cyle said to tell you orange box." Lily says.

I don't want Zoe to need an orange box. I want her to have a normal, happy life not plagued with colors and flashes. I bite my tongue to keep from saying this, and instead ask, "How long have you known?"

Lily and Chaundra exchange a look before Chaundra nods, telling Lily to answer the question.

"Since the beginning. The day of my birthday party."

My entire body goes rigid with both fear and fury. They've known all this time and haven't said a word to me about it? The betrayal stings.

"What the hell? Why didn't you tell me? Did you know the flashes weren't from me and let me think I was losing my mind all this time?"

Chaundra grabs my hand. "I'm sorry. We did what we thought was best. Lily told me in the beginning, and I saw it, too, later on. We didn't want to make this any harder on you than everything you were already going through."

I jerk my hand away from her grip. "You should have told me. You know I was freaking out thinking my flashes were back forever."

Jonas sits on the other side of me and grabs my hand. I turn toward him with my jaw clenched.

"I know this is upsetting," he says, "but really, what difference would it have made had you known? It would have only worried you—us—more."

I want to scream, but a part of me knows he's right. Even if I'd known from day one, there would have been nothing I could do about it other than obsess and worry. How can I be angry at them for keeping this from me when they did it to protect me?

"You're right," I say, barely louder than a whisper.

Jonas squeezes my hand. "I know it's scary, but we've got this, hon. She will *never* go through the things you went through. We will love her and believe her, first of all. She will never be as alone and isolated as you were. There is no one better in the world to help her through this."

I shut my eyes and let my body relax, trying to believe his words. Chaundra hands Zoe back to me and I cradle her close. She looks up at me and everything clicks into place. Her eyes are not the typical blue of newborns, they are the loveliest, brightest shade of green—the exact color of my flashes.

Jonas leans in and surrounds us both in his arms. I don't know how or what the future holds, but we will see her through this. She will never feel unloved or alone.

Liam's voice interrupts our sweet moment. "Mom, can I go to the vending machine? I'm starving."

"You know I don't want you out of my sight right now," Chaundra says.

Liam stomps his foot. "Stop treating me like a baby! It's right down the hall, and we're in a hospital!"

Chaundra sighs loudly. "Fine. But come right back here." She digs through her purse and hands him some money.

"Grab me something too," Lily says.

I chuckle when he glares at her and sticks out his tongue before leaving the room.

"Hey, guys! I forgot to tell you, but Micah is going to stop by if that's okay. He wants to see Zoe and drop off a few gifts. I forgot to bring them before we headed over, so he stopped by the house to pick them up. We won't stay long." Chaundra's smile beams from ear to ear.

"That's fine with me," I say, still riding high from the burst of oxytocin now that Zoe is back in my arms.

"Good, because he texted to say he'd be here in a few minutes."

I stare at this little bundle of heaven in my arms and can't believe she's ours. Yes, I worry about what a burden she'll carry from her gift, but I also can't wait to see exactly how it's different from mine. I know beyond the shadow of a doubt that hers is much more powerful and doesn't necessarily come from only touching people. I also look forward to discovering who she becomes. We have so many adventures ahead of us.

My attention is jerked away from Zoe when I hear Chaundra yell, "Lily, what's going on?"

Lily is in a trance-like state, trembling from head to toe, staring at the door to the room. Her mouth hangs open as if she's trying to speak but can't get the words out.

Chaundra shakes her arm. "Lily, talk to me. What's happening?"

Tears stream down Lily's cheeks as she points to the door. "Liam... he's got Liam."

Chaundra jumps to her feet. "Who has Liam?"

"The bad guy. He's here."

CHAPTER 50

Chaundra bolts out the door, yelling Liam's name. Jonas wraps his arms around Lily as I snuggle Zoe closer. Lily has to be wrong. It's not March nineteenth yet—there's no way Bryan is here at this hospital right now.

Zoe begins to cry, and I suddenly remember. I saw him during labor, even though I convinced myself it was my imagination or a hallucination. A knowing settles over me—it *was* him outside my door.

"Jonas, I saw him. I thought I was imagining it, but it was him." The words pour out of me frantically. "Go help Chaundra find Liam. Tell her what I saw."

When Jonas opens the door, Chaundra's wails bounce off the walls, and her excruciating anguish slices through me. Once the door closes again, I am aware of Lily's sobs.

"Come sit next to me, Lily." I pat the bed.

As soon as she's next to me, I dry her cheeks with a tissue. "It's okay. Mommy will find him. He'll be okay."

"I can't..." she hiccups back a sob. "I can't see him. I don't know where he is. Why didn't I see this coming?"

I rub her back. "It's okay, Lily. They'll find him. He'll be okay. You couldn't see what was going to happen with Zoe, yet she's fine.

Liam will be too." As I say the words to console her, doubt fills me. What if they don't find him?

As I pull her into a hug, Lily touches Zoe's cheek and freezes, mouth gaping open.

"Lily, what's going on?"

Before she can answer, the door bursts open, and Bryan enters with Liam in his grasp. Bryan is wild-eyed and frantic with sweat glistening across his forehead. Liam struggles to break free from Bryan's grip.

"Let him go!" I shout, pulling both Lily and Zoe close to me. Lily trembles so badly the whole bed shakes.

With his free hand, Bryan pulls a gun from his waistband, pointing it directly at my head. *Oh my God!* My mind races as I try to figure out how to keep Liam, Lily, and Zoe safe. I just had a baby. There's no way I stand a chance at fighting off a gun-toting maniac.

"Please let me go!" Liam screams, his eyes widened in fear.

"I can't. I need you to bring my boy back," he mutters.

"Killing these children will not bring your son back. He's gone. He can't come back to you," I say, trying to keep my voice calm, yet confident.

Where are Chaundra and Jonas? Please let them come back to help.

"Shut up! I don't care what you say. I listen to God, and God alone. He's the one who called me to resurrect my son. Renamed me Ezekiel. Through His power and might, Sam will return to me. These bones will walk again. God will breathe life into them." He looks at Liam and says in a much calmer voice, "I'm sorry. But you are needed for this sacrifice. Please forgive me."

My mind scrambles as Lily buries her head against my chest and Zoe's cries grow louder, more urgent. What can I say or do to stop him? My eyes frantically search for the call button, but it's on the side table, just out of reach. I don't want to make any abrupt movements that could startle Bryan and make him shoot.

"It's not yet March nineteenth—your ordained day to kill. Perhaps God won't use your sacrifice if it's not performed on the date of Sam's death."

Bryan's face flames bright red as he pushes Liam to the ground and rushes toward me. "You keep my son's name from your lips. You are not worthy! I've been watching you. Saw you go talk to my wife and then followed her to your house. I know what you're trying to do—stop me from collecting all the pieces to return my boy to me. Stop me from fulfilling my destiny. You are acting on Satan's behalf, trying to interfere with the will of God." He's so close, his spittle wettens my face. "But, you see, you failed. All you did is help me find the next sacrifice. The next vital piece of the puzzle." He points to the corner where Liam cowers with his head buried in his arms.

Everything suddenly clicks into place as he speaks. Chaundra *did* sense him near when we were at the restaurant and when Cora was visiting. He was watching us from the shadows. In my mind, I shout out to God. *Take me. But protect these kids. If someone has to die, let it be me. Show me what to say or do to stop him from killing anyone else. Help!*

Bryan raises the gun, pointing it less than a foot from my head. If he shoots now, he could miss me and hit one of the kids. Is this why Lily couldn't see if Zoe was going to be okay? And why Lily and I both saw her in our vision with the other murdered children? Is she going to be killed on the same day she entered this world?

Zoe wails uncontrollably, and Lily reaches out from beside me to grab Zoe's tiny hand. I suck in a deep breath and prepare for the inevitable. He's going to shoot, and perhaps I'm going to die. I will gladly give my life if it means the kids will be spared. I lean forward and kiss Zoe on the head. She quiets instantly as a green flash and a sense of serenity flood me. *A flash?* I don't have time to ponder as peace settles in my soul despite the chaos of our current situation.

"Bryan, you need to put the gun down, and turn yourself in. I'm sorry about Sam. It's not your fault that he died, but you have to end this madness. You must stop killing these innocent children. They don't deserve to die. It will not bring him back." I'm surprised by how calm and confident I sound.

Bryan's body quakes as though a jolt of electricity is coursing through him, and then he goes completely still, staring at Zoe. I hold my breath, terrified to see what he does next. He drops the gun on the floor next to the bed and crumbles to his knees.

Suddenly, so many things click into place. I understand part of Zoe's gift. Memories zoom through my mind. The first time we met Micah, and he didn't believe me about my powers and Tatum. Then, the green flash came, and he suddenly accepted what I was saying.

Our meeting with Ranger Ferguson, who wasn't going to give us the information we needed about the park rangers around the time of AJ's death. But then, I had the green flash and touched his hand. Suddenly, he was cooperative, giving us everything we needed.

The day in Jonas' office, after Chaundra saw the gruesome painting I did of Liam. I had the green flash, and suddenly she knew, without a doubt, I would never hurt him and that, together, we would stop the killer.

Because of Zoe and her gift, I was able to push my thoughts and desires into others and force them to do what I was asking. This time the push involves stopping Bryan and making him step away from his delusions long enough to see reality.

With no more time to ponder, I shout, "Go Liam, now! Get help!"

Liam dashes out of the room.

Bryan buries his head in his hands, sobbing. "I'm so sorry. Sam, I tried, but I can't do it anymore. I can't hurt anyone else. I never meant for you to die. I wanted to see you again. I'm sorry I couldn't save you. I'm sorry I couldn't bring you back," he wails.

His sorrow cuts straight through me—his grief and despair hang in the air like a storm cloud. The death of his son broke him. The killing kept him from grieving. But now, it is all crashing down around him. The truth. Everything he's done and the atrocities he committed.

As he sobs, I clutch Zoe and Lily to my chest and whisper a thank you to the heavens. I am certain that Zoe's abilities shifted to me, and I was able to compel Bryan to finally give up his fight and delusions.

Security guards rush in the room, followed by Micah and other police officers several minutes later. Bryan doesn't put up any fight as they cuff him and drag him from the room. His eyes meet mine one last time. When he was in my mind, overpowering my thoughts, all I could see was a monster that killed children. Now, standing before me, is only a man—one broken by misery and desperation. A tear slides down my cheek for Bryan and Cora. Sam's death was a tragic accident that they didn't deserve.

CHAPTER 51

Once they've removed Bryan and remanded him into custody, Jonas returns to the room, red-faced and sweaty. He rushes over to the bed and encircles Lily, Zoe, and me in his arms. "I'm so glad you guys are okay. I never should've left you."

"We're okay. None of us could've known or predicted this."

Jonas swipes tears from his cheeks. "Poor Liam! He had to be scared out of his mind."

"Liam, is he okay?" Panic races through me.

Jonas kisses Zoe on the head before answering. "He is. Chaundra is talking to the police and will be back when she's done to get Lily."

Jonas holds out his arms and I reluctantly hand Zoe over to him. "Tell me everything that happened."

I tighten my embrace around Lily, and she relaxes against my chest. "Let's just enjoy our little girl. We've been through enough. We're okay, which is all that really matters."

Jonas sits in the rocking chair and cradles Zoe close as he glides back and forth. The motion calms me. Now that everything is over, my adrenaline crashes, and my eyes drift closed.

Zoe lets out a wail, and my eyes snap back open. I laugh—the sleep deprivation has already started. Jonas pats her on the back to try to calm her.

"She's probably hungry." I hold out my arms for her.

Jonas brings her to me and sits on the edge of the bed next to us while I feed her. We both stare at her in awe. She's perfect. I haven't told Jonas all the details yet, but she is the one who saved Liam's life, along with so many other children. If not for her… I can't even finish that thought.

Yes, I'm scared about what she'll have to endure because of her gift. But I also know that she is so special. Her gift has already been used for good. She's going to change the world.

PART III

AUGUST

CHAPTER 52

I'm adjusting to life as a mom and loving absolutely every moment. Well, almost every moment—I could definitely use more sleep. I never knew how much a baby would change my world and my perspective on life. My fear over Zoe's abilities has transformed into determination to make sure she has the best life possible, and that she's able to learn to celebrate her differences to use them for good. Time will tell exactly what her gift entails. I know for certain that her gift is much stronger and more powerful than mine, though. Sometimes that thought scares the crap out of me, but I'm working on accepting and embracing it. No matter what she goes through, Jonas and I have her back.

Bryan Benson is now behind bars, so Jonas and I are cleared of every suspicion. Most of Bryan's home was a shrine to his lost son. Sam's pictures plastered the walls, along with articles about his death and scriptures. They also found stacks of Bryan's journals describing each murder and his rambling thoughts. There were a few snapshots of us at the restaurant with Cora as well as several pictures on his phone of our house with her car parked in the driveway. He had renamed himself Ezekiel and truly believed his mission was ordained by God— he was directed to kill these children so that his son could live again. In his basement, they found a partially erected skeleton made from the bones of the murdered children. He confessed to nine murders and directed the agents to where their remains could be found. Chase, Anna, AJ, Tatum, Leah, David, Stephanie, Dominick, and Scott have all been returned to their families. They are now laid to rest, and their families have a tiny bit of closure, although I doubt that true healing will ever be possible.

His lawyers have claimed insanity as a defense. As much as I hate mental health issues being used as an excuse for such deplorable actions, I believe it is true in his case. I was inside of him, or perhaps it was him inside of me. He didn't want to hurt those children, but losing his son fractured his mind. Mentally, he really was no longer Bryan Benson, rather Ezekiel, who believed he was called by God. He needs help and to grieve his son properly.

I hold Zoe to my chest and can't imagine the pain of losing her. The guilt that must have consumed Bryan after Sam's fall. I know that grief, guilt, and pain can destroy a person, as it did him. Sadly, it destroyed the future of nine children too. But because of Zoe and her gift, Liam's life was spared, along with many more children who escaped falling prey to him. Before she was even born, she started serving such a powerful purpose. She has this gift for a reason, exactly as I did.

I gaze into her sparkling green eyes now as she studies my face. There's a knowing there—a deep understanding, far beyond her years. She sees parts of me that I probably haven't even yet seen myself.

She reaches up and puts her little hand on my cheek and smiles. A green flash whooshes through me and Cyle's smiling face appears before me. I can hear his voice plain as day.

"Tessa, I want to tell you I love you and you're doing a wonderful job as a mommy. Zoe is perfect. Please don't be upset, but I have to go now."

I'm so stunned that I can see and hear him again that it takes a few moments to find my voice. "Go where?"

A kaleidoscope of calming yet vibrant colors surrounds him, along with children. Children whose names and faces I know, each smiling and looking completely at peace. Sam, Chase, Anna, AJ, Tatum, Leah, David, Stephanie, Dominick, Scott, and Aiden.

"It's time for us to move on from this world. We've served our purposes, and we're ready to go home."

I choke back a sob. "I love you, Cyle."

"I love you too, Tessa. I'll see you again someday."

He picks up Aiden and carries him as they all walk away into the sea of colors. Peace and serenity consume me. They all deserve to move on, away from this world full of pain, agony, and heartache. I hate that I'll never get to see my brother again this side of heaven, and that Lily will no longer get to hang out with Aiden; but, as Cyle said, I will see him again someday. A tear trails down my cheek as Zoe removes her hand from my face, and I'm back in this room with only her.

Her entire face brightens in a smile.

I wipe my tears away and snuggle her to my chest. "My precious girl, you are so beautiful and strong. Your gift will change the world," I say and kiss her on the head. "Mommy and Daddy will be here with you every step of the way."

I believe every word. Her future is wide open, and while her path is uncertain, I'm privileged to be a part of her journey.

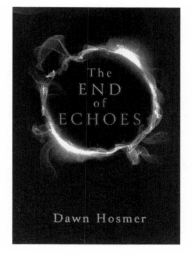

Two families, forever linked by tragedy.

Ruby Dunkin is in an abusive marriage. Her best efforts aren't enough to shield her two children from an abusive father whose cruelty knows no bounds. Their volatile situation ends in tragedy when Ruby's eldest son, Billy is torn away from everything he loves. Consumed by hatred and self-loathing Billy becomes the thing he hates the most— his father.

Chelsea Wyatt, a senior in high school, goes missing after work one night, never to return. Her parents are devastated, only knowing this kind of tragedy from the news. Crimes like this are unheard of in their quiet, midwestern town. Consumed by the tragic fate of their friend, family member and neighbor, their lives and futures are forever altered.

For over eighteen years, no one knows the connection between Ruby Dunkin and Chelsea Wyatt. A journey through time reveals the common thread stitching their heartbreak together. Yesterday echoes throughout each character's life as they decide how, and if, they will break the chains of the past.

Will they continue to leave a legacy of pain and loss for future generations? Will they break the cycles of abuse that have destroyed so many lives?

My name is Mackenzie Bartholomew, or at least it was. I'm staring at my dead body, lying in a casket. I was a healthy, thirty-nine-year-old, mother of three.

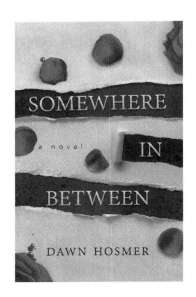

I have so many questions but very few answers. Was I murdered? Did I commit suicide? I don't know if I'm in some sort of purgatory or if I've gone straight to hell.

I'm stuck somewhere in between life and death, forced to travel back in time to relive moments from my past, ones I'd rather forget. I'm desperate to piece together the details surrounding my death. If I don't, I fear my soul will never find rest.

Chock full of family drama, secrets, betrayal, and lies, ***Somewhere in Between*** is a Psychological Thriller with wicked twists that will keep you hooked until the last page.

Mosaic is a collection of very short stories, ranging from scary pieces to those full of hope. Through these stories, I hope to provide glimpses into what it means to be human. Each of us is made up of many different pieces that, when fit together, make a beautiful, messy whole. Those tiny pieces in and of themselves don't mean much and are easily overlooked. But, when we put them all together, a full picture of what it means to be human starts to form.

Bits & Pieces

Tessa was born with a gift. Through a simple touch she picks up pieces of others. A chance encounter with a stranger traps Tessa within the mind of a madman. A "flash" of color devours her—the only indication that she's gained something new from another person. Will she be able to find the killer and help save the next victim without losing herself in the process?

ACKNOWLEDGMENTS

As I write the acknowledgements for my fifth book, I realize how blessed I am with such supportive people in my life who encourage me on this writing journey. It takes so many people to help create the best book possible, even when you are independently published.

I'd like to thank my husband, Steve, for always believing in me and this crazy dream of mine. Also, my children—Jesi, Krystyna, Dominic and Gabriel—you all are my why and keep me going on the darkest of days. And to my beautiful granddaughter, Alayna, who has brought such joy and sunshine into my life. I am also so grateful for my mom, Joyce Boyer, for loving me unconditionally and offering unwavering support.

There are many people who've read this book in its early stages who have provided me with invaluable feedback to help improve it. Thank you to Kate Yelland for her amazing editorial assistance and feedback. You have made this book a thousand times better. Also, thank you to all my beta readers who took the time to read my work before it was completely polished: Eileen Hammond, Jen Yan, Bradley Poage, Eve Corso, Anne Waldon, Alain Davis, and Bethany Sammadar. Your insights, feedback, and friendship have been invaluable. I hope you are all pleased when you see how I have incorporated your feedback into the final product. Also, thank you to all of you who have volunteered to read an Advanced Reader Copy of this book—early readers and reviews are so important to a successful launch.

I am also so grateful for the #BookTok community and the Kind Valkyries who have welcomed me with open arms. You all have given me a new zest for writing by offering such amazing support for me and my books. I now consider many of you dear friends.

A continued thank you to the Writing Community on Twitter for your support, encouragement, and friendship. So many of you have been huge champions of my work (and me)—I'd be lost without you.

I am so grateful to each and every person who has read my work. Without readers, this would all be in vain. *Pieces & Parts* would not exist without the love I've received for *Bits & Pieces*, which to date is my bestselling novel. Your desire to know what happens next in Tessa's journey is the only reason this book is now in the world.

Thank you to everyone who has shared a review for any of my books on social media and/or review platforms. Taking those extra few minutes to do a review makes more of a difference than you'll ever know.

Independent authors rely on reviews to help spread the word about our work. Please take a moment of your time to leave a review on Amazon, Goodreads, Bookbub, and/or social media. Thank you!

ABOUT THE AUTHOR

Dawn Hosmer is the author of psychological thrillers and suspense. She is a lifelong Ohioan. She received her degree in Sociology and spent her career in Social Work; however, writing has always been her passion. She is a wife and the mother of four amazing children. In addition to listening to true crime podcasts, drinking coffee, and coloring, Dawn is busy working on her next novel.

For more information, visit www.dawnhosmer.com or follow her on Twitter @dawnhosmer7, Instagram @dawnh71, Tiktok @dawn_hosmer, or Facebook. Dawn can also be found on Goodreads and Bookbub.

Made in the USA
Monee, IL
05 July 2022

99104280R00180